I WILL FIND YOU

A Mother's Love Never Dies

Lorraine O'Byrne
18/11/2023

I Will Find You

Published 2023 by the estate of Lorraine O'Byrne

Print Edition
First Edition
Copyright © The estate of Lorraine O'Byrne
ISBN: 978-1-916544-11-6

Publishing Information
Design & publishing services
provided by JM Agency

www.jm.agency
Kerry, Ireland

I WILL FIND YOU

A Mother's Love Never Dies

LORRAINE O'BYRNE

Chapter One

Louisa

1950

I tiptoe past the beds, groping my way through the dormitory. The gloom my shield. Latest victim, Pauline, lies curled up in a foetal position on a mere sheet, sniffling in her sleep. Something rankles. Poor sod must have wet the bed again. I throw the blanket over her and then melt into the corridor. Silent as a wraith. The Virgin Mary leaps out at me from her sanctimonious perch on the windowsill amid intangible threats that lurk elsewhere in the shadows. Shoes squeak from a room to the left. A pungent odour of antiseptic wafts through the air. Someone flicks on a light from behind. It's Sister Mary Theresa pushing a trolley heaped with towels and sheets. She'll recognise me. I've got to get out of the open.

Finding a door at my shoulder, I shove it aside, stumble into a closet and wait for her to pass. Sister Mary Theresa has the hearing of a flea, but she can smell fear a mile away. Sweat pools behind my neck and slithers down inside my clothes. I twist my hands, powerless to block the overwhelming panic about to drown me. The light goes out, and murk descends in the hallway once again.

I'm so cold, goosebumps prickle my legs and arms, and I can see the vapours from my breath billow into the frigid air. I straighten and will myself to think through the fog that fugs my mind. It will be morning soon, and they will be searching for me. Hugging myself to keep warm, I glance down at my stained brown smock that is almost threadbare from constant use. At my knuckles, skinned from scrubbing concrete floors. Flinching at every rattle and floorboard creak, I squeeze the Claddagh locket suspended from a chain around my neck, close my eyes and recite a prayer in my mind my grandmother taught me when I was little to give me courage.

Angel of God
My Guardian dear
To whom God's love
Commits me here
Ever this day
Be at my side
To light and guard
To rule and guide
Amen

My breathing slows, and I scrutinise the little room with new eyes. A black habit dangles from a hook to the right, and below that, a tunic, wimple and gleaming black shoes. My hands are shaking so much I struggle with the baggy habit and stuff my hair into the wimple. It's just the right fit, tight against my skull.

In my haste to escape, I knock a small bag of linen to the ground, so I pick it up to cover me in case anyone questions what I'm doing. Heart pounding, shoulders back and striding with a confidence I don't feel, I emerge from my place of hiding, praying that no one will see me.

A weak shaft of light filters through the grimy windows overhead, revealing a dismal grey sky beyond, a promise of the day to come.

The habit is so long I step on the hem, stumble and drop the bag. A voice stops me cold.

'Sister, goodness, where are you going at this hour?'

My gut clenches, screaming to flee, and it takes every last ounce of willpower not to lunge for the stairs just four feet away. Rigid with fear, I turn. My hands twisted in a ball at my side.

Sister Mary Theresa's glasses rest askew halfway down her bulbous nose, biscuit crumbs muddy her tunic. She glances up as I turn around and squints. My mouth goes dry.

'Bit early for deliveries, isn't it, Sister Augusta?' she clucks. 'What's the world coming to – delivery vans at half seven in the morning. Lord save us and guard us.'

I'm so relieved that she doesn't recognize me; air whooshes out of my body. I shrug in reply, hoping to God she'll leave it at that, but needn't have worried as she's off grumbling to herself down the corridor. Rosary beads swinging, still shaking her head in bafflement.

Clutching the bag full of washing, I rush downstairs to the basement. One ear cocked for activity upstairs. Out of breath, I toss the bag on the ground and spring to the door. Cobwebs cling for dear life to crevices overhead. A pump hums in the corner. Empty boxes are tossed upended in a pile. The sound of clanking pipes.

The bolt jams at first. I yank it back, my hands slippery with sweat, and it opens. Cold air hits my face like a bucket of iced water. Nothing ever felt so good. As soon as I am free of the confines of the institute, I bolt up the street and lose myself in the maze of the town.

A Volkswagen Beetle ploughs through a puddle drenching me. I gasp and jump back onto the pavement for safety, just as a green bus advertising Kellogg's Cornflakes on the side and belching smoke out its rear end trundles to a stop not far from where I wait. The bus is my knight in shining armour. Arriving to my rescue in the nick of time. I scan the destination overhead. *Letterfrack*. My heart skips a beat.

The driver, rounded and bearded with black hair, steps out for a smoke. I hop on when he's not looking, huddle at the back, and pray that my good fortune will hold out until I get home.

Babbling girls in school uniform get on the bus, forming a wall in front of me. A weary sun dapples anaemic hedges scattered throughout the estates as the bus meanders along cobbled streets and squares, stopping now and then to let more passengers on. Heat sears my face; finding it hard to breathe, I tug at the wimple.

At the next stop, the girls disembark, and a small slight middle-aged woman carrying a loud orange handbag, and a folded newspaper tucked under her left arm, boards the bus. She sits down opposite me, scans the headlines, then puts the paper down and stares out the window. The town slowly chugs to life. Up ahead, the steeple from St. Mary's Church pokes into the sky like a beacon towering above the houses directing me where to go.

I don't have the luxury of resting. My heart is racing. At the last stop, I jump out. Pull down the wimple, and gasp at my reflection in the glass as the bus sputters away; my colourless cheeks and limp stringy brown hair.

I blink, momentarily disorientated at the warren of houses around me. I have to keep moving. So, I head west towards the village. Head bent against the biting wind.

My feet ache from walking; the shoes are pinching my toes. People are glancing curiously at me as I pass. Pointing and whispering. My head can't take it anymore. If only Gran were alive, she'd know what to do.

At last, I reached the village post office. Less than a mile to go from there and I'll be back home. I keep picturing Mum's happy face when she sees me, hugging me up, telling me how sorry she is. Everything will be okay; I just know it.

Mottled grey clouds scud across the sky, muscling out the sun. After a few minutes it begins to get chilly, and then it buckets down. A gull swoops to the ground. Church bells chime out the midday hour. Banging, clattering and hammering from a nearby building site stunts my hearing, so when a Garda car pulls to the curb, I register the arrival too late. A guard jumps out, bull-necked and cross-eyed. He marches towards me.

'Louisa Hannon, stay right where you are.'

I spin on my heel, but the long habit hampers my escape, and I collide into two elderly ladies in headscarves carrying shopping.

Chapter Two

Carrie

1976

C arrie jerked awake, yawned and knuckled the sleep out of her eyes. She'd been out for a drink with friends the night before to celebrate turning twenty-six, and it had been all hours by the time she got home.

Normally, the wild mountain bracken and bleak limestone escarpment of Connemara's rugged coastline took her breath away, but after ploughing through roads upon roads of cow shit, dodging numerous potholes, and narrowly escaping a collision with a tractor, it wouldn't have bothered her if she never set foot in Connemara ever again.

She parked at the end of a grass-topped lane, twisted her hair back into an elastic band, and then disappeared back into the car to get her keys, notepad and camera.

Right, she thought, straightening her jacket. Here goes.

She trudged up to the cottage. It was a simple stone house. Green paint flaked from the low-sized wall out front, and the tiny lawn was submerged in weeds. She unlocked the door, turned on the light and went inside. The living room comprised of a red brick fireplace, narrow casement windows with faded net curtains, muddy mustard floor tiles, and a pine dining table and chairs covered in dust stood in the centre.

Stepping over a broken ceramic vase, she sat down to jot down some notes, then went on to inspect the rest of the house.

Another door through the living room led to the kitchen. Two people couldn't stand in here it; was so cramped and dark. Anyone who'd buy this place would need to install another window or skylight. This is what she would be advising the new prospective owners. A white fridge was squeezed into a corner beneath a tiny narrow window obscured from view by thick cobwebs and dirt, a free-standing cooker, three presses, a gas heater and a square Belfast sink. She twisted the taps but got no water. She made a note to check the pump.

Adjusting the lens of her camera, she set the flash then took a few snaps of the backyard with its dismal clothesline and also a shot of the vegetable patch before finally heading upstairs to finish.

There were three rooms on the first floor, one of which was a mint green bathroom, tiled from floor to ceiling, with a toilet, a chipped handbasin and a shower. The first bedroom looked bright and airy; it had a double bed, matching pine lockers, a towering oak wardrobe to the side, an oval mirror, peeling yellow wallpaper and frayed blue carpet. She rolled off some photos and then went into the second bedroom.

This bedroom was cosy and small, and she loved the way the beams of the ceiling veered downwards at an angle. There were two single beds, faded pink flowery wallpaper, a fairy light in the centre, and a white dressing table complete with wooden stool that sat next to a small square window overlooking the garden out front.

She was about to head downstairs when she heard something rolling along the floor directly above her in the attic.

'Oh my God, what is that?'

She pulled down the ladder and went up. The gabled roof was so low it almost touched her head. Immediately the stench blasted her. *Jesus, is there a dead animal rotting under the floorboards?*

A weak shaft of light filtered through the smudged window onto a small cast iron bed cloaked with cobwebs. *An attic bedroom. How come this wasn't included in the plans?* On a crooked shelf sat a miniature chipped porcelain doll upended inside her black pram and, directly underneath, a brown-stained locker. Carrie rubbed her arms, regretting not having worn a coat, unable to comprehend how temperatures could have plummeted when it was warm just five minutes ago. Her breath billowed in the frigid air, and her toes felt like ice in her thick socks.

She opened the locker, knocking a rusted locket and a one-eared teddy to the floor. She picked up the locket and was attempting to prise it open with her fingernail when she felt a sudden draught lift the hem of her suit.

A whisper. *Carrie.*

'Who's there?'

A ball rolled, stopped at her feet, then suddenly bounced.

Her heart flapping like a frantic bird desperate to escape, she staggered out of the attic, stumbled down the ladder, and ran to her car. Then drove off in a screech of brakes and didn't stop until she put at least ten kilometres between her and the cottage, and her breathing began to slow. She stopped outside a community centre and snapped open the glove box, pushing papers, tapes and manuals aside until her fist closed around a jar of tablets. Twisting off the cap, she swallowed two pills, then tipped out her last Marlboro cigarette onto her lap.

Her hand shook each time she tried to strike a match. Thumping the wheel in frustration, she flicked the spent matches out the window, brooding on what just had happened. And whether or not she should confide in Tom. He'd say she imagined it. No one would believe her. There's no such thing as ghosts. Just a trick of the wind, a symptom of exhaustion. Had to be. Hadn't it?

She shuddered. *No, no way! I refuse to believe that it is happening again. I just need to sleep, that's all.*

It was going on for two when she got back to their shared office. The door opened, and Tom shuffled in, scruffy as ever. Brown biscuit crumbs clinging to his white beard, he brought out the Connacht Tribune and sat back to read the paper.

'We're out of coffee,' she said. 'Do you want anything?'

'Digestives, oh, and sugar,' he said, taking off his chunky jumper.

She headed out and bought coffee, sugar, a packet of chocolate digestives and Marlboro. Then, turning up the collar of her waxed jacket hastened down the street back to work, anticipating a downpour. When the first drops of rain landed, she flew past the butcher's shop, the mini market square and dodged an elderly couple crossing at the pedestrian lights. Rain battered the ground for several seconds, then tapered off as the sun came out. Soaked to the bone and still dwelling on her weird experience, she collided with a man in a hoodie hurtling around the corner.

'What the fuck!'

Momentarily blinded by the impact, pain rocketing through her eye, she dropped the biscuits and sugar. Crows dived for the crumbs. The sugar bag burst, and the grains spread like a blanket of snow onto the pavement.

'Christ, your head's like granite,' the man groaned, rubbing his jaw. His hood fell aside to reveal shoulder-length dishevelled dark brown hair, thin, sallow cheekbones, a stubbly chin and he looked to be about thirty-five. Green paint blotted his Led Zeppelin t-shirt, and there were holes in his jeans.

Carrie bristled. 'Well, if you were watching where you were going instead of being glued to the newspaper –'

His hands shot up, palms out in a placatory gesture. 'You're right. I'm sorry.' He rummaged in his pocket And handed her a pound note. 'The price of a packet of biscuits.'

'What about the sugar?' her olive-green eyes twinkled.

He pulled out his pockets. 'Have mercy. I'm skint.'

Carrie touched her throbbing eyelid, wincing through her smile.

'You might want to put an ice pack on that,' he said.

'Think I got the worse end of the stick?'

'I've a thick skull,' he said with a smirk. 'Don't bruise easily.'

'Got to go; this is where I work,' Carrie said, avoiding further conversation.

He looked up and read the sign overhead. *Clancy & Gillespie Auctioneers Ltd.* 'Nice one. How about a drink in O'Driscoll's Saturday – say around eight?' His words came out in a rush. 'To make up for it. The name's Jack, by the way.'

'Carrie. Thought you were skint, Jack?'

He grinned. 'Payday, Friday.'

'Here's your pound back.'

'Keep it. I won't starve.'

She turned to head back inside.

'Hey, you didn't give me an answer.'

'It's no…sorry.'

His face fell. 'All right then – another time, maybe?'

'Bye, Jack.'

She left Jack and unlocked the door, slapped an ice pack to her eye, then finished typing up her report on the cottage. She found it impossible to concentrate. The words had merged into one another, becoming a blur on the paper. Her trousers were welded to her skin from dampness, and she could feel a chill coming on. The gas fire doing nothing to lock in the heat, she got up to put on her coat.

'What happened to you?' Tom chuckled, putting the telephone back in its receiver.

'Bashed heads with a stranger.'

'Looks nasty. Put anything on it?'

'An icepack.'

'You know that cottage you visited today?'

The hackles rose on the nape of her neck. 'Yeah – what about it?'

'Someone's shown an interest in the place.'

'Already? That was fast. I've only just completed the bank evaluation.'

'I said you'd meet him there on Friday morning.'

She stared at him, her heart thumping and swallowed. 'Can't you...only my eye doesn't feel so good?'

'No, I can't, sorry. I promised Claire I'd take the boys to the zoo before they go back to school. Besides, it's three days away. The swelling will have died down by then.'

She took a deep breath and, after a moment, unclenched her hands.

I won't show him the attic.

'Fine. Who's the client?'

'Jack Hannon.'

Chapter Three

Louisa

1950

There is no window in this basement. I can't see my hand in front of my face. The nun's robe has been ripped off me, and I'm shivering in just my underwear. Alone and isolated from the others. The cold seeps up through my toes from the hard concrete floor. I pace up and down, try to rub circulation into my arms. My teeth chatter. Hunger pains gnaw at my belly, and I'm desperate to use the toilet.

I run to the door and bang on it with my fists. 'Let me out, please. It's freezing in here.' I keep pounding the door, but my cries go unanswered, and after many long minutes, I sink to the floor and weep.

Hours pass.

I get up, cock my head, listening out for scratching sounds. Bile rockets to my throat at the thought of black furry putrid bodies with sharp teeth gnawing my toes, just as hungry and desperate as I am. In blind panic, I lunge for the door again and batter it. My voice ragged from shouting.

I'm hollering so much that I don't hear the rattle of a key twisting in the lock. A fumble, then a clang as it drops to the floor. Another key inserted. The door judders open, admitting a narrow shaft of light. Long enough to see a brick chimney, a metal bucket in the corner and a mattress. No rats. Just a crow. Weak with relief, I stagger.

Rough hands clutch my elbows.

'Louisa, it's me, Mary.'

I peer through half-slitted lids as she gently pushes me back into the room and closes the door. A soiled grey dress stretches over her swollen belly, and she smells of bleach. Her ankles are like balloons. Dirt beneath her fingernails. Clumps of blonde hair sprout on bald patches on her scalp, but her large eyes are shining.

We embrace. She darts a furtive glance over her left shoulder. Swivels back. Finger to her lips, warning me to keep quiet. Then places a plate of dripping, ham and a husk of dried bread on the floor next to a jug of water, and out from under her arm, unfolds a brown dress, socks and shoes.

'I'll bring some more food tomorrow soon as Sister Emmanuelle finishes her inspections.' She looks down at the keys in her hand. 'Gotta put these back before someone finds them missing.'

'Give them to me,' I gasp, lunging for the keys. 'I won't tell anyone.'

'No, Louisa,' she cries, recoiling as if I'd just slapped her. She clamps the keys in her fist and hastens back to the door. 'They'd kill me, have to think about this little 'un…I'm sorry.'

The click of the lock, and she's gone.

Grateful to get the clothes, I throw on the dress, socks and shoes. The dress stinks of mould, it's too big, its coarse material itches my skin, but glad of the warmth I put up with it. I gorge on the bread, toss the dripping back my throat, wolf down the ham, and gulp the water so fast I almost choke. The food has revived me. Inching over to the metal bucket, I relieve my bladder, then curl up on the mattress.

I've no idea of time passing. Humming from a pump breaks the silence. Doors open and slam elsewhere in the building.

Muffled cries of pain, grief and loneliness echo from the walls. My prison.

How long are they going to keep me in here? God has forgotten me. Even my own mother doesn't love me. There's no escape. I'm going to die here.

The Reverend Mother's words ricochet in my brain. 'You're a wicked sinner. The devil's spawn. No one wants you.'

Maybe she's right. Maybe I am wicked. After all, my family don't want me either. The man who had raised me hated my guts. I remember, whenever my siblings got into trouble, I was always the one who got the blame. My youngest sister Martha broke my mother's prize antique clock by accident; she twisted the hand too tight and burst the springs. Despite pleading with him that it wasn't my fault, he went after me with a stick and leathered me until I was black and blue.

My mother had begged him to stop, but he just ignored her and snarled, 'Your brat is good for nothing. A wicked, selfish child.'

I was more hurt by those words than by the beatings he gave me. It was against the law to throw a child out on the street, but I think he would have if he'd gotten away with it.

I remember thinking there had to be some truth to what everyone was whispering about me. You see, sometimes I see ghosts, dead people walking around. I started getting visions when I was twelve. It could happen anywhere, any time of the day or night, but mostly when I least expected it. Visions of various people, some old, some young. Each longing to be heard.

At first, they were very scary. One time, I saw their bones, faceless empty sockets where their eyes used to be. I was terrified. I'd leapt from my school desk screaming. A kind old lady staying in a caravan near home told me that they just wanted someone to talk to, a bit of comfort before they passed. In time, I came to realise she was right, that they couldn't harm me.

In school, however, the other kids grew afraid of me. 'It's not my fault they can't see what's right in front of their eyes,' I told my mother, but there were further complaints of disruption in class, so some of the children refused to come to school. I got the stick from the headmaster, and my stepfather was called to come in.

I'll never forget that day. It was a cold, wet, foggy January. I sat huddled in the cloakroom, knees drawn up to my body, fear in my belly. I heard raised voices, then a door being slammed, marching thunderous footsteps from the hard shoes I recognised so well, and the cloakroom door being wrenched open.

He pulled me to my feet, his grip pinching my arm, and pushed me out the door to the waiting cart where the donkey stood, ears drooped, coat rough and almost emaciated. The donkey looked how I felt at that moment. He bundled me onto the cart and didn't say a word. I braced myself for the first punch, but nothing came. Not a word spoken the entire five miles back.

When we returned home, I saw the reason why he didn't attack me. Father O'Shea had come to visit. His bicycle propped against the wall of our house. It was decided. I was not allowed to return to school but forced instead to slave for 'Moses' (on account of his long beard) McGrath, a local dairy farmer. He made me do all the washing, cleaning and cooking. My back broke from hauling coal, got blisters from boiling water and from scalding my fingers on his rusted stove. Aching joints from overreaching to dust shutters, from dragging heavy buckets to feed his pigs. By the time I got home in the evening, my clothes stank, and I fell to bed exhausted. But at least I was away from my stepfather.

I'd been working for Moses for three years, turning fifteen, when one evening on my way home, I collided with Nathaniel, my step-uncle, staggering home from the pub.

'Well, if it isn't my favourite girl,' he'd slurred. Looming over me. Iron grip on my arm. Bulging out through his open plaid shirt. A scapular hugged his beefy neck, and greasy black hair flopped into grey flint eyes. 'Come 'ere an' give yer ole uncle a kiss.'

Chest pounding, I twisted away from his grasp and kicked him as hard as I could in the balls. He clutched his crotch; his face contorted in a grimace of agony. I spun to flee but instantly felt pain explode in my scalp, where he'd hauled me back by the hair. His mouth pressed to mine, bruising my lips, forcing them open.

I'll never forget the foul stench from his sour whiskey breath.

Chapter Four

Louisa

1950

Craving release from my memories, I close my eyes and pretend I'm in Granny's quaint pebble dash cottage by the sea. Water tinkles from a stone swan fountain in the middle of the lawn. Six Rhode Island hens strut around the corner, their beaks poking the ground rooting for worms. I take a slice of bread out of my pocket, break it up and toss it to them. They descend upon me in a flurry of excitement. Each hen out for herself. Granny's farmyard houses a gaggle of geese, a cow and a Clydesdale in the paddock out the back. I head to the outhouse, inhale the rich aroma of hay, then sit on a three-legged stool to milk the calm, ever-docile Delilah. Milk sprays into the galvanised bucket, then some minutes later, full to the brim, I scoop up the rich, creamy mixture into a metal cup, bringing it to my mouth, and guzzling every last drop, bask in its warm, delicious taste.

Gran's bay Clydesdale juts his head out over the low laurel hedge and whinnies. I pick a carrot from the vegetable garden to give him and rub his soft nose as he munches. He nuzzles my shoulder as I stroke his neck, leaning in to soak up his heady horsey scent.

I'm climbing the stairs to my bright primrose bedroom. I've got a writing desk with a lamp on top and an assortment of pretty frocks in my very own wardrobe. An antique ballerina jewellery box sits on my dressing table; a hairbrush, six pieces of multicolour lipstick, a hand mirror and a bottle of perfume.

I sit on the edge of the mattress and apply lipstick to my lips, tracing the actions with my two fingers as if I'm doing it for real. I smack my lips to get even coverage of the rouge and survey myself in my pretend mirror. View my hair as it once was. Long and lustrous with a healthy sheen.

Outside my grandmother's home, the sun is blazing hot, and the birds are singing. Far below my window on the narrow strip of concave beach, waves pound the shore. I head to the beach with my dog Sam. Toss him a ball and watch him splashing into the sea to retrieve it. The sand is warm under my feet, and the sea feels cool and refreshing.

I open my eyes feeling chilled, achy all over and disorientated. The escape and subsequent capture hurtle back into my mind, and I groan in despair. Cover my face. My scalp's still throbbing from the thrashing I'd received earlier. I feel the stickiness of the blood on my fingertips. Get up and pace the basement. Probe the walls for loose cavities or holes but find nothing.

My chest tightens. I sway, dizzy, fling out my hand to the wall for balance. Rest my brow against the cold block, eyes closed. The dizziness subsides, and I slide to the floor. Head lowered on my raised knees, I mumble a quick prayer, begging for forgiveness, the chance to start again and make amends, then tear at my itchy scalp and imagine flakes of dandruff cascading to the floor.

Music floats through the air, faint at first, then increasing pitch.

Step it gaily; on we go
Heel for heel and toe for toe,

Arm in arm and row on row
All for Mairi's wedding.
Over hill ways up and down
Myrtle green and bracken brown,
Past the sheiling through the town
All for sake of Mairi.

I gasp. Suck in my breath and, scrambling to stand, reach out to grasp the vision before me. Of Ellen, my grandmother jigging to that very song. Eyes shut. Humming to the music. Our song. Bony elbows, legs kicked out. She looks much younger. Wisps of grey-blonde hair curl to her shoulders. I watch in delight and wonder as she twirls around the living room, and I glide along the concrete floor in unison. Just like I used to do when I was small.

Lost in the trance, I don't hear the footsteps nor the key fiddling the lock. The vision fades as the door opens, but I continue to dance, oblivious.

'What in the name of God are you doing?' Sister Augusta marches in and grabs me by the ear. 'You're needed in the laundries. Come on, move!'

Mumbling under her breath, 'Dirty bitches,' she drags me out of the basement and up a flight of steps to the main building, rosary beads swinging as she walks. Her fingernails pinch my arm, but I've been pinched so many times I don't feel it anymore. I blink at the light streaming through the grimy windows overhead, hear clanging sounds from the kitchen as we pass, running water from a tap, one of the nuns barking orders.

Pictures of the pope amid a deluge of holy statues leer down at me like gargoyles in the grey, grim corridors. She hustles me into the laundry room where some girls I recognise are slaving, red-faced and tear-stained, mumbling *The Our Father.*

The smell hits me straight away. It's the familiar scent of desperation and despair. The air is foul with it. There are other stenches too. Bleach mingled with sweat and unwashed bodies.

'Get to work,' Augusta barks, prodding me forward.

There are ten of us girls in the steaming room. We're all just puppets, our movements jerky and stiff, dipping shirts, towels and blankets into boiling water, loading sheets into machines, folding them when the cycle is finished, then pressing them using heavy irons to make sure there are no creases. Condensation steams the windows. I'm baking from the heat, fit to pass out, and I've only just started. We don't speak. We barely acknowledge one another. Such is our existence. Each day like the one before and the one before that. We work. We pray. We eat. The nuns watching us like gulls.

Sister Augusta languishes in an armchair at the top of the room. She picks her nose, thumbs through the *Connacht Tribune*, one foot resting on a low stool, throwing an eye over at us every time she turns a page. There's an open box of Cadbury's Dairy Milk chocolates by her side. She plucks a sweet with her sausage fingers and nibbles it slowly, savouring every morsel like it's her last, then licks her fingers. I clench my hand, itching to ram the box down her throat, to watch her fall to the floor, writhing, about to choke, but I avert my eyes and continue my work in case she notices me watching.

Augusta keeps glancing at the clock, checking to see if we will make the deadline. We never see a penny for all our hard work. Nobody cares. Not the government, not the church, not the Social Services, not even our parents. There's nobody to stand up for us. We're forgotten, and there's nothing no one can do about it.

Joan Fitzsimons, a tall willowy girl about my age with long blonde hair, screams suddenly, holding her hand like it's about to fall off. The other inmates stop what they're doing and stare, slow to react, terrified to say anything. I rush to Joan's side.

'I b…burnt my hand.'

She cries, tears streaking her chalk-white cheeks. The red knuckles look sore and will surely blister later.

Augusta slams down her newspaper and, storming over to us, grabs Joan's hand to inspect it.

'Ow, you're hurting me!'

'It'll hurt even more by the time I'm finished with ya, can't see anything wrong with it,' she said, flinging her hand aside. 'Now get on with your work.'

'Sister, please,' Joan said, her hand shaking. 'Help me; it hurts so bad.'

'Put ice on it,' I say, then glance at Augusta. 'If it gets infected, she won't be able to do anything.'

Augusta's face turns mutinous, and I'm starting to regret opening my mouth, but then she growls, 'Come with me to the kitchen.' She yanks Joan out the door by the arm.

The minute she leaves the room, we drop what we're doing and descend upon the open box. Our eyes, feverish with excitement, feast upon Turkish Delight, soft caramel, strawberry mousse, fudge and juicy liquorice. The soft pink chocolate reminds me of summer. I savour the sticky sweetness in my mouth, cram in three more, then hide one for later.

'She's coming back,' squeals Hilda, tiny, waif-like girl, gaping in horror at the empty box.

Chapter Five

Carrie

1976

Agaggle of white, honking geese shuffled across a winding country lane into a farmyard on the left just as a red Massey Ferguson tractor rumbled past to collect trams of hay in a meadow nearby. Wooden chimes rattled from a gnarled oak by the farm entrance, while across the paddocks, a field gate thumped against a concrete post. A blue Ford Cortina turned into the driveway. Max, a black-and-white border collie, bounded up the yard to meet Carrie as she got out of the car, showering her with licks. She crouched to give him a bear-hug before opening the door to the house. She tossed the car keys on the kitchen table and ran to the shed to fetch wood.

Pushing the door shut with her toe, she proceeded to the living room, where she dropped the fuel into a basket beside the stove and began to light the fire. She popped a lasagne into the oven, waited forty minutes, then tucked in. After chucking the carton into the bin, she fed Max, knocked back the rest of her wine, then went to inspect her eye in her bedroom mirror. The swelling had gone down a bit. It should be gone completely by the time she's to meet Jack Hannon on Friday. Brushing away a familiar feeling of unease, she decided not to dwell on the cottage visit any further.

The wind had calmed, weak shafts of sunshine filtered through her curtains, so throwing on black leggings and a grey sweater, she called Max and headed outside for a brisk walk. She was about to turn left as she always did when the cry of a wheeling Shearwater pulled her towards the marina.

She spotted her neighbour. 'Hi Nuala, nice evening.'

God, those bloody blue rollers add decades to the woman and always the same vintage housecoat too.

'Would you whist! Can't ever seem to get these clothes dry what with ducking in and out of showers all day.' Hand on hip, she observed Carrie with a frown. 'What in the name of God did you do to yourself?'

'You shoulda seen the other guy,' Carrie said.

'It's no joke. I remember when my Davey walked into a door, he couldn't see for weeks. Come 'ere an' I tell you. Had a coffee this morning at *Lily's*, you know *Lily's* café on Main Street?'

Carrie sighed and nodded.

'Ice cold it was, and the second one too. Won't be going there again in a hurry. Noonan charged me a fortune to get these dentures replaced,' she said, poking at her tooth. 'You know, they fell out this morning right in the middle of me breakfast. And if that wasn't bad enough, just as I was reaching up to fetch a towel from the press, I got a ladder in me tights, my last good pair. I'm raging.'

Carrie edged away from the wall. The woman could gab for Ireland.

'Adam's home. Did you know?'

She shook her head. 'How is he?' She hadn't clapped eyes on him since the accident, and it rankled that he hadn't bothered to keep in touch in all that time.

'Came back last night. On the hunt for a place in Galway. Told him he could move back here, but he won't hear of it. "The house is too cramped, Mam," he says, and it only meself and his father living here; but, no, nothing's ever good enough. And the price of houses these days, and he just a carpenter, I said –'

'Sorry, but I'd better keep going, Nuala,' Carrie said, looking pointedly up at the bruised clouds. 'I want to get a walk-in before the next shower.'

'Right so. Come 'ere, Davey will fix your fences if you like – and cut those paddocks too. Sure, one would think there was no one living there - the state the place is in!'

Carrie rolled her eyes, then counted to five before replying. 'Thanks, but there's really no need. I can manage. Bye.' Tugging Max on the lead, she hurried away before Nuala could stick her beak out any further, turned right and made for the harbour. She knew Nuala meant well, but sometimes she just got on her nerves.

Despite the evening sunshine, there weren't many about. She was strolling past pea-green boats, pink-painted timber, white, cream, little skiffs and fishing vessels, all moored up on the quayside, when she heard a squeal of laughter, looked up and felt a stab of longing. A young family were tangled together in a game of *Twister* on the deck of *The Merry Maiden*. She kept going, tossed a ball, watched Max dive into the water to get it, grab it and bounce back to her again. Sopping wet, he shook the water from his coat, dropped the ball on the grass and wagged his tail.

And then, all of a sudden, she saw it. *Oh, Jesus.*

Her mind swept back to her seventh birthday when she stood with her father on the deck, one hand on the mast and one in her father's hand. He was steering the boat and let her have a go at the wheel.

The earth tilted. She closed her eyes, and wrapped her arms around herself, desperate to block the tidal wave of grief threatening to topple her over the edge. *Get a grip. You don't want to end up back in the loony bin again.*

'I'd rather you didn't have to face their death alone,' was what the doctor had said.

It had been fifteen months since she'd been a patient in St. Pat's Psychiatric Unit. Memories barged to the surface: Of a cold, wet February morning, heading down the corridor to the bathroom, towel, soap and fresh underwear in her hand. Two female patients in their fifties passing her with vacant expressions. Of the woman with long braids and huge eyes sitting on the window seat nursing a baby doll to her chest. Rocking back and forth as she cooed. The teenager in the corridor examining himself in a mirror, talking to his reflection. How nobody paid any heed to him, not even the stern nurse with straw hair and round spectacles pushing a trolley of medications into the cavernous lounge to songs from Vera Lynn drifting from the kitchen.

The stink of piss and vomit was no stranger to the hospital. It seemed to stick to every crevice no matter how many times the wards and corridors had been doused with disinfectant. She recalled scrubbing her skin so hard she'd drawn blood. The water tepid, almost cold. The food hadn't been great either. Soggy scrambled egg on burnt toast for breakfast. Then sequestering herself as far from the others as possible - in particular, a gawking moustached scruffy patient. Hearing the scrape of his chair and feeling relief that he was leaving, then panic when she saw him loping towards her. Her mouth burning from guzzling the tea down so fast that she leapt out of her seat. Toppling her chair with a bang as it hit the tiles, then making a swift escape. Sitting outside the consultant's room, her foot jigging up and down from nerves. Eyes darting from the large colourful aquarium on the cabinet, then back to his door every few seconds. And thinking Christ sake, hurry up.

The consultancy room looking a lot bigger than she'd imagined. Potted plants trailing to the carpet. A long indigo sofa and three plump matching armchairs. The doctor's deep hypnotic voice.

'Come in, Carrie, close the door.'

That he was tall, dark and shockingly handsome, and she had blushed like a schoolgirl.

'Please take a seat.'

'Tell me,' he said, steepling his hands together, 'How are you feeling?'

'Fine.'

'Let's see –' He peered down at his notes. 'You were admitted on the tenth of February with acute anxiety, six days ago. I believe all you needed was rest and I feel it has done you a power of good.'

Nodding, a whoosh of relief surging through her that they were on the same page.

'But perhaps another three days would ensure complete peace of mind?'

Staring at him incredulously as she sprang to her feet. 'No! I came here of my own volition and intend on leaving that way with or without your consent.'

'Of course. You are free to leave anytime you wish. Please, sit down.'

Complying, ears reddening.

'I'm going to increase the anti-anxiety tablets by 20mg to help you get through this difficult time. Here's a new prescription for one month.'

She folded it and put it in her pocket. They only helped numb the pain for a while, then she was right back where she started. Dulled senses and disconnected from daily living.

'Is there anyone at home you can talk to?'

'No. Just me.'

'Bereavement of this magnitude can trigger a relapse at any time, which could send you right back to where you started.

So, I will make one suggestion,' he said, hands laced behind his head. 'I want you to check in with one of my counselling staff at least once a week to ensure that you are coping okay. Here is her number,' he said, tearing off a sheet from his notepad.

It was a big eye-opener but one she never wanted to experience again. A biting sea breeze ripped through her. Hands in pockets, she headed back home. Deciding on an early night, she filled a hot water bottle to take to bed with her and mulled over the day's events. Tossing a paperback on *A Pictorial History of Magic and the Supernatural* on the four-poster bed, she crossed to the window to draw the curtains, discarded her slippers, and sank her feet into the plush red carpet. She was whipping off her clothes when something fell out of her pocket and landed on the floor. She bent to pick it up and frowned. It was the silver locket from the attic room.

She placed it on her locker, climbed into bed then scanned her messy room ruefully. Cobwebs clung to the globe lightshade that dangled from exposed wooden beams crisscrossing the ceiling. A large, knotted pine wardrobe was crammed into one corner. An assortment of dusty shoes, boots and sandals lined a wooden rack beneath an oval mirror. Various perfumes, hairbrushes, and cosmetics cluttered a square table, and, over by the window, dirty socks poked from a laundry basket.

She tugged the bedspread up to her chin and reached for the locket. Inside was a black and white grainy photo of an elderly lady holding a little girl's hand. The girl looked to be about seven or eight. Carrie turned over the locket and saw an inscription on the base:

To Louisa, with all my love
Granny xxx

Chapter Six

Louisa

1950

'Who scoffed 'em?' Sister Augusta demands, striking her stick against the table. 'Well?'

I flinch, eyes lowered, praying that none of the girls is stupid enough to own up to the theft as we all stand in a line awaiting our fate. I'm rattling my brain to come up with an answer when Sister Bernadette shuffles past the open door, nibbling an eclair. There's a barely audible collective sigh. The tension lifts from my shoulders, and we're ordered back to work.

'Sister Bernadette should get her own sweets and leave mine well alone,' says Augusta grumbling to herself.

She sits down, flicks through *Ireland's Own* and clears phlegm from her throat. While she's engrossed in her reading, I inch over to where Joan is hunched, loading a mammoth-sized washing machine. She pauses what she's doing to tie back her hair with an elastic band, her red face slick with sweat.

'How's the burn?' I whisper.

She glances over at Augusta, then back to me.

'Still sore but not as bad. Did you take her chocolates?'

'We all did,' I grin.

We labour for another thirty minutes,;my hands are cracked and red from the hot sudsy water and daily constant scrubbing with carbolic soap. Work, work, work. Nothing else. Fit to pass out from the scorching steam and stink from the detergent. Each of us lost in thought. About the lives, we used to have. I almost weep in relief when the bell rings, announcing breakfast. I count sixty girls lined up in rows at the long tables, all dressed alike in plain brown threadbare uniforms, in a vast echoing hall, the windows so high you'd need a ladder to get up to them. Most of them I know from slaving in the laundry, but there are others I don't see as much who slog day and night sewing sheets and mending collars in another room further down.

Two are twins, Elsie and Maude, both mute, abandoned by their parents. They are petite, have immaculate porcelain skin, huge hazel eyes. Of the two, I like Elsie more; she's always smiling and is generous with her bear hugs. I gobble the lumpy meal of cold porridge and dried bread. Longing for a cup of tea and not just lukewarm water, when all of a sudden, a mouth-watering aroma wafts through the air. I peek behind me, my eyes widening at the delectable assortment of sizzling sausages, crisp rashers, button mushrooms and black pudding on the nuns' table. I lick my lips, the temptation to grab a plate so strong I have to turn away.

The girl sitting next to me, Hilda, has a noticeable bump. Waif-like with green eyes, she picks at her spots, drawing blood, pushes her bowl aside and stares down at the table. Suddenly, she puts her hand to her mouth, bends over double, clutches her stomach and pukes. The contents of her gut splay out onto the floor, followed instantly by the scraping sound of a chair being pushed back, then the rapid clatter of shoes towards our table. Reverend Mother Emmanuelle bears down on her like a bull as she cowers beside me.

'Clean that up, you ungrateful little wretch,' she snaps.

While Hilda scuttles to the kitchen for a dustpan, I tip her uneaten food into my bowl and ram it back before mass begins. After breakfast, we are marched to a pokey chapel at the rear of the building, heads down, hands clasped together in prayer, not allowed to even look at one another, let alone speak. We're directed to separate pews to discourage conversation and forced to kneel on hard surfaces while the nuns have cushions. The priest, a stout bald man, drones on for what feels like decades. Preaching about God, sin and lust. Often, I feel like passing out. When I'm not thinking about my belly, I'm concocting a plan. A means of escape. And figure that the time to do that is just after mass when the chapel is still open to the outside world.

We file up to the altar for Holy Communion behind a procession of nuns to the chorus of *Ave Maria* sung by members of the public. It's the only occasion we get a glimpse of 'real' people.

I glance across and observe their style of dress; sleek matching suits, long elegant dresses, flared skirts, Celtic brooches and pearl necklaces. My chest tightens in misery.

I feel so ugly. I guess we all do.

My breath quickens. A lad with a round, boyish face, ginger wavy hair, brown trousers, and unbuttoned navy blazer is staring over at me, but I'm now at the top of the queue and can't turn around without the nuns noticing.

Mass drizzles to an end. Father Biggins thanks the choir and bows, then goes into the sacristy to remove his cassock, followed by Elsie at his heels to collect his dirty laundry. The rest of us are herded out the door, back to drudgery. I watch the choir walk out of the foyer one after the other, imagining them going home to a normal, loving family life and stifle a sob of bitterness. At that moment, the boy looks behind him and smiles at me, uplifting my spirits a little. Someone prods him on at the rear for fear that he might catch something just by looking at me. Then, sandwiched between an older couple, he shuffles out of the chapel and vanishes from view.

I glimpse over at the sacristy and notice that Elsie is still in there. Afraid she'll get into trouble, I creep back up the centre aisle and go inside when Emmanuelle's back is turned. My nose twitches at the heady odours wafting from incense candles dotted throughout the room. I glance around. Our Lord peers down on me above a great shiny teak cabinet. A long wide picture of the last supper suspends from a peg in the centre of the wall, while, on the other side, a statue of the Virgin Mary embraces baby Jesus. The priest's cassock hangs on a rack along with six identical others; tucked away in a corner, a kettle and two cups stand on a shelf. But there's no sign of Elsie. Conscious now of Emmanuelle spotting my absence, I head for the door that's closed on the right, thinking that maybe she exited the vestry that way. The carpet swallowing my footsteps, I turn the knob and open it.

I gasp and palm my mouth in shock.

Father Biggins's revolting bare arse is cocked in the air doing unspeakable things to Elsie on a couch. His grunts stop as soon as he registers the interruption, then without a moment's hesitation, wheels around and yanks up his trousers.

'GET OUTTTT,' he roars, fumbling with his belt.

Elsie stares up at me wide-eyed; her rumpled dress is pushed up, exposing red welts across her white thighs. Tears blurring my vision, I burst from the vestry, stumble on the altar steps, and collide headlong into Emmanuelle.

Chapter Seven

Louisa
1950

She grabs my forearms and shakes me. 'Where have you been?!'

'I saw Father Biggins with his pants down doing dirty things to Elsie.'

She slaps me hard across the face. I palm my burning cheek; blink back hot tears.

'I'm…I'm telling the truth.'

'How dare you make up such a vile story,' she screams, rattling me like I'm a rag doll. 'You wicked, wicked heathen. Perhaps a whole day on your knees polishing the chapel floor from top to bottom without any food will put a stop to your filthy lies.'

She hauls me by the ear out of the chapel over to the storage cupboard and points to a shelf where a galvanised bucket, polishing tin, cloth and scrubbing brush are sitting idly by. She waits while I fill it to the top with water and add disinfectant, then supervises me as I drag it back to the chapel.

'I want every bit of this floor spotless by this evening. Sister Claude will supervise you.'

She gives a curt nod to the nun in a navy skirt and cardigan who's just entered the chapel, then exits, her cloak billowing out like *Dracula*.

'Begin on the first aisle,' Claude instructs.

I don't realise how huge the chapel is until I'm forced to clean it on my hands and knees. My punishment for telling the truth. Tears drop onto my nose. I scrape them away angrily. Claude busies herself rearranging flowers at the altar. The sacristy door is closed. I wonder if they're still inside. The image of Father Biggins's bare arse will be imprinted on my mind forever. She waddles to the first pew in the right aisle, and that's when I spot the black cap on the floor under the seat in front. She genuflects, kneels down for several minutes, hands joined in prayer, then sits back and reads her Bible.

My back hurts from having to crouch and scrub the floor. I'm cold, and my joints ache all over. I'm halfway up the centre aisle; my hands reddened from the bleached water when Emmanuelle strolls in. Her eyes look bloodshot. She gives one cursory glance at how much I've done, purses her lips and kicks the bucket over.

'Mop it up!'

Bitch!

Reeking of drink, she struts past me out of the chapel.

I stare aghast at the mounting flood of water, and molten rage welds me to the ground. I want to stuff the cloth into Emmanuelle's mouth until she chokes on it, then drive a stake through her chest and run.

Sister Claude looks up and frowns.

'The floor won't dry itself. Get to work.'

'It wasn't my fault. *I* didn't kick the bucket over.'

Her eyes flash. She puts the Bible down and rolls up her sleeves.

'What did you say?'

I swallow. My courage failing me again.

'Nothing, Sister…'

'Get on with it then!'

I clean up the mess. The cloth stinks, wringing wet by the time half the water has been squeezed out of it back into the bucket. The sweat pours off me from the effort it takes to mop everything up, and my knees are skinned from bending on the rough flagstones. I collapse onto the hard stone, legs splayed out in front of me as a tsunami of pent-up suffering rocks my body, dissecting my emotions into thousands of little jagged pieces that threaten to rip me apart.

A door opens up ahead on the left. I don't hear the footsteps until he is towering over me. I look up and blush. It's the same boy from earlier. I scramble to my feet and press down my dress, conscious of my ragged appearance.

'Forgot my cap.'

'Oh, right. It's over there.'

I hear the snores and glance at Claude. Her head is bowed, her double chin almost touching her chest in a deep sleep. He fetches his cap, and I think that'll be the end of it when he comes over to me and sits down.

'It was just an excuse to see you,' he smiles.

I can't relax. I keep expecting the nun to wake up or Emmanuelle to march back in at any moment.

'I'm Luke. What's your name?' he whispers.

'Louisa.'

Luke looks around him.

'Are you allowed out at all?'

I shake my head, ears reddening. What must he be thinking? Claude shifts in her seat. I hold my breath, but she doesn't wake.

'How many of you are there?'

'About sixty, I guess.'

His clothes are immaculate. Gleaming black shoes, hair combed and clean. I observe his nails and see no dirt; there are no callouses on his hands either. My throat thickens. This boy comes from a proper home, something I'd give my right arm for.

'Those people you're with – they your parents?'

'Yeah, and my little brother.'

Claude stirs again.

'You have to go. If she sees me talking to you, I will get into big trouble.'

He stands.

'You're real pretty.'

I can feel my face turning red. No one's ever told me that before.

'Can I see you again?'

My heart beats fast. I like him. He has kind eyes.

I smile. 'Yeah – that would be great.'

Luke leaves just as Claude grunts awake.

I can hardly stand up. I'm so tired and weak from hunger. Dinnertime has passed me by. Sister Bernadette replaces Claude. Pots clatter in the kitchen. I hear the patter of footsteps as the girls return to the laundry. At the end of the last aisle, I hear the sacristy door open. Father Biggins stares down at me contemptuously, then stomps out by the same side exit. I wonder if Elsie is still inside but decide to say nothing, head bent polishing the floor. Just seconds after Biggins, Elsie emerges, spots of red flushing her cheeks. Sister Bernadette pays her no heed as she descends through the chapel, clutching a laundry bag in her left hand.

'Elsie?'

She doesn't turn but plods past me out the door.

Choking back a sob, I fire the brush into the bucket, where it makes a loud splash, vowing that when I escape, I will tell the media and anyone who will listen everything that goes on here. Feeling dizzy, I stagger to my feet. I cannot do any more. I need to rest. I need food.

Sister Bernadette pins me with her scrutiny, throws down her embroidery with a vexed sigh, then accompanies me to the kitchen to get the leftovers. I'm so hungry I don't care what I eat. The bread smells wonderful. I stuff down almost an entire loaf. Even the pork dripping is manna to my taste buds. She locks the kitchen.

'You did good work today. Go to bed before Reverend Mother finds something else for you to do.'

I look at her in surprise.

'Don't stand there gawping like a goldfish. Go on, before I change my mind.'

'Yes, Sister, thank you, Sister.'

I flee down the dimly lit corridor for fear of meeting the witch, but I needn't have worried. The Reverend Mother has other things on her mind and doesn't even see me. She's supporting poor Mary, whose face is crumpled in pain, her tummy swollen like a hot-air balloon, guiding her by the elbow out the door to the waiting ambulance that will take her to the hospital. Poor Mary, I hope she'll be okay.

'For goodness sake, relax, girl,' Emmanuelle snapped. 'It'll be all over soon. Crying won't help the baby one jot.'

Chapter Eight

Carrie

1976

Friday morning rolled around. Carrie left the office at nine thirty and drove to the Connemara cottage. She had styled her long brown hair into a French plait, diamond stud earrings, a turquoise trouser suit and matching heels completing her look. Black clouds dominated the skyline, and the air was pregnant with more rain to come. All of a sudden, hailstones pummelled the roof of her Ford. She shook her head. *Jesus! Irish weather is just so unpredictable; one never knows what to expect.*

Pulling up outside the house next to a green Land Rover, she waited for the deluge to pass before getting out of the car. Jack joined her at the doorstep, looking dapper in a smart burgundy leather jacket, black turtleneck and mustard seamless trousers, his dark brown hair tied back.

'We meet again. I see your eye is looking better - sorry again about that.'

'Yes, the bruise has almost disappeared,' she said, shaking his hand self-consciously.

'Bet you weren't banking on seeing me this soon!'

'No, I wasn't,' she admitted, unlocking the cottage door.

'I have some connections with this place, you see,' he said, stepping across the threshold, 'and when I saw it was on the market again, I couldn't believe it.'

She turned on the light.

'As you can see, the living room needs a lot of work.'

He nodded, followed her through to the kitchen and gazed around him.

'You know, there's scope here for a much bigger space. I could knock this partition and make it all-in-one.'

'Good idea – I was going to recommend you do that. Would you like to see the upstairs now?'

'Sure. Lead the way.'

She could feel her heart thumping louder with each step up the stairway. Standing aside to let Jack go through each room, she listened for odd sounds, but heard nothing. Her hands shook so much she had to stuff them in her pocket.

Stop being ridiculous, there's nothing to worry about.

As it turned out, everything was normal. Jack was enthralled by the cottage and said he would buy it. He loved the bedrooms, outlining all the plans he was going to make. His enthusiasm was infectious, and by the time they went back down, Carrie had recovered her usual form and was giving him tips on how to improve the house, including installing a skylight in the kitchen. She finished the viewing by showing him the outbuildings and the land, which included its own well, and finally, the garden, before they started to walk back to their cars.

'What business are you in, Jack?'

'I'm an artist.'

'Oh. What kind of art?'

'Come to my gallery sometime and see for yourself. Here's my card.'

'Thank you, maybe I will.'

'Actually, I'm having an open exhibition on Sunday if you're around?'

'I could be.'

'The address is on the back of the card. You're more than welcome.'

He looked back at the cottage and gave a sigh of contentment.

'I can't believe this house is going to be mine at long last. Thank you for the tour,' he said, sliding behind the wheel. 'I'll swing by during the week to sign the papers.'

'Perfect. Goodbye, Jack.'

She trailed him for three miles, then branched right for Clifden feeling like a weight had been lifted, relieved that he didn't ask about the attic. She took out Jack's card to check the address, noting that the gallery was in Salthill, not too far away.

There was a mountain of paperwork piling up on her desk when she got back. Tom had taken the afternoon off, leaving it to her to finish the filing. Flinging her bag on the floor, she pulled out a chair and knuckled down to sorting through the load, then opened a folder labelled 'Connemara Cottage' and added her assessment report to the file. Winding an elastic band around the folder, she pulled out the drawer and went to drop it in when one of the photographs slipped out of its plastic pocket.

Carrie picked it up and frowned. *I didn't take any picture of the attic – yet here it is.* She squinted. *What is that?* Turning on the desk light, she rummaged in the drawer for a magnifying glass, peered at the image again, and drew a shuddering breath. A sickening sensation formed in the pit of her stomach as she registered a faint shadow of a girl holding a ball in her hand, staring straight at the camera. Her heart thumped, transfixed by the image she held her breath, unable to tear her eyes away until the sound of a noisy engine passing the window broke the spell. She gazed up at the clock and took a deep breath. Closed her eyes and looked again, this time seeing nothing.

Vexed at her overactive imagination, she shoved the photograph back into the folder, tackled the next file and kept slogging through the load until only three remained to be catalogued. Then made herself a coffee, nicked one of Tom's digestives and took out the photograph again. Rubbing her eyes awake, she scrutinised the spot where she thought she had seen the apparition.

'Could I have imagined it?'

'Talking to yourself again.'

She jolted, hand to her heart.

'Hannah! How did you get in?'

Twenty-six-year-old Hannah was her cousin and close friend since childhood, with only three months between their birthdays. Inseparable as kids, they did almost everything together.

'I rang earlier, but the phone was engaged. Anyway, the door was open,' she said, peeling off her fleece jacket.

'What's wrong? You're like a sheet.'

'Look at this and tell me what you see.'

'I will if there's a coffee going?'

'I'll make you some.'

Hannah's short-cropped russet hair glistened with raindrops as she inspected the photograph.

'Here's your coffee.'

She took a sip, pulling a face. 'No sugar.'

'Oh, I forgot, sorry,' passing her a bowl.

Dropping in six cubes, she stirred the coffee.

'So, what am I meant to be looking for here?'

'Just anything unusual.'

'Stop pacing. You're making me dizzy.'

Hannah threw the photograph aside.

'That's the ugliest photo you've ever taken, you know. There's nothing here but a hideous bed, a locker and a shelf.'

'Are you sure? Look again,' handing her the magnifying glass.

'I don't have to. I've seen it already. Look, Car, you're just tired and overworked – that's all.'

She handed her back the photo. Carrie studied it again, concentrating hard on the entire image but could still see nothing. *Jesus, am I losing my mind – has the medication addled my brain that much?*

'Are you going to tell me what's got you so rattled, what it is you think you're seeing now?'

Carrie dropped the Connemara cottage folder into her briefcase and belted her coat.

'Come on, I'll explain later.'

Chapter Nine

Carrie

1976

They staggered out of Fogarty's pub just before midnight, doubled over in convulsions laughing.

'Oh God, Car, I think I've wet myself.'

Tears of laughter rolled down Carrie's cheeks.

'The look on yer man's face was priceless.'

'No, don't get me started again. You and your bloody ghosts. And he took you seriously.'

Arm in arm, they teetered across the street in four-inch heels and short sequin dresses.

'Aw Car, I thought we were going to the chipper. You know I don't stand a chance of getting inside that door.'

'You'll be fine. Come on. I'm dying for a dance.'

'Dying!!'

More howls of laughter followed; they sobered up at the entrance to the discotheque, where a strapping security man eyeballed their unsteady approach.

'How old are you?'

'She's a gnome.'

The bouncer folded his arms.

'Aw come on, let her in.'

'Look, I've got ID, it's in here somewhere,' she huffed, rummaging through her clutch. 'Got it!' she declared triumphantly, flashing him her license photo.

He squinted at the photo and, after what felt like forever, grunted, 'Go on.'

'Woo-hoo,' they squealed.

They went through to wiggle and jive to flashing disco lights along with about eighty others, and after a good hour of sweating, they found a seat away from the dancefloor where they could talk. Hannah bought a Guinness for herself and Carrie.

'Thanks for getting me in, Car.'

'No prob.' She gulped the pint. 'How's Auntie Tess?'

'Oh, you know Mum, nothing fazes her.'

'I must call in. It's been ages.'

'Best leave it for a while. Hasn't been herself since the stroke – she's rambling a lot lately – but worse than that, the doctor said she could have dementia triggered by the stroke.'

'Poor Tess. That's rough. Must be hard seeing her gradual slide downhill.'

She shrugged. 'She experiences a lapse in memory now and then, but most of the time she's okay. You know, she called me Louisa yesterday.'

Louisa... that rings a bell. 'Probably just a slip of the tongue. Did you ask her who this Louisa was?'

Hannah sipped her drink, then wiped the froth from her upper lip. 'The phone rang, and I didn't get a chance. I told her about my interview for the National Symphony Orchestra; she seemed to remember how important it was to me.'

Carrie smiled. 'Bet she was proud. I always knew you had it in you. I could listen to you play the cello all day.'

'No, you couldn't.'

'Okay, maybe not *all* day, but I envy your talent. I don't know how you do it! I haven't got a musical bone in my body.'

'What can I say – some become lowly musicians, and some go to college to become hotshot auctioneers.'

'Christ Hannah! Have you forgotten how hard I worked while you were out getting pissed? Don't say it just fell into my lap!'

'Sorry, forget I said anything. It's just the drink talking.' She made a face. 'I'm bursting. Back in a tick.'

Carrie watched her wobble to the toilets and scowled. *I thought we were over all that jealousy crap.* She sighed and turned to gaze at couples swaying to Abba's 'Fernando', arms wound about necks, bodies pressed close together. Feeling a sudden pang of loneliness, she thought again about Jack - about reconsidering his invitation.

After another hour of dancing, they collapsed into chairs. A lad of average build in a cowboy ha, swaggered over with a lopsided grin, his boot spurs clinking as he approached.

Oh my God.

Doing her best to keep a straight face, Carrie watched him smooth his brill-creamed hair aside, then hook his hands into his belt loops.

'Lovely ladies – would you like a drink?'

She almost choked on her pint, giggling so much that some of the froth shot up her nose.

His self-assured smile faltered. 'Was it something I said?'

'Sorry,' she gasped, thumping her chest, 'went down the wrong way. Thank you, I'll have a Guinness.'

He looked at Hannah.

'Me too.'

He returned moments later with the drinks as they scooched up on the couch. He was positioning himself next to Hannah when his friend called him.

'Pa, I'm heading off. You coming or what?'

'Now?

'Come on.'

'All right, I'm coming! Sorry, ladies. Another time?'

'Sure. Hey, thanks for the drink,' piped Hannah.

'Thank Christ!' Carrie exclaimed as soon as he'd gone. 'Did he think he was at a fancy-dress party? Not to mention that bloody bog accent. Jesus!'

Hannah snorted; her belly shook from so much laughing, tears streamed down her cheeks.

'Your mascara is running. Here's a tissue.'

'Thanks,' she wiped her eyes. 'Haven't had this much fun in ages.' She observed Carrie and then, after a moment, said, 'You were spooked when I called earlier.'

'What do you mean?'

'You know, the ghostly house,' Hannah said, covering her head with her white cardigan.

Carrie burst out laughing, spilling her drink in the process. 'Oops.' Her face turning serious, she said, 'And hearing voices, do you think I'm going potty?'

'What? Finding it hard to hear you with this loud music.'

'Never mind. I want to go home. I've had enough. You coming?'

Hannah nodded and followed her to the cloakroom, where they retrieved their coats. The stars were out in abundance like twinkling white dots in the sky. Arms linked, they strolled home together. Except for a few stragglers tumbling out of late bars and the odd passing taxi, the street was almost deserted.

'Discos are so overrated. That bloody Abba song keeps going round in my head.' She glanced at Carrie. 'You're quiet. What's wrong? Still mulling over what you saw or thought you saw?'

'I almost lost the run of myself on Wednesday. I went down to the marina.'

'You should have called me, Car.'

'I was okay, honest. It's just that it still feels so raw, you know.'

'God, Carrie, what did you expect? It's only been five minutes since your parents died!'

They turned in the drive to Carrie's house. Max had been sleeping at the front door and galloped up to meet them. Once inside, the kettle on, the fire lit, they curled up on the sofa, facing each other - one on either side. Carried cleared her throat. 'Forgot to mention it earlier, but you know that guy I bumped into during the week?'

'Hmm.'

'His name's Jack. I met him again today; he wanted me to show him the cottage.'

Hannah's eyes widened. 'The *ghost* cottage?'

'The very one.'

'What did you say?'

'I gave him a tour. I had no choice. Tom wasn't available.'

'You didn't show him the attic, did you?'

'He didn't ask. I don't think he even noticed the trap door.'

'At least you don't have to go back there anymore.'

'Amen to that!'

Carrie took the empty mugs over to the sink, gave them a quick rinse, then opened the hot press and brought down blankets from the top shelf. 'Hope these will keep you warm. Gets chilly in here at night, but the fire should last for a few hours.'

'Thanks.' Hannah spread them out on the sofa. She studied a photo frame of Carrie sitting astride a bay horse, a rosette clipped to its ear, her mother's hand on the horse's mane, smiling for the camera. 'You know, you don't look a bit like your mum.'

Carrie glanced at the photo. 'Of course I do. Look, we have the same button nose and dimpled cheeks.'

'Who else has got those eyes? No one I can think of.'

'I'm unique, what can I say. Here's a pillow.'

Hannah stretched out on the couch and pulled the blankets up to her chin. Left arm beneath her head, she asked, 'Seen much of Adam lately?'

'He's been away a lot, just got back yesterday. Looking for a place in West Galway, his mother said.'

'Adam's a good catch. Have you ever thought of –'

Carrie snorted. 'The only thing that Adam's good at catching is a horse's reins. He worked me to the bone, pushing me to my limits.'

'But he was the best trainer in all Ireland though.'

'Yes, he was.' She looked at Hannah. 'He never once gave me a second glance. God knows I was as subtle as a charging elephant at dropping hints.'

'Maybe you need to lay it out on a plate for him. Some guys just can't see what's in front of their noses.'

'Nah, that was ages ago. Water under the bridge.' Carrie yawned. 'Oh, I forgot to ask, are you free Sunday evening?'

'No, sorry, I'm on babysitting duties. Matt's meeting up with some of the lads from work. Did you have something in mind?'

'Jack invited me to see his art gallery exhibition. I'm thinking of going.'

'Oh my God! You like him, don't you?'

'He's all right,' she admitted, blushing.

'What time is it on?'

'Seven.'

'That's early enough. I might be able to wangle my way out of babysitting. Not promising anything though. Listen, I'll head off as soon as I get up, which will probably be early.'

'No prob. Night, Hannah. Hope you sleep okay.'

Chapter Ten

Louisa

1950

Christmas Eve falls on a Sunday this year. We're allowed to finish early in the laundry to help the nuns put up the decorations. And for once, no one is punished for talking out of turn. My mood is uplifted in anticipation of the Christmas festivities and a respite from back-breaking labour. Together, we carry a huge pine tree into the chapel foyer. Joan hauls a refuse sack of gold baubles, red tinsel and Christmas lights up to the altar. We pluck the baubles from the sack and hang them on the tree, the nuns watching us like gulls, ready to swoop in at the first sign of 'trouble'. I haven't seen Elsie since that day in the sacristy and hope that she is all right.

Sister Claude summons me over to help her with the life-sized crib that is being set up next to the baptismal font, along with two other girls, one of whom is Mary. I position the shepherd statuettes and kings beside the manger while another girl winds tinsel around the top. I'm placing Joseph next to his beloved when, all of a sudden, Mary wails at the top of her lungs. She startles me so much I drop Joseph, but the make-shift grass around the crib breaks his fall, and he's still intact. Mary rocks the infant Jesus and continues to howl.

'Stop that! Stop that horrendous screeching this minute!' Claude bellows.

She flings the plaster cast of baby Jesus to the ground as if she's suddenly realised it's just a small sculpture she's holding. We pause what we're doing and stare, stunned, as, with a deafening crack, its head snaps off and rolls to the side.

'I want my baby!' Her dull black fringe poking her puffy eyes. 'Please,' she begs, tugging Claude's sleeve, 'give him back to me.'

My heart is racing. I must do something before Emmanuelle sees her like this. Too late, I hear the door swing open and hit the wall with a bang. Reverend Mother Emmanuelle thunders into the chapel. The clatter of her shoes echoes on the flagstones as she storms over towards Mary.

Just then, my ears start ringing. A strong scent of lemongrass gusts through the air. All of a sudden, great thick, shiny icicles seem to just emerge from the altar, and cleave to the walls and seats. Paralysed by fear, I glance over at the others to gauge their reactions, but they continue to decorate the tree, unaware. A young woman in a sweeping black habit materialises before me, kneels in front of the crib, and blesses herself. Emmanuelle stumbles over her prostrate body just as the woman looks up at me. As her kind eyes mirror pools of sadness, she fades from view after a moment, and the frigid air in the chapel returns once again to normal.

There is no time to consider the apparition. Emmanuelle flings out her arms to stop herself from falling, grabbing the only thing she can lay a hand on, the tree. She shrieks, shielding her face, just as the Christmas tree falls on top of her. Claude and Bernadette rush to her side.

'Don't just stand there gawping,' Sister Bernadette yells, 'go fetch a doctor.'

'I don't need a doctor,' Emmanuelle snaps.

She staggers to her feet and brushes pine needles from her robe, eyeballing each of us in turn.

'Which one of you little bitches tripped me?'

'But it was an accident, Reverend Mother,' says Joan.

'No, it was no accident.'

She turns to Mary, springs towards her and pokes her in the chest.

'It was you, wasn't it? All that screeching - had to be you.'

Mary balls her fists. Sparks of anger and defiance shooting from her eyes. Her mouth wobbles.

'Yes, it was me.'

'No, Mary!' I cry.

Emmanuelle wallops Mary so hard across the mouth she cuts her lip and Mary falls to the floor, but the nun isn't finished with her. She hauls her up by her hair and drags her out of the chapel. We all stand and stare in shock. Why did she take the blame? Hot tears scald my eyelids. I'm disgusted with myself for letting it happen. But what could I have said? You tripped over a ghost!

I hate this place. I hate this place.

'Finish decorating the tree,' Claude barks. 'I want this chapel spotless before mass tomorrow.'

'Yes, Sister,' we chorus.

We stand the tree upright and rush to finish decorating. Augusta shuffles in with a naked doll and thrusts it into Claude's pudgy hands.

'For the crib,' she pants, tottering out again.

A bell gongs in the convent announcing dinner. We finish what we're doing and walk in single file to the hall, heads down, subdued, worrying about what could have happened to Mary.

As we're taking our seats, she walks in. I look up, startled, not expecting to see her so soon. She doesn't have a scratch. Only her lip is bleeding. She pulls out a chair beside me and sits down. We drone Grace before Meals collectively and await our usual pork dripping. But because it's Christmas, Cook gives us portions of chicken, a potato, sweet tea, and brown bread with butter on it.

After I've eaten, I whisper to Mary, 'What did she do to you?'

'She would have thrashed me if my daddy hadn't just come in the door and caught her.' She touches my arm. 'You shoulda seen him, Lou. He whipped the cane out of her hand and snapped it in half.'

'That's the best news I've heard all year.'

'But there's more,' she says in a sing-song voice, 'I'm going home tomorrow. My mammy's coming for me.'

'Oh, that's wonderful, Mary. I'm over the moon for ya.'

I hug her, thrilled that at least one of us will leave this hellhole and have a happy ever after. But I'm really wishing it was me.

Chapter Eleven

Louisa

1950

Mary has transformed overnight. Her cheeks are rosy, her hair looks clean and combed, she has a dreamy look in her eyes, and she hums as she walks. She tells me because she has to pack her things to get ready for leaving the convent, she won't be able to attend mass. It's my turn to do the wash-up after breakfast. I soak the dishes in sudsy water, my mind in faraway places, while Joan dries and stacks them on the shelves in the press. Augusta calls us out of the kitchen and hands us a frock each. I stare at it in wonder, like it's an alien. Mine is long, velvety soft and light blue, with white flowers sprinkled throughout and has a lace collar. She gives Joan and the others a green one that doesn't look as nice.

'This is only for Christmas, mind. Go, put them on.'

I hold the dress up to my nose and breathe in its spring cotton freshness, then slip it on. It pinches under the arms, but the length fits okay. I pretend that I'm going to a dance and do a twirl in front of the towering glass cabinet outside Emmanuelle's office. Then I pause to frown at my reflection no pretty dress can disguise: my dull, red-rimmed eyes, ragged curls, and sick complexion.

At the sound of the second gong, I wipe my eyes and hurry down to the chapel to take my place along the first aisle. The door opens, and the choir press inside. I crane my neck to see if Luke is among them and spot him standing next to his parents and younger brother. The choir commences, and I wait for Father Biggins's appearance. Only it's not him but a different priest.

I'm rattling my brain to engineer an opportunity in which I can meet Luke when, suddenly, I hear a baby cry behind me. I stiffen. My hand involuntarily cups my stomach, rendering me immobile for several moments as my mind hurtles back to that morning, 16 August, when my little girl was wrenched from my arms.

I'm nursing my beautiful bonny angel. Cooing to her as she suckles. Stroking her soft downy skin. Marvelling at the miracle that I've created. She grabs my little finger, and I smile. But it's a smile of heartache. I smooth back a brown curl from her brow and commit her tiny red, dimpled face to memory; her olive-green eyes, cute button nose, how she weighs six pounds, eight ounces. I can't bear it. I can't let them take my baby. I have to get out of here. I don't care if my parents don't want me. I will take her somewhere else. Somewhere far, somewhere safe where no one can bother us.

Adrenalin pumps through my veins in the realisation that I can do this. The urgency to escape is so overwhelming it almost paralyzes me. I must get moving now before the nuns return. I look down and see my baby is sleeping. I extricate her gently from my breast and place her on the bed. I hunt frantically for my clothes, but then, too late, I hear the curtain rail being pushed open around my cubicle.

My heart pounds impossibly hard. It's the Reverend Mother, and she's with a stranger. A tall posh lady in a long teal gabardine, with matching hat and gloves, regards me warily. I lunge for my child. Clasp her tight to my chest. Grit my teeth.

'She is *my* baby. I won't let you take her.'

Emmanuelle turns to the woman.

'Would you mind waiting outside for a moment?'

'Of course.'

'See this form,' she says, brandishing a sheet in front of my face, 'here is your signature giving your consent to put this child up for adoption.'

'No! You're lying. I would never do that.'

My world collapses around me. I can't breathe. Nurses move about in slow motion. Sounds seem far away. The only thing that's real is the scent of baby powder, the thud of her heartbeat, her soft pudgy skin and the warmth of the little life huddled up to me. As if sensing the tension in my grip, the baby squirms and starts crying. Emmanuelle picks that moment to reach over and snatch her from my arms.

'Pull yourself together,' she snaps, rocking her back to sleep. 'She is going to a good home. Better than what you could ever have hoped to give her.'

I am numb. Wrung out, I stare into space. The curtain twitches aside, and the stranger comes in. Emmanuelle hands her my child. She glances cautiously at me. I shoot daggers at her with my eyes. She flinches. I turn away and, hands trembling, gather my things.

'I promise we'll take good care of her.'

My eyes blur. The pain in my chest so immense, that for a moment, it renders me speechless.

'What did you name her?'

I choke back a sob but don't turn.
'I call her Carrie.'

Mary and I both had babies stolen from us. How many more girls have to experience the same cruel injustice in this soul-destroying place? With clenched hands, I clutch the seat in front until my knuckles turn white; I promise myself that when I get out of here, I will find my daughter and protect her from all the badness in this world if it's the last thing I do. Then, I look to where Luke is sitting up ahead, my ticket to freedom.

Chapter Twelve

Carrie
1976

The phone blared from the hall, waking Carrie up. Rubbing the sleep out of her eyes, she looked at the clock. 'Shit, it's midday, can't believe I slept in again,' she said, running downstairs to answer it.

'Hello.'

'Did I get you out of bed?' Hannah asked.

'Not at all. I've been up ages.'

'Listen, I won't be able to make it this evening. Matt refused to be manipulated.'

'It's okay.' Carrie yawned into the phone. 'I'm bushed. Might give it a miss anyway.'

'No. You won't. You've been single far too long, girl. You've got to get out there and play the field before you shrivel up like an old prune with just cats for company.'

'I don't have any cats.' She heard shouting in the background.

'Have to go; my two are tearing strips off one another.'

'Should I place a bet?' Carrie asked, listening as the children argued in the background.

'Ha, ha, very funny. Hey, tell me how it goes. I want every detail. And don't forget my cookery class this Thursday.'

'Yes, Teach. Bye.'

After a long hot bath soaked in Radox, she padded into the kitchen, threw pedigree nuts into a bowl for Max and made herself some toast and coffee. The alarm pinged on the radio, a reminder to take her medicine, but when she tipped open the jar it was empty. She blew a disgruntled sigh. Another trip to the doctor. She'd been taking anti-depressants for as long as she could remember. Her mother's idea to repress all the bad dreams and unwanted hallucinations she'd been having. Lately, however, she had grown to realise she had become a shadow of her former self; old friends claiming she was no fun. The pills stunting her personality to the point she was unable to form a deep connection with anyone anymore. She had become too dependent on them, resolute in the belief that they were helping her and that she couldn't live without them. And God, always bloody tired too.

That ends now.

She was tossing the empty pill jar in the bin when the doorbell rang. Max started barking, wagging his tail. Putting the mug on the table, she went to open the door.

'Thought there was nobody in. I was just about to go.'

'Morning, Adam, what can I do for you?'

He'd grown a beard since she'd last seen him. His steel cap grey boots were smudged white from cement.

'Mum asked me to give you this.'

He handed her a small tub of purple Tulips.

'For the grave,' he added, putting his hands into his khaki pants.

'Oh, that's a lovely, kind thought, thank you. Are you coming in?'

'No, better not…another time.'

'Tell Nuala I said thanks.'

He started to turn away, then said, 'How have you been?'

She smiled, grateful that he asked. 'I'm getting there, day by day.'

'Good to hear.' He cleared his throat. 'Bye, Carrie.'

'Bye, Adam,' she replied faintly, went to shut the door, then remembered something. 'Have you managed to find anyone else to train?'

'I'm working on it.'

'I miss competing,' she murmured, sighing wistfully.

'It's not too late, Carrie – you're still a great horse rider.'

'Maybe, I was once.'

'Well…better go. See ya 'round.'

At half past six, she threw on a short-sleeved red printed dress, cardigan and flat shoes, raked a brush through her long hair, applied some lipstick and hopped into the car. Traffic was light, and she made it in good time. Soothed by lilting waves and a fresh breeze that ruffled her hair, she strode up to the art gallery. She had never been to this gallery before and was struck by how bright and airy it was; the coral-coated walls, gleaming wooden floors and domed glass ceiling that revealed a vast azure sky beyond.

People, young and old, milled about, a drink in their hands, laughing and talking. She felt glad she spruced up for the occasion as everyone here was smartly dressed, and she didn't feel out of place. She craned her neck over the numerous heads to catch a glimpse of the host, but there were too many crowds, so she concentrated instead on his paintings.

They were really good. Landscapes depicting various mythical creatures dominated one entire section of the exhibition. Moving along slowly, she studied each one in detail, wondering how much they cost. At another wall she was drawn to a dark seascape, mesmerized by a forlorn naked woman rising from the depths of the water, an infant in her arms.

'You like it?'

She jumped at the deep voice and spun, surprised to see him dressed down for the special occasion in black pants and black shirt sleeves turned up to the elbows, his hair loose to his shoulders.

'They're amazing, Jack. Where did you get your inspiration from?'

'Oh, my love for nature, I guess.' He twisted to take a glass from the tray a passing waiter was holding.

'Have some sherry. There's cheesecake and salted crackers to go with that too.'

'Thank you,' she took a sip and glanced around. 'A lot of people here. Congratulations.'

'Most of them are here for a gawk, nothing more.'

They circled the room. Jack pointed out various paintings in his collection, offering explanations for each one.

'What does this one mean?'

'The woman and infant signify mother nature. The water is the birth canal.'

'And this one?' she said, pointing to another painting.

'What do you think?'

She studied the kaleidoscope of distorted images.

'Haven't the foggiest.'

'Know anything about abstract painting?'

She shook her head, 'Not really'.

'Well, this is it. It can signify chaos, loss, madness. Take your pick.'

He showed her the last paintings on display. By this time, the crowd had dwindled to a few hangers –on, then finally, it was down to just two.

'Thank you for coming, Carrie. I wasn't sure you would.'

'I'm glad I came. You have a wonderful talent.'

'Don't suppose you'd like to take a walk with me on the beach after I close up?'

'I'd like that,' she smiled, tucking a rib of hair behind her ear.

'Great, just give me five minutes, and I'll be with you.'

He set the alarm, locked up, and together they headed down the steps to the beach front.

'So, how long have you been an auctioneer?'

'About three years.'

'Do you like it?'

'Yeah, I suppose…'

'That doesn't sound too convincing.'

'I wanted to be an architect but didn't get the points.' She glanced at him sideways. 'How about you – did you always want to be an artist?'

'Ever since I was a kid. My uncle loved to sketch portraits and landscapes; you name it, he could do it. You should have seen his work, Carrie – he brought portraits to life and helped restore the magic of nature.'

'What's his name?'

'Daniel Hannon.' Jack said softly, 'He's got cancer. Anyway, I asked him to teach me how to sketch, and that's how it started. You know that cottage I just bought?'

She nodded.

'That used to be his.'

'Oh, so that's the connection you'd mentioned before.'

'Yep.'

'Do you live in Salthill?'

'I'm renting an apartment here until I move into the cottage. How about you?'

'Born and bred in Clifden.'

'My dad's from there – he knows almost everyone in the parish. What are your folks' names? I could ask him; maybe he might know them?'

Oh God, why did I open my mouth? She knew that she'd have to tell him about her parents' accident sooner or later, assuming they meet each other again, just not now. *Relax. Breathe.* 'Don't think he'd know them; my parents moved away from Clifden a long time ago.' *She lied.*

'Oh, okay.'

Winking stars speckled the night sky one by one. A pigeon plucked a chip out of a discarded snack box, then flew away when they came near. Gentle waves wrinkled the shoreline amid green, maroon and orange canoes that bobbed on the water. She whipped off her shoes so she could feel the sand beneath her toes. A sea breeze lifted the hem of her dress as she stepped into the water, squealing at its icy coldness. Jack did the same, rolled up his trousers and waded in.

'God, it's breathtaking.'

She closed her eyes and tilted her face to the breeze, unaware of his sneaking glances at her long bare legs.

'Don't know about you, but I think something's just bit me,' he shrieked suddenly, dashing out of the water. He looked down and gasped in shock. A reddish-brown crab was clinging onto his big toe as he shook his leg about trying to knock it off.

She laughed and walked onto the beach, then bent and, scooping up a sharp rock, whacked the crab off his foot.

'There.'

Jack peered down at his red, skinned toe and grimaced. 'That's gonna hurt later.'

'You big baby! Try stepping on a jellyfish!'

He grinned and rolled down his trousers. 'Thanks, I owe you one.'

She looked at her watch. It was ten thirty. 'I've got to go; work tomorrow.'

'How about a drink, just as a thank you for *saving* my life?'

She paused to consider, then replied, 'Yeah, all right. Friday night, okay?'

'Friday night's perfect,' he beamed. 'Meet you in Quinn's, say eight o'clock?'

'See you then,' she said, smiling shyly.

Chapter Thirteen

Carrie
1976

Carrie tapped the steering wheel in a staccato beat to *Love, Love Me Do* from the Beatles, feeling uplifted and positive for the first time in ages. A cool sea breeze floated in from the open window. She took a left turn and headed west where up ahead; a massive billboard welcomed families to Renvyle. She was instantly taken back in time. She's five, wearing a sleeveless peach summer frock, and her neck is turning cherry red from sunburn. She's hitting a ball back and forth against a wall with the palm of her hand; a warm sea breeze tickles her bare arms. Gentle waves whoosh in and out, and there are a lot of dog walkers. She pockets the ball, grips her mother's soft hand, and together they skip along the promenade. Her mum's spotted headscarf blows off, and she dives to catch it before it lands in a muddy puddle.

She didn't see the girl until she was standing directly in front of the car. Eyes huge with shock, Carrie slammed on the brakes. The car skidded across the road just as the deafening blare of an oncoming truck bore down upon her. Its flashing lights illuminated the inside of the car. Her heart rate revved to two hundred. She floored the accelerator, and with a screech of tyres, the Ford Cortina nose-dived off the verge into a deep dyke.

The truck kept going.

Blood oozed from a cut in her temple. With shaking fingers, she fumbled with the seat belt only to discover that it was stuck. She went to turn her head to see out onto the road and was blinded by a sudden sharp pain in her neck. Her breath hitched as panic started to set in.

Fuck, it's the middle of the night – what's going to happen to me?

She tugged at the belt again. The same result. The cool breeze had turned cold. Her teeth chattered from bitter draughts that billowed in from the Atlantic. Anxiety curdled in her belly.

What happened to the person on the road? Oh God, please don't say I hit them.

She leaned on the horn. The only thing that seemed to work. Its loudness pierced the still night. Harsh and repetitive. She felt she had been pressing it for hours. She heard at least twenty vehicles in the last hour, each of them travelling at high speed and out of view. All of a sudden, water from the dyke began to gush through a hole beneath the gearbox, swirling around her feet. Her seat belt dug into her skin, and her fingers felt numb.

She tried the horn again, only this time it didn't work at all. She slammed the steering wheel in frustration then tested the lights. And bingo! One still operated. She turned it on full blast. More water pooled around her feet. The clock on the dashboard read midnight. Giving in to exhaustion, her head drooped to her chest.

Then. The sound of an engine. Full headlights. The patter of running footsteps. Frantic running and heavy breathing. The passenger door wrenched open.

'Jesus, Carrie!'

Adam produced a penknife, sawed through the belt and cut her loose. She opened her eyes to see his pale, worried face peering down at her. A wine jacket zipped up to his neck and black trousers.

'Oh, thank God. Are you hurt?'

'My neck.'

'Can you move your head?'

She turned. Palmed her neck. 'Ow.'

'Could be whiplash. You should see a doctor.'

'What about the girl –'

'What girl?'

'I hit someone with my car. You've got to help her!'

'Carrie, there's no one there. See for yourself.'

One glance showed her that the road was indeed empty. Nothing lying on the verge either. She looked back at him in confusion. 'But I saw her. She was right there in front of me.' *Wasn't she?*

'Come on; you've just had a horrible ordeal. I'll take you home.'

Adam called the doctor, who came straight away. He was stooped, wore a hearing aid, and he talked with a lisp. He gave her antiseptic for the cuts, examined her neck and reassured her it was nothing to worry about and that she'd heal in a few days.

Pounding headache. Sore throat. Aches. It was half past six in the morning. She lay back. What happened last night? A girl standing in the middle of the road. The car skidding. Oncoming lights of a truck. A screech of brakes as the Ford derailed into a dyke flooded with water.

Chapter Fourteen

Louisa

1950

Luke glances in my direction but is forced to turn away when his frowning mother tugs his arm, shoving him out the door. Disappointment flares in my chest, and a heavy depression weighs down upon me. But at least we do not have to break our backs slaving in the laundry today. We are led to the darning room after mass like a procession of cows to the milking parlour. The only concession to our lack of freedom is a brown wireless on the windowsill. Sister Augusta switches it on and sits next to Claude, who's warming her hands by the fire. We are ensconced in various threadbare armchairs mending sheets and shirts for the Hardiman Hotel and the parish priest when a speaker comes on the radio and announces the anniversaries.

"Today we celebrate the fifth anniversary of Sister Pauline Sullivan, late of Mullingar and The Sisters of Mercy Convent, Galway."

'May she rest in peace,' Augusta murmurs, blessing herself.

'Sister Sullivan was always pushing for reform,' says Claude loudly, 'Do you remember?'

Augusta nods, 'Sure if it wasn't for the tuberculosis, she'd still be here giving orders.'

The apparition I saw in the chapel, I wonder if was that her. She looks over, sees me earwigging and frowns.

'Mind your business, Hannon and get on with your mending.'

'Sorry, Sister Augusta.'

I avert my eyes and stab the shirt with the needle, imagining it is Augusta's bloated puss.

'Just think,' Claude continues, 'if Sullivan got her way, we'd have no laundries, and then who would do all the work?'

'I agree. A disaster waiting to happen. Now,' Augusta says, patting her knee, 'don't fret yourself; nothing's going to change. Reverend Mother will see to that, I promise you.'

Claude lurches to her feet, face contorted in pain. 'Blinking corns are killing me; I'll be back in a moment.'

I keep dropping stitches, upset by the conversation I'd just overheard. As soon as Claude leaves the room, helped by Augusta, I throw down my needle and turn up the volume on the radio, only to hear the squeaking voice of the Archbishop of Galway giving a spiel about the vital role of the church and the positive spiritual impact it has on its growing community. Then to twist the knife even further, going on to crow about the glowing work carried out by *The Sisters of Mercy Convent* and how so many fallen women in their care have been redeemed and reformed.

'What about us?' I shout at the radio. 'We've done nothing wrong.'

'Shut up, Louisa,' Joan hisses. 'Someone will hear you.'

'I want someone to hear me, Joan, but nobody will listen.'

She glances back at the door – touches my arm. 'Please, just not now.'

I shrug her hand away and go back to my sewing. They're frightened. We're all frightened, but sometimes I can't help feeling they're spineless too. Where's the fight in them? Is Mary the only one who'll stand up for herself?

'Lord bless us and save us. Turn that down, can't hear myself think,' Claude sputters, shuffling back into the room, Augusta at her heels, hobbling in with a walking stick.

'Sorry, Sister Claude,' mumbles Joan.

'Did you hear the news?' Sister Bernadette squeaks, bounding in the door. With a sparkle in her eyes, she fills four glasses up to the top with red wine. 'The Taoiseach has heard about our good work and is coming to visit us.'

'Goodness, gracious,' Claude palms her mouth. 'I don't know what to say.'

My ears prick to attention. This could be my opportunity!

'It seems to be a day for surprises,' beams Emmanuelle, who'd just walked in, 'we just got another bulk order from the Hardiman Hotel.'

'Oh, that's wonderful,' Augusta claps, 'truly wonderful.'

'Here's to the Magdalen Laundries,' Claude sings, raising her glass. 'And to a prosperous future for *The Sisters of Mercy Convent*.'

Emmanuelle leaves the room then breezes in moments later with a plate piled high with sandwiches in one hand and an assortment of Cadbury Roses in the other.

'I've decided to celebrate the hard work you've all done this year with some treats,' she says. 'Come on, girls, tuck in.'

I stare at her in disbelief, my antennae on the alert. Since when has she ever been nice to us? Augusta enters the room with a tray of glasses fizzing with lemonade and sets it down on the table. I can't believe it. Maybe there's some good in them after all.

'Gather around, come on. Don't be shy.' Augusta clucks.

We approach the table, eyes round as saucers marvelling at the quantity of delectable delights ripe for the taking, and we don't even have to feel guilty, but a worm of unease slithers down my spine. If it's too good to be true, that means it usually is. Nevertheless, I'm not one for looking a gift horse in the mouth, so I take a sandwich off the plate.

It's roast beef, and it's delicious.

'Try the turkey,' Joan pipes. 'Tastes just like… home.'

'Beef is my favourite,' another girl squeals.

I take some more before she scoffs them all. The lemonade trickles down my throat, setting my taste buds on fire. It's ice cold but delicious. I guzzle every last drop bursting for a second glass. Claude and Augusta encourage us to sing Christmas carols, and some of the other nuns join in, including Reverend Mother Emmanuelle. She's like a different person. Her eyes are merry as she sings *Come all ye faithful* at the top of her lungs. We glance at one another in astonishment at this whole new side to her. It's the first glimpse I see that things may be about to change for the better.

Visitors arrive to celebrate Christmas Day, but no one comes to see me. I'm in the kitchen scrubbing counters when I hear squeaks of delight, followed by sobbing and pleading to go home. It's cruel of these parents to visit and pretend that everything is still the same, to say that they love and miss their daughters, but then go away and abandon them yet again. It makes it impossible to forgive. It would be better if they didn't come at all.

The girls sniffle at supper. Maude, in particular. She seems to have shrunk in the last few weeks. Her cheeks are gaunt, and a rash has broken out on her hands and face. She's half the girl she was when I met her, and I know it's because of Elsie, her twin, from whom she's never been separated. I wonder again at what happened to her and resolve to ask Sister Bernadette when I can get her alone. We should be getting heaped turkey sandwich rolls on Christmas Day, not leftovers fit for stray dogs. One sausage, one rasher each is our ration. I stab the burnt sausage with venom. My lips are chapped and sting when I eat, but it's all we're going to get, so I force myself to chew. This morning's music and singing and munching tasty sandwiches seems monstrous now. A lifetime ago, that only comes once a year.

Too soon, the day's festivities are over. We kneel on the hard concrete and rattle off our prayers before climbing wearily into bed. Mary, I notice with a frown, is still here. Fully dressed, sitting on the edge of her mattress. Grey suitcase by her feet.

'Are you okay, Mary?' I whisper. 'Did something happen?'

'Thought your ma was bringing you home today?' says Hilda looking healthier after her brief sojourn in hospital.

'She's going home tomorrow,' I snap. 'Right, Mary?'

Mary doesn't reply but clamps her long green scarf and stares off into space. I start to go over to her when I feel Joan's hand on my back and look up. She's shaking her head.

'Leave her be. Her mother's not coming,' she murmurs.

I stare at her in shock. 'What! How do you know?'

'I overheard Augusta and Claude talking about it this morning.'

I glance over at Mary, every bone in my body heartsick and boiling with rage at how her parents have treated her. At the injustice of the system. And at this corrupt government for washing their hands of us. Anguish and grief surge through me for her. I want to hug her tight but know that nothing I do or say will ease her pain, so I go to bed, too wound up to sleep, but exhaustion finally claims me at 3 am.

The chapel bell chimes eight-thirty. I splutter awake on St. Stephen's Day, shivering from the cold with no blanket covering me, to an enraged Reverend Mother and her posse of glaring nuns. She screams for us to get up. We jump to her command and wonder what the hell we've done now to deserve this treatment. Our bodies still warm and lazy after a full weekend of extra food and rest. She shakes a bundle of white sheets in the air, spittle flying from her mouth. A blob lands on my cheek. I rub it away in disgust, shifting from one foot to another in an effort to get the circulation flowing back into my frozen feet.

'See these sheets. Take a good look.' She shoves them under our noses.

I notice the stains and holes, and I squirm.

'While you were all busy merry-making on convent money, this batch was returned this morning with a note.'

She paces in front of us like a sergeant major, a maniacal gleam in her eyes, clenching and unclenching her fists as if longing to strike us.

'Take a guess at what the note said. You, Hilda,' prodding her in the chest.

She looks down at the floor. 'I don't know, Reverend Mother.'

'Well, I'll tell you, shall I?'

"Dear Reverend Mother, we are very disappointed and surprised to have just received dirty, damaged laundry from your convent. We

are cancelling our order and, as of January 1st *will no longer require your services."*

I flinch; her voice is so sharp it would cut through metal.

'Where do you think you're going, Hilda?'

'To the bathroom, Sister.'

'Why don't we all go?'

I gape at her in confusion, then turn away as we are marched by the nuns into the cubicles down the hall. Dread blooms in my gut as I sense that this will not go down well.

'Strip now,' Claude commands.

Hilda pees on the floor.

'Clean that up,' Emmanuelle bellows.

She rips off toilet paper and dabs the puddle. I take off my nightdress until I'm down to my underwear. Conscious of the bruises and scars on my chest, I cross my arms to hide them from view.

'Take off everything,' Augusta yells, pus oozing from angry red sores on her neck.

We look at one another, stricken and don't move.

'No, we won't do it.'

'What did you say?'

Emmanuelle's voice is low and deadly. She's standing so close I could pluck the hairs jutting from her pointy nose.

'No,' I reply, lifting my chin in defiance.

Emitting a guttural roar of outrage, she seizes Augusta's walking stick and strikes my legs. Over and over. The pain blinds me. I buckle but don't fall. Holding back tears, I remove the rest of my clothing, as do the others, and stand naked while she circles us and pokes and prods our bodies. Disgust rears inside me as shame and desperation compete for room in my head. She pinches Joan's plump breast, cackling at the stream of menstruation blood running down her inside leg. Then turns the hose upon us, drenching us in ice cold water. Her lips crimped in disdain, she watches us dance and scream in horror.

Numb from the freezing water, I can't feel my legs. It's as if I've gone into paralytic shock. Blood oozes from a deep gash on my left thigh where she struck me. I hear Mary's cries. A fog descends, muddies my brain, and I black out.

Chapter Fifteen

Louisa

1951

I wake up disorientated in a lather of sweat and shivering. The room is dark. The curtains are drawn, and some-one has placed a cold compress on my forehead. Sister Bernadette snores by my bedside. I move my leg, wince at the sudden pain then drift back into oblivion. When I come to, hours later, my body is aching, my leg throbs, and I'm parched. The door opens. I struggle to sit up, feel a wave of dizziness and fall back against the pillow.

Joan comes in with a tray and sets it on the bed beside me. 'Eat the soup. It's Oxtail.'

Sister Bernadette jerks awake. 'Do as she says. I'll come back and check on you later.'

Joan helps me to sit up. I finish the soup and the bread, then peel back the blanket to look at my leg. It's swollen and wrapped in thick gauze.

'You won't be able to walk on that, let alone stand.'

'What happened?'

'Don't you remember – Emmanuelle lashed you real hard.'

I close my eyes. The memory is seared into my brain.

'No, I mean, what happened afterwards?'

'Sister Bernadette brought you here after you passed out. Emmanuelle was in a tearing mood. She stormed out of the convent and hasn't been seen since. Things are different when she's not around – the nuns don't watch us as much, and we can talk freely – won't last long though she's bound to come back sooner or later.'

'How's Mary and the others?'

'Hilda and Maude are crying all the time; no one has seen Mary.'

'Do you think she ran away?'

Joan shrugged. 'I don't know.'

'Hope she's all right.'

'She'll turn up when she's hungry.'

I look at the empty bowl and sigh. I start to get up when she pushes me back down gently.

'Play it down a little – this is the only rest you're ever going to get. I'll bring you some more later if I can.'

'Thanks.'

'I'd better go; the others will be wondering where I am.'

Every bone in my body throbbing, I snuggle down under the covers, but sleep eludes me. I can't help thinking about the other morning, the way we were treated. Disgust coils in my stomach. Nausea bubbles to the surface. I stumble out of bed and make a run for the bathroom, then puke up the soup. What Emmanuelle and the nuns did was barbaric, and I want them to pay but how?

I get a flashback of Augusta boasting about the Taoiseach's impending visit, and I have my answer. But first, I need to get my strength back if I'm to put my plan into action, so I climb back into bed, close my eyes and try to sleep.

By dinner time I am feeling more rested but starving, so I get dressed and limp down to the dining hall. I pass Emmanuelle's office and overhear two nuns talking.

'Have you heard from her at all, Sister Augusta?'

'No, not yet.'

'I think we stepped over the line this time.'

'Who's going to know?' Claude replies stiffly. 'At least it frightened them so much they won't be careless again.'

I hear a chair being scraped back and hobble to the dining hall, my heart in my mouth. The others are sitting there looking pale and subdued and don't even turn to look up. Hilda's face is blotchy, and tears fill her eyes. I sit next to Joan.

'Thought you were staying in bed,' she hisses.

'It's okay. I feel better now.'

I glance behind me as the nuns, all eleven of them, sit at their long table. One chair is empty. Rain lashes the windows; the single light bulb makes a buzzing sound, and soon we're thrown into darkness. There's a loud gasp from the girls.

'Eat your food; it's just a blown bulb, that's all,' says Claude pushing back her chair.

Sister Bernadette and Claude leave us to go to the basement and replace the bulb. Light envelops us once again; we breathe sighs of relief and continue chewing our small portions of leftover ham and bacon.

The mood at the table is subdued as the girls pick at their meagre portions. Even the nuns are quiet and don't bark orders. My leg doesn't throb as much, but psychologically I feel I'll never be the same again after what happened.

Just as we are clearing away the plates, Emmanuelle strolls in. She crosses the hall to the other nuns and doesn't look at us. Her habit is dark blue, and a long crucifix around her neck swings side to side as she walks. Her cheeks are glowing, and wisps of grey-black hair jut from her wimple. I collect the dirty dishes and head to the kitchen while the other girls scuttle to their dormitory to safety.

Joan scrubs the plates and hands them to me. I dry them with a tea towel and go to stack them on the shelves when I hear them talking. I cock my ear to the door and listen.

'They accepted my offer,' Emmanuelle says, relief colouring her voice.

'Heaven be praised,' Augusta whistles.

'And the girls, what do we tell them?' sounds like Sister Bernadette.

'We tell them nothing. It will teach them a lesson if nothing else.'

'But…'

'I said no, Sister Bernadette. We can't afford to let this happen again. Let's be grateful that they've given us a second chance and leave it at that.'

'The Taoiseach John Costello will be visiting us on January 18th, so we need to prepare.'

'This place will be a hum of activity for his arrival, Sister Augusta, don't fret. Mark my words, I will have everything in order by then.'

Chairs slide back, I hear footsteps, the plate slides from my hands and smashes onto the grubby tiles. I spring from the door expecting a tirade of abuse, but no one comes bothering us.

Joan stoops to help pick up the broken fragments. 'What did you hear?' she whispers.

'Not sure, but I think Emmanuelle made some sort of deal that she doesn't want us to know about.'

'What kind of deal?'

'I don't know. Look, we have more important things to think about. The Taoiseach is coming.'

'So?'

'Don't you see – he might be able to help us.'

Joan stands on her tippy toes and stacks the last dish on the aluminium shelf. She wipes her hands on her apron and turns around. 'They won't let us near him to say anything. You know that.'

'Well, we can sure as hell try.'

'Mind your language, Louisa.'

The door opens. Claude pokes in. 'Finished yet? There's work to be done in the laundry, and we're one body short.'

I look at Joan with a worried frown. Where's Mary?

I limp to the steaming laundry room along with the others. My thigh throbs, but it's not as bad as before. Emmanuelle refuses to look me in the eye as she rushes past. I feel tired and weak and regret coming back so quickly. Joan was right, as usual. I should have spun it out a bit longer. At least I would have got more rest.

Joan irons the sheets while Hilda folds them from her place on the chair. She is quiet and pale and much bigger; I can see the strain on her face. It's boiling in here. There are no air vents, and the heat from the machines makes me fit to pass out. We break at three and are escorted outside for some fresh air. I don't know which is worse, the intense heat or the cold wind biting through our clothes. We are marched out to the back haggard military style, our faces red from icy winter chills. The back of the laundry is surrounded by high walls; all that's missing is the barbed wire to prevent our escape. I lag behind the others, my thigh chafing me as I move. Sister Bernadette patrols the grounds. She is wearing an overcoat and takes out a cigarette, and lights up. I arch my brows in surprise, particularly when one of the girls asks her for a pull, and she agrees.

I rest on a stone and try and embrace the cool fresh air, but my thoughts are on Mary and what could have happened to her. Suddenly I feel a wet nose against my bare leg, give a squeal of fright and glance down to see the most beautiful black puppy. I look up and around for his owner, but of course, there would be no one here at the back of the convent. The puppy licks my hand and jumps onto my lap. I cuddle him, press my face up to his hairy neck. Drink in his scent. I never had a puppy of my own, but Martha, my sister, did. Martha got everything.

The border collie pup followed me home across the field. She was black, white and tan and about ten weeks old, had no collar and no name tag, and I begged my mother and stepfather if I could keep her, but they said no and told me to drown her in the Connemara lakes. Incensed and horrified, I hid the little pup in the barn, slipping her bits of bread and food whenever I could, going out to her at night and sleeping next to her to stop her from howling and alerting my parents. I called her Bella, and for weeks no one knew she existed but me until one evening I bumped into Martha as I was bringing food out to her. I always knew Martha was a daddy's girl and that she had asked for a pet and was still waiting on an answer. She followed me to the barn and saw Bella lying on the straw. Squealing with excitement, she lifted her up and cuddled her, stroked her silky soft coat, then ran back inside. I swore her to secrecy, but Martha could never keep a lid on her emotions, and I knew sooner or later, she would spill the beans. I had no choice but to let my Bella go. Daddy would catch her and drown her if I didn't, so before Martha blabbed, I hunted Bella off down the fields begging her to go as far as she could, away from me and the farm. I even threw stones at her to make her go, the pain ripping me in two at her hurt face.

Chapter Sixteen

Carrie
1976

C arrie was tidying the living room when a book poking out from underneath the cushion fell to the floor. The library book she'd forgotten to return last week. Sitting cross-legged, she skimmed through the chapters hoping to find something that would help and found what she was looking for in the last chapter.

A medium can only channel spiritual energies when the mind is open and fully receptive. In other words, for this to happen, the individual cannot have any barriers or obstructions to sluggish the mind, i.e., medication.

Christ, it was the pills all along!

Feeling bitter at her lot, she put the photograph back into the file and closed her briefcase with the knowledge that this was not going away. Whatever or whoever it was had to be confronted whether she liked it or not. The ghost had to be connected to the Connemara cottage, she reasoned, as that's when it all started. The cuckoo burst out of the cuckoo clock, causing her to jump as it sounded eleven times.

As she hadn't received her replacement car yet, she decided to walk to the local church. Max wagged his tail and started yelping. She debated whether or not to leave him home, then fetched his lead from the hook next to the door. If there was a problem, she could tie him up outside.

Rain glistened on the road from a previous shower, but the sky looked blue and welcoming. Huddled in a long lemon raincoat, she turned left up the narrow winding country lane sloshing through puddles and tractor muck. She trudged up the hill to the quaint parish church overlooking the entire village.

The church, where her parents got married two years before she was born, had cobblestone grounds, an ancient yew tree at the entrance, a community hall squeezed in beside it and a smattering of graves out the back. Though Max was a good collie, she didn't want him running through the graves and barking and scaring off mourners, so she fastened his lead to a rusty ring jutting out of the side of the church and went down to visit their memorial headstone. She hunkered down to pull the weeds recalling the day that had changed her life forever.

Early June. Red, blue, yellow and pink balloons dangled from the trees. A red and white bunting hung across the centre of the living room, congratulating the happy couple on their 30th wedding anniversary. The house exploded with light and laughter. So many people waiting expectantly for their return. Auntie Tess, in the prime of her health, wearing coral chiffon trousers and a flowery top, stood baking apple pies, scones, and chocolate muffins. The delicious aromas wafting through the air were heavenly. Buddy Holly and Elvis Presley belted out poignant songs from the record player. Carrie dashed back and forth in a peach dress setting the table for their arrival. Close neighbours and friends gathered around; Nuala, Dave, Adam, the parish priest, Hannah and her two children and many more crowded into the small house, waiting for them to come home.

Carrie heard a car and spun to the others excitedly standing behind her. 'Hide, quick! They're coming! Someone turn off the lights.'

The house was thrown into darkness just before the car turned in the gate and stopped outside the door. The doorbell rang. Mum must have forgotten her keys *again,* she thought with a smile. Motioning for everyone to be quiet, she opened the door to the loud declaration of surprise from the gang behind; only it wasn't Mum and Dad but two guards.

She stared at them, confused for a moment, then shut the door behind her.

'Miss Gillespie, we are sorry to give you this bad news.'

The other guard placed his hand on her shoulder. 'Your parents drowned in a freak boating accident at one am this morning. They hit a bad storm on their way home, the boat overturned, and they were swept out to sea. We are very sorry for your loss.'

Her parents were lost at sea, their bodies never recovered. A part of her longed to believe that they were still alive and that they'd return someday. She stood up, brushed the dust from her pants and headed into the church.

Father Finnan was dropping mass leaflets into each seat. His belly protruded over his navy seamless trousers. Black hair greyed at the temples; he was wearing a light blue fleece opened to reveal a familiar white dog collar. His face was florid, and he was known to take a tipple or two. Organ music floated through the church. Daffodils, crocuses and tulips brightened up the altar, and sunlight streamed in through the high stained glass windows.

'Father, may I have a word?'

'Carrie, how lovely to see you. Of course, you may. Please join me for a cup of tea in the sacristy.'

'I don't want to take up too much of your time.'

'Not at all. I always have room for my parishioners. Come, this way.'

She followed him across the vestibule, where he showed her into a cramped room to the right of the altar and put on the kettle. Now that she was there with him, she couldn't help cringing at what she was about to say next. *He's going to think I'm barmy.* While he fiddled with the kettle, she gazed around her in interest. It wasn't at all what she expected. There were no holy pictures. The room was stark, linoleum on the floor, a sink, two chairs and a round table in the centre. The kettle hissed to life, rocking on its stand. He brought down two mugs, took the chipped one for himself, then emptied a packet of fig rolls into a plate. He placed a pewter milk jug, spoon and mugs next to the biscuits and sat down.

'Oh, do you take sugar?'

'No, thank you.'

'Nothing like a good cup of tea to start the day. I love this time of year, don't you?'

She nodded and sipped.

He placed his mug on the table, sat back and surveyed her. 'Haven't seen you at mass lately. How have you been?'

'I don't know how to explain this, Father; it sounds ridiculous.'

'Whatever it is, you're clearly troubled – it's written all over your face.'

She told him about the voice, the phantom photograph. She waited, her hands clenched at her sides to see how he would react.

Father Finnan took a deep breath and studied her for a moment. 'And there was no one else with you at the time to vouch for what you saw?'

'No.'

He chewed the last fig roll averting his eyes for a moment. 'You have been under a lot of stress, Carrie, sometimes –'

'I didn't imagine it,' she said coldly and stood up to leave. 'Sorry for wasting your time.'

'Please, sit down. I didn't say I didn't believe you. Put yourself in my shoes; these are questions I have to ask.'

She felt her face flame and sat back down. Sheep bleated outside in the meadow, and a vehicle rumbled past. It was hard to believe that she was even contemplating these bizarre events.

He steepled his hands. 'When did these strange phenomena occur? Can you think of anything that triggered them?'

'It all started in a cottage in Connemara that I was assessing and getting ready for selling - and things just got worse from there.'

'You've experienced something like this before?'

She nodded. 'Yes, when I was much younger. I could see shadows of dead people, feel their anguish.' She paused. Reddening up with embarrassment. 'You must think I'm cracked.'

'If you think you could commune with the deceased, who am I to say otherwise. Just take care who you tell this to, though. Not everyone will react the same way.'

'No one would believe me, you mean.'

'I believe you would have a difficult time convincing people otherwise, yes. Did you tell your parents about this?'

'Yes.'

'I gather from your expression they weren't receptive to the news.'

'No, my mother warned me never to mention it to anyone, and I haven't until now.'

'It must have come as quite a shock to you all the same when the visions first started. I'm having trouble getting my head around it, to be honest.' He paused to reflect, then said, 'However, since the foundation of the Catholic Faith, we have started to embrace more and more new possibilities, and supernatural incidents though rare, have not gone completely beyond the realm of our beliefs. Take our Lord for instance; he was born of the Virgin Mary.' Realising that he was going off on a tangent, he cleared his throat and said, 'Were you ever able to speak to the deceased?'

'I only saw blurred images, visions of people who had passed or wanted to pass on a message to their loved ones. There was never direct communication and much of my experiences came from dreams but nothing as vivid as what I've been experiencing lately.'

'Right, right. Dreams. Now that's something I could understand.' He grew thoughtful. 'In Connemara, you said?'

'Yes.'

'And have you been back to that cottage since?'

'Yes, but everything was normal.'

'What's the name of the townland?'

'Dunas.'

'I see.'

She didn't.

'And then you saw the ghostly image in the photo.'

'Yes, Father. All sounds crazy, I know.'

Someone knocked.

'Come in.'

The door opened, and a wizened grey-haired woman with a pointy nose, and floral headscarf, entered the room. She looked at Carrie. 'Excuse me. The McGinleys are waiting for you, Father.'

He clapped his hand to his forehead. 'Goodness gracious, I completely forgot. Tell them I will be with them presently.'

'They're already waiting ten minutes.'

'Then they won't mind waiting just another few more, will they.?'

Flinching at his thunderous expression, she hastily retreated from the room and shut the door.

'She's a good caretaker, but sometimes she takes her responsibilities too far.'

'I'm sorry, I've taken up too much of your time already. Thank you for listening.' Carrie shoved back her chair and got ready to leave.

'Wait, just a minute.' He pulled out a drawer and, rummaging through it, brought out a faded diary and thumb flicked through a list of contacts. 'Ah, here it is. Take this number down,' he said, handing her a piece of paper. 'I may not have been able to help, but this man might – Father Adrian O'Dea. He was the parish priest of Dunas at that time. If anyone can shed some light, he can.'

'Thank you,' she murmured, folding the paper into her purse. 'This means a lot.'

'God be with you, my dear. I hope this will bring you some peace of mind and some closure.'

Later, at a coffee shop, she searched for Dunas in a phone book. A waitress set a porcelain pot of tea and matching cup with saucer on the table, then fetched her scone and brought it over.

'Thank you.'

Stirring the tea absently, she calculated the distance in her head and took a bite of her fruit scone. It was delicious and warm, with jam in the centre and a slather of cream on top. A bell tingled above the door as another customer entered, and soon the café was full with the tinkle of laughter and undertones of conversation. This was her favourite place. She liked the red and cream chequered tablecloths: the picturesque paintings, the bright coral walls, and the light, airy atmosphere of this quaint café. Rose, the owner, had dimpled cheeks, wore a wide smile, and loved the chat.

She checked her watch. *My replacement car should be ready.* She thanked Rose and headed up the street.

The garage man handed her the keys to a 1971 Volkswagen, hers to keep for a fortnight until her insurance came through and she could get another vehicle. The Beetle interior was spotless; the leather cream upholstery gleamed, and everything smelled spanking new. She was almost afraid to sit in, for fear of creasing the material and dirtying the floor with her shoes. She turned the key, and the engine purred to life. It sounded a lot louder than her own car. She glanced around her sheepishly, but everyone was going about their business.

Removing a road map from her bag, she scanned the area again, then folded it and set off cautiously down the street until she got the hang of the different buttons and gears. At the traffic lights she pressed the brake too hard, shot forward and almost hit her head off the dashboard. Colouring slightly, she eased off on the pedal and inched forward once the lights turned green, paused at the next junction, then took a right into open country.

Feeling more relaxed, she fiddled with the buttons until she found a radio station and hummed along with the Celtic music. Wild, rugged mountains formed a gigantic wall on one side and rolling meadows on the other. It didn't take her long to reach her destination; she arrived within twenty minutes. She drove past quaint, multi-coloured houses lining the roadside on the left, a fountain, grocery shops, a school, and there up ahead on the top of the hill hemmed in by towering conifer shrubs was the church she was looking for.

She parked in a small churchyard, got out and locked the door. This church looked very old but beautiful. There were stained glass windows over the main entrance, the steeple stretched into infinity, and the stone walls looked mottled with age.

There was no one about. Two baskets sat on a round table in the porch, and there were mass leaflets placed neatly beside them. She opened a glass door and walked inside. Her footsteps echoing on the flagstones, she gazed around at the familiar pews and confessional boxes on either side. The scent of incense filled her nostrils as she took in the altar covered with lace trimmings. She looked up at the vaulted ceiling and gasped at the splendidly detailed carvings of Jesus Christ and the exquisite colourful mosaics depicting his life.

'Can I help you?'

'They are truly stunning.'

The woman smiled. A crucifix hung from her neck, and she was dressed from head to toe in black. 'Yes, it is beautiful.'

'I'm looking for Father O'Dea. Is he here?'

'Father O'Dea has been retired years.'

Carrie's face fell.

'But if you come back this afternoon, Father Owens will be here.'

'I really needed to see Father O'Dea, my parish priest Father Finnan said he would be here.'

'Oh, goodness, why didn't you say? Sure, I know Father Finnan well. Come with me,' she said, beckoning Carrie towards a window. 'You see that two-storey across the road?'

Carrie nodded. 'Yes.'

'You'll find Father O'Dea there, no doubt resting by his open fire.'

'Thank you.'

The house lay near the road, and she could see in through the windows from the gate where she stood. A neatly trimmed hedge spanned the length of the wall, and the lawn was cut out front. Ivy trestles climbed to the gable. There was the cheerful melody of birdsong, and Red Admirals flitted in and out through pink roses on either side.

The biggest dog she ever clapped eyes on bounded around the corner, making her run for the gate.

'It's all right, Bess won't harm you.' Father O'Dea was stooped; wrinkles creased his weather-beaten face, and his hair looked snow white. His navy cardigan was buttoned wrong, and his blank pants were streaked with grass stains. He peered at her through bi-focal glasses, one gnarled hand clutching a cane.

'That's a huge dog!'

'You've never seen an Irish Wolfhound then. What can I do for you?'

'My name is Carrie Gillespie; my parish priest Father Finnan said you might be able to help me.'

'How is the old bastard?'

She blinked at him in shock.

He smiled and chuckled. 'Apologies for the bad language. Take no notice. Damien and I go back years. Come on in. I was just making a cup of tea.'

One hand nursing his hip, he hobbled in the door to the smell of woodsmoke and the delicious aromas of baked pies and herbs. The kitchen was dark, flagstone floor, a square mahogany table, open fire with a kettle suspended from a hook. The walls painted a maroon colour added to the darkness, and the ceiling was vaulted. Carrie found it comforting and not garish like many modern kitchens today.

Old shoes with holes and Wellington boots littered the ground. Chewed soft toy rabbits jutted from a dog bed coated in hairs. Geraniums and begonias spilled from clay pots by the door. A large wooden crucifix hung over the kitchen sink. She could see a well-tended garden through the wide window in the centre of the room.

He placed a china pot of tea and a plate of scones on the table. He poured the tea into chipped cups and pushed the scones towards her. 'Help yourself; made them myself.'

'Thank you.'

The scone was mouth-watering and still hot from the oven. She took two.

Father O'Dea sat back, patted his belly in contentment then threw a piece of scone to the dog. He looked at her and said, 'I'm guessing you didn't come here because you heard I'm a great cook?'

Carrie blushed. 'Sorry, no, I didn't, but they were the best scones I've ever tasted.'

'Thank you.'

'Truth is, I don't know where to start; it all sounds so crazy.'

He sat up straight. She'd got his attention. 'Take your time.'

She told him everything from the beginning, finishing with her experience on the road and once again felt her face burn. *What must he be thinking? A total nut – a fruit cake!*

A shadow fell over his face. He pushed back his chair abruptly and stood. 'If what you're saying is true, there's nothing you can do but pray for the poor unfortunate's soul.' He scrubbed his eyes. 'Now, if you'll excuse me, I'm rather tired, and Bess needs her walk.'

She followed him out and thanked him for his time, heard him shut the door behind her and headed across the road to her car, frowning in puzzlement. That was quick, she thought. It was like he couldn't wait to get me out of there!

Chapter Seventeen

Carrie

1976

'Have you seen my keys?'

Carrie looked up from the typewriter at Tom towering over her. His hair was dishevelled as usual; glasses askew, looking like he'd dressed in a hurry; his waistcoat was buttoned wrong, and his trousers were creased.

'They're in the drawer.'

'Claire was just saying she hadn't met up with you in ages. Call over to the house later for a drink; she'd love to see you.'

'I can't, sorry – maybe next week?'

He turned at the door, eyebrows raised. 'Got plans?'

Her face reddened. *Please don't ask me who it is.*

'Anyone I know?'

'Nope. Stop fishing.'

'Me? Wait 'til you hear Claire. Right, have a good one. See you Monday.'

'Bye, Tom.'

The door slammed behind him on the way out. The clock on the wall gonged four just as the gas fire flickered, then died, and the temperature nose-dived. Shivering, Carrie plunged her arms into the sleeves of her woollen cardigan, then pressed the button on the side to get it to light again. But the bottle was empty, so she filled out her schedule for Monday, grabbed her bag and left the office.

A grey overcast sky greeted her when she stepped outside. She spotted Adam in deep conversation with an older woman, a redhead, on the way into a bar. He didn't see her. Quinn's pub was on the other side of the street. A delicious shiver of anticipation thrilled through her at the prospect of her date as she backed out of the car parking space, heading home.

The church door was open, so she decided to do what Father O'Dea said and nipped in on her way home to offer a prayer for the soul of her unknown visitor in the hope that it would give her some peace and leave her alone. She also said a prayer for her parents and felt calm upon leaving the church.

Having fed Max and gobbled up the rest of the chicken curry she had made the evening before, she grabbed a quick shower and then sorted through her wardrobe for something to wear.

She shook her head. *This won't do. I really need to buy some new clothes.* After an hour of trying on jumpsuits, skirts, tops, and dresses, she still couldn't make up her mind. The phone rang.

'Are you excited?'

'I've nothing to wear, Han.'

'You still got that gorgeous peach satin dress from Jamie's wedding?'

Jamie was an old school friend now living in the UK whom she met once a year. 'Doesn't fit anymore.'

There was a pause.

'You still there?'

'I know – the dress you'd on the other night – that was fab.'

'No, that's way too flashy for a pub.'

'Got any other suggestions?'

Carrie sighed. 'I hate dressing up.'

'The mother-in-law has just arrived. Talk tomorrow.'

With only half an hour to go, Carrie had butterflies in her stomach and still no idea of what to wear. She eyed the sequinned dress she'd worn out clubbing with Hannah critically. She clipped her hair back into a chignon, dabbed on a smidgeon of maroon lipstick and slipped into black patent heels.

'Well, Max, whatcha think?' she asked, doing a twirl.

The dog looked up at her for a second, then lowered his head to his paws and sighed.

'My thoughts exactly, but it'll have to do. See ya later, boy,' she said, closing the front door behind her.

She was glad she'd worn a dress as the temperature had soared to 21 degrees, and her skin was beginning to feel flushed from the heat.

Quinn's looked deserted when she pulled into the car-park across the road. Just as she was about to cross, a great lumbering bus passed by, splashing into a crater of a puddle, drenching her dress.

'Oh, Jesus, I'm soaked!'

A ladder of dirt blotted her tights, and her dress was wet across the front. She ran back to the car, heaving and spitting her outrage. Spying an old jumper on the back seat, she cleaned off the dirt and wiped her dress, debating whether or not to call it a day and not show up. She sat in the car with the full blast of heat turned on for at least ten minutes. Her tights didn't look too bad, a bit muddy, but nothing you would see in the dark, and her dress had almost dried. Carefully scanning the road in both directions, she scooted across and entered the pub.

It was a typical traditional Irish publican house; the bar to one side, a fire lit in the centre, leather stools, a black flag-stone floor, mahogany tables, a snug, wooden wall panelling and beamed ceiling. No sign of Jack.

Two gentlemen staring into pints of Guinness propped up the bar. The younger of the two, round and moustached, gawked at her openly while his bleary-eyed companion eyed her up and down, smirking.

Wishing she had brought her coat, she took a seat at the other side, in view of the door.

'Hello, Carrie. Haven't seen you around in a while. How are things?' The bald bartender wore a white shirt rolled up to the elbows, moon-shaped glasses that had slid halfway down the bridge of his bent nose, and he had a pudgy friendly face.

'Up the walls, Kevin. I've been looking forward to this drink all day. Did Sile have the baby yet?'

'Tomorrow, please God.'

'It's your first grandchild. You must be so excited.'

'You should see my wife – you'd swear she was having the baby herself,' he said, rolling his eyes and chuckling. 'What are you having?'

'Just a beer, thanks.'

'One beer coming up.' He finished polishing the glasses then raised the volume to a match being played out on the telly.

The door opened, and Carrie glanced up. A group of six young lads staggered in, talking and laughing loudly. One had his arm around a stick-thin brunette in a mini who glanced over at Carrie, sniggering into her hand. More people came in, and soon the bar grew crowded and full of smoke. She threw an eye at the clock and was not happy to see he was over a half hour late. *Face it, girl, he's stood you up.*

'Can I get you a drink?'

It was the man with the tweed cap. He was standing too close; she could smell his breath and his bad body odour too.

'I'm just leaving,' she said hurriedly, pushing back her stool. She burst out onto the street, chest heaving with indignation. *I can't believe he stood me up.*

Back home she whipped off the dress, bunched it into a knot and tossed it into the laundry basket. She took Max for a short walk towards the village, then headed home and wriggled into a pair of pyjamas.

I could be at Tom's house now, drinking wine and having a laugh, not sitting here miserable, stuffing my face with ice cream.

TV was crap, with nothing on but a wildlife documentary. She got up to put on a video when Max rose from the floor and started to growl. He ran to the door and pawed the wood.

'What is it, Maxie boy?'

Rain pummelled the windows. She heard a thump on the door and jumped. Max started barking.

'Who is it?'

'Jack. Please let me in. I'm drowning out here!'

She unbolted the door and rushed him inside. His sopping hair was plastered to his brow, and his blue denim shirt clung to him. A puddle started to form on the floor. 'How long have you been standing out there?'

'Ten minutes, give or take. I thought nobody was home. This is for you.'

She looked at the sagging daisies in his hand and couldn't help thinking he had just picked them from the side of the road but not to appear ungracious, thanked him and put them in a tall glass.

He snuffled into a handkerchief, then stuffed the wet rag into his pocket, rubbing his arms while he gazed around him.

Max circled him warily, sniffing his legs. Jack bent to pat his head, and the dog backed away with a growl. He sneezed four times in succession.

'Wait there,' Carrie said. She fetched pants, a shirt, and a jumper from her father's wardrobe. 'Put these on, they were my dad's.'

'Thank you.'

Turning away to let him get dressed in private, she filled the kettle at the sink, plugged it in to boil, then put together ham and cheese sandwiches, all the while wondering what the hell he was doing outside her house and how did he know where to find her? When she turned around, he had on brown corduroy pants with a chequered shirt. She smiled and wondered if her father would approve. 'Suits you,' she said, bringing the plate of sandwiches over to the table. 'Sit down.'

'These sandwiches are good. Haven't eaten anything all day.'

Tucking her legs under her, she waited until he was finished before asking. 'So, spill, Hannon.'

'Just so you know, I didn't forget our meeting tonight.'

Ouch! Meeting now, was it? 'What happened to you, then?'

'I had a row with my dad over one of my paintings. You see, I owe him quite a bit of money and was planning to pay it back this week, only the buyer reneged on the deal and pulled out. When I told him that it would take a little longer to pay him back, he flew off the handle, kicked the side of my car and damaged the door.' Anger flashed in his eyes. 'To top it all off, the car wouldn't start, and I had no way of contacting you. I had to wait for mum to come home so I could borrow her car and - so here I am.'

'You still haven't told me how you knew where I lived?'

'Oh, that was the easy part. I bumped into Tom, your business partner at the store, he knew who I was, and I went from there.'

Twenty questions on Monday so.

'I truly am sorry.'

'Never mind, you're here now.'

Max continued to size him up and hadn't stepped an inch nearer.

'Come here, boy,' he called, slapping his thighs.

Max wandered over to the table and rested his head on Carrie's feet. 'He's not usually unfriendly,' she murmured, ruffling the dog's ears.

He glanced up, his gaze travelling over her terry muslin robe, pink cotton pyjamas. 'I like your pyjamas; they look snug.'

She blushed beetroot and looked away, got up but stumbled over the dog at her feet right into his arms.

He held her tight to prevent her from scurrying away, his eyes twinkling in amusement at her embarrassment. He lowered his head to kiss her on the mouth. Within a few seconds, Max started to growl, then howled at the top of his lungs.

'What is it, boy?'

'Leave him.'

Max continued to stare at a point in the wall directly above them. He started keening softly, his eyes white with fear, then pawed at a spot only he could see. His body shaking, he curled around Carrie's legs, whimpering and growling at the same time.

Jack gave a goofy grin and reached out to pull her into his arms again when suddenly there was a knock on the door and loud screeching. 'Oh, for the love of God,' he exclaimed, raking his hand through his hair. 'What now?'

Carrie groaned.

She opened the door, and Hannah tumbled inside. 'What took you so long?' She saw Jack. 'Oh, didn't know you had visitors, sorry.' She strode across the room and pumped his hand. 'I'm Hannah, this one's cousin. Great to *finally* meet you.'

He grinned as Carrie squirmed. 'I should go.'

'You might want to change first,' Carrie said.

'Oh,' he said, glancing sheepishly down at her father's old corduroys.

Hannah sized him up, her brows rising at what he was wearing. 'Aren't they your -?'

Carrie felt her cheeks redden again. 'He got wet, so I gave him a loan of Dad's.' Taking the clothes off the radiator, she handed them to Jack. 'They're dry.'

'Thanks, I'll put them on in the living room.'

As soon as the door closed, Hannah rounded on Carrie, her eyes sparkling. 'He's quite a dish. How long has he been here?'

'Just a little while, that's all.'

Jack emerged from the living room. 'Thanks for the change of clothes. These are nice and dry now. By the way, I'm having a house party Friday week to celebrate my new home. You both should come.'

'Terrific,' Hannah beamed, linking arms with Carrie, 'we'll be there.'

Jack stalled at the door, shuffling his feet. 'Right, then, I guess I'll be off.'

'Here, take my umbrella,' Carrie said.

'Cheers. Bye.'

Chapter Eighteen

Louisa

1951

At the sight of a hare, the pup leaps from my lap and darts across the overgrown patch of grass, wriggling under a hole beneath the wall until all I can see is his butty tail. I hear him yelping in excitement and imagine the hare bolting across the field to safety. I hope he doesn't catch him. I don't like animals getting killed.

Sister Bernadette stomps out the cigarette with her shoe and turns to head inside. I run up to her.

'Has Mary gone home, sister?'

'Yes, her parents came for her when you were sick.'

I notice she doesn't look me in the face and figure that maybe it's because she feels uncomfortable at the reminder. A drizzle cloaks the landscape in perpetual gloom as we shuffle back inside to complete our tasks for the day.

Joan and I are on wash-up duty again this evening. Sister Claude leaves us to our own devices and swings the door shut behind her.

'Isn't it great that Mary has gone home?'

Joan stops what she's doing and looks at me. 'She couldn't be. Her case is still here, and so are all of her things.'

'Maybe they left in a hurry, and she didn't get time to bring them.'

She shrugs. 'I don't know. Mary would never leave without saying goodbye; it's just not like her.'

'You hear the Taoiseach's coming next week?'

'Augusta promised us extra rations if we behave,' she snorts.

'I'm going to tell him everything,' I say, putting the plates on the shelf.

'How are you going to do that? Emmanuelle will be watching you.'

I frown. Why does Joan have to be so negative all the time? 'I don't know, but I'll think of something.'

Saucepans mount up on the draining board. Joan twists the tap, but no water comes out. 'We're out of water again. Better go down to the boiler room to check if the pump is still working.'

'I'll go.'

It seems like a lifetime ago since Emmanuelle had dragged me down here and locked me into the basement. My footsteps echo on the stone steps. I go to open the door to discover that it's already unlocked. The smell hits me straight away. It's so strong I have to hold my breath and block my nose with my sleeve. I push open the door expecting to see the rotting corpse of a rat.

And scream in horror.

Mary is dangling from a beam; her long green scarf is knotted around her swollen purple neck. One of her shoes is on the floor beneath the chair she stood on. Her face is greyish-yellow. Her fingers tinged with blue as she stares through unseeing eyes, swinging gently side to side.

I can't stop screaming, not even when the nuns rush to the basement emitting gasps of horror. Sister Claude and Bernadette cut her down and lay her out on the floor. Emmanuelle joins them, hand to mouth in shock, and pushes me out the door.

'Do not breathe a word of this to the others,' she says quietly. 'You've just had a terrible shock; take the rest of the afternoon off and say a prayer for Mary's soul.' Her fingers pinch my arm. 'Not a word, Hannon!'

Wrenching my hand away, I take the basement steps two at a time, race up the stairs to the dorm, throw myself on the bed and break down and cry for the remainder of the day. I can't put those dead eyes out of my mind, nor her swinging corpse. I know that every time I close my eyes, I will see her bloated body, not the girl I admired and loved. Oh, Mary, what have you done?

The door opens, and Joan shakes my shoulder. 'You've missed supper. I brought you some.'

'Go away. I'm not hungry.'

'What happened – I waited ages?'

'Leave me alone.'

I hear the creak of the mattress as Joan gets up. 'Fine, suit yourself. I could have gotten into trouble sneaking away this food – you know.'

Emmanuelle had warned me not to tell anyone, but Joan was my friend, and I couldn't keep this from her. 'Joan!'

'What?'

'Come 'ere, something I want to tell you.'

She walks over.

'Shut the door.'

'Why?'

'Just do it, please.'

I sit up on the bed.

'You look terrible.'

Sobs wrack my body. I lower my head to my knees.

'Lou, you're scaring me.'

I wipe my eyes and stare at her through blurred vision. 'Mary's dead. I just saw her.'

'How…how do you mean dead? What! No, that's not possible!'

'Keep your voice down. The others will hear.'

'Why shouldn't they know?'

'Emmanuelle warned me not to tell anyone. She killed herself, Jo.'

'Oh, Jesus, poor Mary.'

I start crying again, and Joan bursts into tears. She wraps her arms around me, and together we rock silently in anguish. I'm still crying when I feel Joan's hand stroking my hair. I don't mind, it's soothing and loving. That's what I need right now.

Soon, the other girls come in, and I warn Joan again not to say a word. Mary is buried the next day and only I am allowed to attend. Her parents come to the funeral and leave just as quick. Mary is buried in a corner of the adjoining cemetery with not even a cross to mark her grave. I steal snowdrops from the chapel and place them on the mound of earth, then say a prayer asking God to take care of her. Tears drop onto my nose. My chest hurts, and it's difficult to breathe.

'I'll never forget you, Mary. You're my friend always.'

Hatred sears through me for Mary's parents. They stood cold and aloof at the grave like she had been a mere stranger. It was only when her mother looked over at me that I could see the sorrow etched in the deep lines across her face, but I'd longed to shake her, call her names, scream, anything.

The laundries continue as before, like Mary had never existed. Life is merciless and cruel, and I'm sick of bearing the brunt of it. Tired of being the victim. I am carrying folded sheets to Emmanuelle's office when I hear voices outside the open door.

'The Taoiseach arrives in the morning; get the girls outside to the garden.'

I must find a way to speak to him.

The telephone rings just as I'm about to rap on the door. Sister Bernadette shoves me aside. 'Leave them here. Go back to work.'

The laundry machine has stopped working, and a plumber is called in to assess the problem. We are ordered outside to pull weeds in the garden until such time that it is fixed and work can resume.

It's chilly, none of us is wearing a coat, but I drink in the fresh air, desperate to fill my lungs with its cleanness and naturalness. Once we're out of earshot, I tell Joan about the Taoiseach's visit and flesh out my plan a little more.

The garden is overgrown with weeds amid clumps upon clumps of carrots, potatoes, cabbage, and wild herbs. It starts to drizzle, but I don't mind. Anything's better than the smelly steam room we work in day in day out, our clothes stuck to our skin with sweat, blistered fingers, and aching backs. The rain feels natural, cool. Maude wheels over a wheelbarrow and dumps the weeds inside. I can hear traffic outside the high walls. Music floats towards us, and now and then, we hear squeals of laughter.

The other girls drift towards the end of the garden, and now that we are alone, I can speak without interruption. 'When Claude rushes us out to the garden tomorrow, I will stay behind and corner the Taoiseach.'

Joan looks at me dubiously. 'What do you want me to do?'

'Distract Claude so she won't do a head count and notice that I'm missing.'

'Where will you be?'

'In the closet.'

She shakes her head. 'I don't know – what if he doesn't want to listen.'

'He's got to.'

Joan wrenches a weed from the ground. 'Hope you're right.'

'So, will you help me?'

'Yes, I'll help.'

Mary has been on my mind day and night. I want to do something to remember her. Joan and I talked about it but couldn't come up with anything that was worthy of her memory. Something occurs to me then as I look around at the hawthorn trees flourishing in abundance. I find Claude in the glasshouse, bent over a potted plant. 'Sister, may I have a word, please?'

She puts down the pot and pulls off her gloves. 'Well, what is it – haven't got all evening?'

'I'd like to plant a tree in Mary's memory.'

I wait.

Her face softens. She picks up a small shrub and hands it to me. 'I was wondering where to put this. It's a small birch, but it will grow big. Needs pruning.'

I look down at the green shrub, resembling a miniature evergreen plant and smile. She'd love it. 'Thank you, sister.'

'It's your responsibility, mind. I'm not going to do the pruning for you.'

'I'll look after it.'

Joan and I plant the shrub where it will get the most sun-light, then carve Mary's name on a piece of wood as a memorial plaque underneath. The sun is going down when we're called back inside. I can hear the plumber banging away at pipes inside the laundry and give a smile of satisfaction. My hands don't know themselves since they've been given a break from the hot sudsy water.

That night, huddled inside our beds, rain drums on the roof and lashes the windowpanes. The ground is struck by a bolt of lightning followed by a bellow of thunder. Hilda squeals in fright, but I love storms and always have done ever since I was a little kid. As I close my eyes, I recall a storm of a different kind that was to rock my world forever.

It was another three weeks before I saw Nathaniel again. Auntie Diane was expecting relations home from England and asked Mum if I would help her clean the house and get it ready for when they arrived as her maid had gone home sick. I was sitting in the corner by the fire, quietly reading my book, and I overheard her talking on the telephone.

'She will of course, Di. Not at all; keep her for as long as you like.'

The phone clicked in the receiver, and Mum turned to me. She wore a pale pink jumper over a brown pleated skirt, black tights, and thick brogues. Her hair was pinned back, making her look a lot older than her forty years. Lines creased her face, and she seldom smiled.

'Head over to Diane's; she wants you to help her clean the house.'

'But it's my only day off.'

She pursed her lips and folded her arms. 'Go on, don't make me call your father.'

I didn't have to be told twice. The mere mention of his name was enough to put the skids under me, so I put on my coat and trudged up the lane to Auntie Diane's. Morning frost glittered on the grass and surrounding hedges. Weak sunshine filtered through the sun-choked canopies overhead as I walked, feeling a little uplifted by the promise of good weather for the day ahead. If I worked fast, I could get out of there by noon, finish my book and maybe get the bus into town and meet Padraig for lunch, so I quickened my pace until I arrived at the imposing gates.

Familiar vast sweeping lawns greeted me at the entrance. Water gushed from a marble fountain. The grass was so springy and well-kept it would almost have done as a bed. It was seldom I came here. I hated this place and all its grandeur. Too neat and manicured for my liking, as if they lived in a palace. I'd heard Nathaniel was away on business, and wouldn't be back 'til this evening, otherwise I wouldn't step foot in the house.

The door opened just as I approached. Aidan, the oldest, a large brute with a mop of red curly hair, a mole on his left cheek, and a goatee, nodded at me and sauntered past, pants riding low as usual. He disappeared around the back as I entered the vast tiled hall, blinded by the chandelier dangling from the centrepiece on the ceiling. The stairs were my favourite. The steps were wide, and the banister curved into the first floor.

'Louisa, how good of you to come.'

I liked Diane. She didn't treat as if I had a contagious disease. She was tall and elegant, wore frocks down to her ankles, sometimes breeches and never swore. Her purple velvet dress strained across the middle; she must be nearly due I thought. I often wondered why she would want another child when she had three already.

'Come this way.'

I followed her into the library where books lay scattered on tables and the floor. She handed me a polishing cloth, her rings glinting in the light from the window. 'Please start on these shelves, just some light dusting. Call me when you're done, and we'll have some refreshments.' She touched my cheek. 'Thank you so much, my dear. You're a lifesaver.'

I wanted to ask her why the others couldn't help, but my tongue stuck to my throat, and I set to work. The library was my favourite room in the entire house. If it weren't for Nathaniel, I'd come here every day when possible. I lovingly caressed the books, breathed in the scents of antiquity. I loved the yellow parchment that felt almost brittle to the touch. I flicked through the pages of a Charles Dickens novel and read the first three chapters.

Doors opened and slammed in the house. I heard footsteps, the sound of a vehicle's tyres crunching in stone and replaced the book quickly and stepped down from the ladder. After spraying the table with polish, I was done; all the books were put back in their rightful places and the library was once again smelling fresh and new.

Auntie Diane offered me lemonade and enquired after my family. 'You have been a tremendous help, dear. Keep *Uncle Tom's Cabin*,' she smiled, 'my gift to you.'

'Really?' I gasped, hands roving over the hardback cover, reaching out to give her a heartfelt hug. 'Thanks so much.' It was my favourite book, *Uncle Tom's Cabin*. I must have read it at least six times, and now it was mine for keeps. I couldn't believe it.

'You're welcome. You deserve it. Now, I have one more room that needs tidying up; when you're finished with that, make sure you come down to the kitchen for some lunch before you go home.'

'I will, thanks, Auntie Diane.'

'Good girl, I can always count on you.'

I couldn't stop smiling, clutching the book tight in my hand as she led me upstairs to do the guest room.

She held her back, frowned in pain, then her expression cleared, and she stood up straight. 'Goodness, this child can kick up a fuss.'

'Are you okay?'

'It's nothing. Let me know when you're finished,' she smiled and glided out of the room.

I stared around me and sighed. The bed was stripped of blankets. Curtains were tossed in a heap on the carpet, and books, magazines, and old broken toys were scattered throughout the room. I found a cardboard box and began by throwing everything into it. Dolls without heads and arms went in first, then faded fire-engine machines, tractors, and toy animals. There were so many of them it took ages, but I was getting through it. The curtains next. It was tedious hanging every piece of material ono the hooks of the wooden rail. I heard the gong for twelve and realised I was still only halfway there. Twice, the hooks fell off, and I had to start again. By this time, my back was starting to ache, and I longed to sit down, but if I did, it would be late when I finished, and I wanted to get home soon. I was putting up the rail at long last when I heard commotion downstairs, the front door opening and shutting with a bang. I looked out the window.

Aidan was bundling Auntie Diane into his car. Her face was crumpled in pain. It must be the baby. I started to rush down to help when I realised there was nothing I could do. She would be in good hands at the hospital, and she would want me to finish the room, so I set to work dressing the bed as fast as I could.

I was sitting on the edge of the bed reading the first page of my book when the door burst open, and Nathaniel staggered in. My heart sank. His red face was bloated. His shirt sticking out from his pants, and he had no shoes.

'Well, well, isn't this a surprise!' he said, pushing the door shut with his toe.

I could smell the whiskey from here and moved to dodge past him when he grabbed my arm, pulled me down and pinned me to the bed, hands either side of my head. *Uncle Tom's Cabin* was still clutched in my left hand.

'Shouldn't you be with Auntie Diane,' I said, whipping my head to the side to escape his rancid breath.

He spat in disgust. 'She is like a whale – but you, you are beautiful, fresh and unspoiled.'

I tried to push him away, but his body felt like a dead weight on top of me. 'Get off me!'

Merriment danced in his eyes. My lips were bruised from his assault. I opened my mouth to scream, and he clamped a sweaty hand to silence me, then resumed the attack. He pulled down my knickers, inserted one knee to prise my legs apart, and slammed into my body again and again. My cries went unheard, and finally he stopped, rolled over onto his side and started to snore.

I didn't see Auntie Di after that. Someone said she had a boy and called him Jack, after his grandfather. Hilda's snoring keeps me awake. I toss and turn, dreaming of revenge and picture Nathaniel's mottled corpse floating face upward in the sea, cast adrift for eternity.

There's no time to hide in the closet. As soon as breakfast is over, we are scuttled out to the garden to pick carrots and other vegetables. It's as if the universe is conspiring against us, and there was never meant to be any justice. The girls are subdued and don't talk much. My hands are numb, my shoes are wet, and I'm constantly getting stung from nettles sprouting up all over the place. Working out in the fresh air had served its purpose. Now we just wanted to get back inside out of the cold.

I'm wondering what time the Taoiseach is due to make his appearance, not that it's of much use to me out here. Just before noon, however, the door is unlocked, and we are all shooed back inside. Something tells me he won't be coming. They wouldn't have let us back into the building otherwise. And I'm right. Just before dinner, I overhear Sister Claude sighing to Sister Bernadette that he had to cancel his visit due to a family emergency. Despair swamps me. He was my last hope. I don't know if I would have been able to grab his attention, let alone convince him of our horrendous situation here in the convent, but at least I could have damned well tried – somehow.

To make matters worse, I hear the laundry machines back up and running. It's back to slavery again.

Chapter Nineteen

Louisa

1951

I'm hoovering the hall when three more girls arrive today, kicking and screaming, pretty much like I was when they forced me into this place. One has long, beautiful wavy red hair, and she looks about twelve. Her face is dirty, and her knees are skinned. Sister Claude and Bernadette grapple her arms and drag her, as she hurls abuse, into a room where they order her to strip and force her into the uniform Mary used to wear. They leave the door open. She sniffles.

'Behave yourself penitent, and we'll let you home in a week.'

'You can't keep me here.'

'Yes, we can. Address us by our proper titles, please.'

'You can't keep me here, *Penguins.*'

Claude slaps her on the face. 'Insolent girl.'

I admire her courage and smile to myself. Sister Bernadette spots me by the door. 'Show this girl the dormitory and laundry room.' She turns to the girl. 'We'll soon put manners into you, go on, get out of here.'

She scratches her arms as she shadows me down the long, dark corridor. I stop and wait for her to catch up. God, she's so young. 'What's your name?'

'Susan. I shouldn't be here. This place is for crazy people.'

'None of us should be here.'

Our footsteps echo in the vast hall. She follows me up the stairway, where I lead her to the dormitory and the bed she'll be sleeping in. I see her gaze around in disgust at the narrow cots, the high windows and imagine what she's thinking.

'This is a prison,' she whispers, diamonds tracking her cheeks.

'Your bed is next to mine.'

'What's your name?'

'Louisa.'

'I'm only going to be here a week. They can't make me do anything.'

'Yes, they can,' I snap, closing the door. 'Get used to it.'

The laundry room is next. Steam hits us the minute we enter. A number of girls wearing the same uniform look up. Their faces hardened and grim. The heat is suffocating, and I back out, the new girl in tow. I explain to her about the laundry and the working hours, but I can see she's not listening as her brown eyes, round with fear, keep flitting to the door, the windows and back.

'The dining room is through here, and two doors down is the sewing room and chapel.'

'I hate it already.' Susan races to the heavy oak door and pounds with her tiny fists. 'Let me out. Let me out.'

Emmanuelle emerges from her office, hears the commotion, and hauls her away from the door. I don't see her again until dinner. I swallow a lump; they cut her gorgeous hair. She keeps her head down and doesn't look at anyone. When no one's looking, I put my arm around her shoulders and squeeze her hand. 'Hang in there, Sue.'

She weeps openly, shoulders heaving, and no one says a word.

'Hannon, you have a visitor.'

I look up with a frown. No one's ever visited me in this hell hole before. Emmanuelle waits by the door to usher me out. Shoulders tense, I brace myself and walk to the small waiting area by her office. She shuts the door behind me. A potted plant sits on a low coffee table. Mint green paint on the walls. A statue of Padre Pio fits neatly into a corner. A woman I know too well sits on one of three metal chairs and rises to greet me.

Her hair is greyer than I remember, thinning on top. Cheap ruby glass earrings dangle from her ears. She wears a scarf, a long grey woollen coat, a chocolate brown skirt and the same familiar black brogues.

She flinches when she sees me, and her face blanches. Tears sparkle in her eyes, and she gets up and walks towards me, hands outstretched.

I step back. I don't feel anything. Only hurt, betrayal and anger. This woman was my mother once. Now, she's just a stranger who left me here to rot. 'What do you want?'

Surprise flickers in her eyes. 'Louisa, I've come to take you home.'

Hope mixed with joy and relief flood my body, but so too do feelings of confusion and suspicion. 'Why now?'

She smooths back a cowlick that was never able to lie flat and crimps her lips. 'I can see that you have learned your lesson. We want you to come home. It's been a long time.'

Euphoria surges through me. They want me back. They're sorry. Things will be different now. They really do love me. I can't believe that I'm going to leave this place, finally, at long last. My family have come for me. They realise their mistake. I'm about to say yes, throw myself in my mother's arms and urge us to leave immediately when she continues.

'Besides, I'm too old to run the farm, with Padraig gone to London and poor Martha frail with her asthma. We need you.' She takes my hand in hers. 'Do you remember when you were little, I bought you those blue sandals you loved, then we went to the park and threw bread to the ducks?'

'I tried to catch a duck and ended up falling into the pond.'

'You were always the curious one in the family – couldn't let you out of my sight for a minute.'

I remembered it well; it had been the best day of my life. I'd just turned seven, and we'd spent the whole afternoon together. Just me and my Mammy. We were laughing and munching ice lollies. Mammy pushed me on the swings. The day was sunny. I wore a short yellow dress to my knees and glittering ribbons in my hair. Dad got a job in London on the building sites and was often away for weeks at a time. It was the only occasion I could relax when he wasn't around to bully and lecture me.

Maybe they've realised their mistake in letting me come here and want to make amends. I'm about to jump at the opportunity to get out of here when I see her peek at her watch and tap the floor impatiently with her shoe, her face now set cold and hard.

Who am I kidding? They don't love me. She didn't even say she was sorry or that she even missed me. She didn't say it was a mistake putting me in here. They just want to use me. I would have to see that brute again, and nothing would have changed. My chest is like a vice. It feels as if someone is squeezing and squeezing the pain is so great. I know that if I go home now, nothing will have changed. I have nowhere to go, and nobody wants me. Not even my own mother. As much as I abhor it, the convent is the only place for me right now. I have no money, no one to rely on but at least we are all in the same boat here. We all look out for one another. At home, I'll be at the mercy of Nathaniel again and Dan. There's got to be another way out.

'You never once told me you loved me. What did I do wrong?'

I remember the day I found out I wasn't my father's daughter. Me and Padraig were having a row. The boys in school were giving him a hard time. Calling me names. That I was a bastard. I didn't know what it meant, and he wouldn't tell me, so I asked my mother. I was only ten, and things weren't good at home. Mammy and Daddy were always fighting. Once when I came home from school, I saw she had a black eye. After that she stopped giving me hugs, and was always snappy when I was around, no matter how good I tried to be.

And just like that, she told me, 'Look, Daniel is not your biological father. Stop pestering me and do your chores.'

'I've no daddy?'

'Everyone has a daddy, silly,' says Padraig. 'Your daddy is a gypsy.'

'Watch your mouth, Padraig!' Mammy said.

'But it's true! I heard you say to Auntie Diane that he was a good-for-nothing gypsy and that you were only glad to see the back of him.'

She looks at my small, devastated expression, and for an instant, her face softens until the door opens, and Daniel stomps into the hall.

'What are you looking at?'

My chest feels so tight I think I'm going to have a heart attack. Somehow, I bring life back to my leaden legs, turn and run out the door, down the road and keep running until my sides ache and my tears are dried up. Things changed after that. The truth was exposed. I guess my mother thought when she didn't have to pretend anymore, she also didn't have to protect me either, and life went from bad to worse. They treated me like a servant in my own home. Mammy kept me at a distance which appeased the man I thought to be my father, and the beatings stopped. But not to me. Not to me! I was blamed for everything.

If I go home now, nothing will have changed. I'll be in a different place but a slave nonetheless. 'No, you just want to use me at home. You don't love me. You didn't even miss me.' My voice rises an octave. 'You don't care what happened to me for the last year – what I have been through in this place. What they have done to me.'

She backs away at the force of my anguish, grabs her bag from the chair and, head up, stalks out of the room without so much as a glance. The door snaps shut. First Mary, now this. Oh, Jesus. I sink to my knees and sob uncontrollably until Sister Bernadette calls me.

Chapter Twenty

Carrie
1976

'Come on, spill, what happened between you two?' demanded Hannah, plonking into a chair.

'Nothing happened. He stood me up and called to apologise, that's all.'

She didn't want to tell her about the *near* kiss. Hannah would make too much of a deal about it.

'Thought you looked a bit flustered when I arrived. You sure nothing happened?'

Carrie shuffled to the sink and filled the kettle. Bringing down two mugs from the press, she set them on the table, then emptied custard creams into a plate. The kettle started whistling, so she poured boiling water into a blue porcelain teapot, added two teabags, and joined her at the table. Max stretched out by her feet, eyeing the biscuits hopefully.

Hannah stirred her tea. 'I interrupted something, didn't I?'

'We talked, nothing more. Was there something you wanted?' she asked, taking a sip from her tea. 'Had to have been important to bring you out in this weather.'

'It's our anniversary next Saturday, could you mind the lads? It's just for a few hours, two at the most, I promise. We haven't been out on a date night in ages. I know they drive you up the wall, but there's no one else to ask.'

'Course I will, and they don't drive me up the wall; they're good kids.'

Hannah embraced her. 'Thank you, thank you, thank you, that's great; give me a chance to wear that new dress I got.' She turned to leave when something shiny caught her eye. 'Nice locket. Where did you buy it?'

'It's not mine,' Carrie said, unwinding it from around her neck she handed it over.

Hannah opened it and glanced at the photo. 'Hmm, pretty. Who owns it?'

'Don't know, that's what I'm trying to find out.'

'Should you be wearing it then?'

'I don't even remember putting it on, to be honest.'

'Okay, I'd best be off. See you next week.'

Carrie closed the door with a weary sigh. She finished her tea, upending the mugs on the draining board. Rain continued to batter the panes, and the house shuddered from the force of a gale gathering momentum. Suddenly, she was thrust into darkness as the power blinked out. Max whined under the table, head lowered to his paws.

Now would have been a good time for Jack to call, she mused, picturing the two of them huddled under a blanket in blackness with just each other for warmth and comfort. She sighed. *Just my luck that Hannah arrived. He would be here with me now only for her.*

Blindly feeling along the kitchen cupboards, she groped in the dark for the sink drawer. Her hand closed over the handle, and she pulled it out but found neither matches nor candles, then closed the drawer with such force a mug tumbled to the floor with a crash. Conscious that she was barefooted, she edged back away from the sink in the direction of her bedroom. The mess could wait until morning.

Max jumped up on the bottom of the bed, where she was comforted by his warm furry presence. She coaxed him to lie beside her and, snuggling under the heavy quilt, closed her eyes.

The storm raged outside, howling down the chimney, loud rain, possibly hailstones. Everything was pitch black. She could just make out Max's shape curled up beside her.

The rain stopped as soon as it arrived, and the wind died down to a murmur. All of a sudden, spasms of pain rocketed through Carrie's body. She was doubled over, clutching her midriff, when a strange woman entered the room and told her to get up for work.

The attic room was stark, sparsely furnished, with just a skylight overhead. Her bed felt lumpy, the blanket thin and coarse, and there were hairs protruding from the material. Maybe it was Max's. She waited for the unfriendly woman to leave, but she just stood there looking down at her with contempt, her mouth a thin line of disapproval. Tired of waiting, she marched over and pulled back the blanket, then gasped in shock.

Her belly was swollen. 'Christ, Louisa. How on earth did this happen?'

Carrie shrank from the woman's anger as if she had just been struck and cowered in her bed.

'Answer me!'

The dream morphed into another image. This time it was of a hard-faced man, big-boned, black beard, towering over her, shouting and waving his arms. 'Whore, liar! Get out of my sight.'

Carrie groaned in her sleep as she was pushed into a black vehicle. She awoke with a jolt, her cheeks wet and her heart racing. The dream still so vivid in her mind. She felt her stomach and was relieved at its flat shape.

Light spilled through the curtains. She checked the clock, still only seven, and turned over on her side to sleep fitfully until after eleven to the sound of Max scratching the door to be let out.

Work was crazy with new clients to meet, accounts to be set up, and constantly on the road travelling to viewings. By the time Friday came around, she was feeling worn out and not in the mood for partying, but Hannah cajoled and begged until she agreed to go. There were jitters in her stomach at the thought of meeting Jack again and maybe continuing where they left off, but all hopes were dashed when she saw the number of cars parked outside. There wouldn't be a chance to talk, let alone get hooked up.

With a sigh, she locked the Volkswagen and traipsed to the back of the house where all the commotion was going on. Wearing navy denims and a pullover, she felt out of place next to Hannah, who'd just arrived, in her glamorous peach two-piece suit, black patent shoes and matching clutch bag.

'I told you to slap on some make-up, but you wouldn't listen.'

'I'm only going to stay an hour.'

She recognised some of the people from her visit to the gallery. God, Jack was popular. People strolled outside holding wine glasses, heads locked in conversation. Jack was lounging on a corner suite outside on a patio, with a burning wood stove beside him. A pretty blonde in a cerise pink chemise snuggled up to him, her right arm draped on the couch behind his head. The Beatles blared from a black Hi-Fi System. All around, the lawn spilled over with people.

Hannah dragged her over to a table and filled her glass, followed by Matt doggedly at her heels. Dressed in a wine-coloured suit, his receding hair was brushed back from his brow. He was the only one wearing a tie. As if realising this, Matt pulled it off and stuffed it into his pocket.

Carrie went over to say hello. 'Hey, Matt, how are you?'

'Can't complain. Yourself?'

He was an inch shorter with a big build and had to look up at her when she was talking to him. 'Good, thanks. Who's minding the kids?'

'Their gran.' He blew a sigh. 'She'll have her work cut out for her. That reminds me, you still on for tomorrow night?'

'Yeah, sure. I'll call about eight.'

'She's been on about that restaurant all week. You'd think we never get out.'

'It's your anniversary; it's special.'

He looked around and hitched up his trousers. 'Have you seen her? Can't stay long, or Mum will go nuts.'

'I'll tell her you're looking for her.'

'Do, thanks.'

As soon as Carrie left, he dived into a plate of salmon and caviar, his sausage fingers picking steak, pudding and rashers from the barbecued grill.

'What about your diet!' Hannah shrieked so loud he dropped the plastic plate onto the grass.

'Keep your voice down!'

'You promised me.'

'I had no dinner. I'm starving.'

'You'll clog up all your arteries with that fat,' she hissed.

He wiped his mouth with a napkin. 'Okay, I'm sorry love. This is definitely the last time. Now, can we go?'

'Not a chance. I want to see Jack's paintings. I'll be back in a minute.'

Carrie found Hannah deep in conversation with Jack as he showed her all his paintings, purring like a cat and batting her eyelashes at him.

'Hey, I was wondering where you got to,' he said, his arms laden with empty bottles and glasses.

'You've done a fantastic job with the house so far.'

'Managed to rope in a few mates to help me but have a lot more to do, though.'

'Where do you want me to put these?'

Carrie turned at the deep voice. Rolls of green wallpaper were tucked under his arm, and brown creosote blotched his large, gnarled hands. His face was lined with a ruddy complexion, his silver hair thinning, but the eyes were the same. Hazel like his son's.

'Dad, this is Carrie. She sold me the house.'

'Hello.'

'Car, I'm heading off. Matt is sick, stuffing his face too much as usual,' Hannah interrupted.

'Thanks for coming, Hannah.'

'Sure, Jack, you know if you need anything – I'll be only too glad to help.'

'Might take you up on that.'

'I've some time on my hands if you like –'

'Really? That would be great.'

'I'll call you during the week, Carrie. Bye.'

Jack wiped his hands on his jeans. 'Right, a cup of coffee is in order.'

'Did I hear someone mention coffee?' A woman in her mid to late sixties entered the room. Her hair was coiffured into a stylish bob. She looked the picture of elegance in a kimono shawl and matching suit, her nails dazzling with bright red varnish. 'How do you do? My name's Diane, Jack's mum.'

'Carrie. I sold Jack the house.'

'Oh, yes, of course, he's beside himself since he got it. Couldn't believe his luck. Do you live locally?'

'Clifden, not too far away.' Carrie smiled, liking her already.

'Come, sit down, tell me all about yourself.'

Carrie pulled out a chair. 'Not much to tell. I'm a junior partner with Clancy Auctioneers. I live alone with Max, my dog. That's it. Nothing exciting.'

'I bet there's more to you than that. Now where does he keep his mugs?'

'I don't know, sorry.'

She radiated warmth. His father, on the other hand… Diane brought out four mugs and placed them on the table. She cleared away papers and boxes to make room, then emptied out digestives onto a plate and called the men.

'The coffee won't stay warm forever, boys. Thank God the place is quiet again.' She exhaled. 'Can't stand crowds.'

Jack's father dumped a load of wood on the floor next to the stove and collapsed into a chair, the springs groaning in protest. She wondered where Jack was and gulped back the coffee. Something about the way his father kept scrutinising her was making her feel uncomfortable.

Jack stomped in and fired his jacket over a chair. 'It's been a long day.'

'We'll head off and leave you in peace in a moment as soon as I finish this brew.'

'No rush, Mum. You're always welcome – you know that.'

'This place is all well and good, but it's only a stop-off point until you get something bigger. Why you'd want to live in the middle of nowhere is beyond me. I had to go five miles just for teabags.'

'I've made my choice. I like it here, Dad.'

'So, you keep saying. Look, I give it one-year tops to do this house up, then sell it on.'

'It'll do,' said Jack, undercurrents of anger in his voice.

'Leave the boy alone, Nate.' Diane took a bite from her digestive then said, 'Any plans for the evening, son?'

'Depends on Carrie.' He winked, 'we might see a movie later.'

That's the first I've heard of it.

'Come on, Nate, drink up and give these kids some space.'

'Yes, dear.' He drained his drink and stood up, towering over Carrie. Feeling heat travelling up her neck, she tried not to squirm and kept sipping; instead concentrating on the inside of her mug, willing him to go away. *What is his problem?*

'Be seeing you, son,' he said, nodding in her direction.

Jack touched her knee. 'Thought they'd never go. You seem a bit jumpy. Are you all right?'

'Your dad is a little intimidating. I don't think he likes me very much.'

'Pay no heed to Dad. He's always like that with my girlfriends.'

Carrie stared at him in surprise. 'Is that what I am?'

'Only if you want to be,' he said, his voice husky as he lowered his head.

Suddenly she remembered the girl she'd seen earlier who had sat so close she was practically on his lap. *What happened her?* She jumped up. 'Thought I felt a mouse at my feet.' It was lame, but the only thing she could come up with. She couldn't put a finger on how she was feeling; she certainly found him attractive. Christ, he was gorgeous. 'It's running late. I have to go.'

Jack raked his hand through his hair. 'There's someone else, isn't there?'

'No…no, not at all.' Scuffing the floor with the toe of her shoe. 'Who was that blonde I saw you with earlier?'

'Sandra Locke. Is that what this is about?' He roared laughing. 'She's just a client, silly goose. Nothing more.'

She felt her face grow hot with embarrassment.

He was bending to tie his shoelaces when rain started to drum on the roof. 'Drat, I wanted to get a walk in, looks like it'll have to wait now. Ah well, I can think of better things to do,' he said, eyeing her suggestively.

She swallowed, excitement churning in her stomach. Then something changed in the atmospheric pressure. A subtle dip in temperature. 'Do you smell that?' she asked, her toes turning numb.

'What?'

'Perfume.'

It appeared that Jack had other things on his mind. He pushed back his chair and, with a seductive grin, started moving towards her when suddenly, he stumbled, hitting his chin off the edge of the table.

'Are you okay?' she asked, hurrying over to help him up.

'It's just a cut,' he said, wiping the blood from his jaw. 'Don't understand it.' He frowned, looking down at his long loose laces trailing along the floor, 'I just tied them a moment ago.'

'Look, I have to go, sorry. I left my dog out in the rain.'

'A bit of water never harmed anyone,' he murmured, reaching out for her again.

'See you, Jack,' she replied, dodging his reach.

'Come to dinner tomorrow – and bring Max, that way you won't be worried about him. Please say, yes, I need your opinion on a painting I'm working on.'

'Okay, yes, that would be great, thank you.'

He hugged her to him then let her go. 'Four pm.'

'Just one other thing?'

'Hmm?'

'This might sound strange, but do you ever experience sudden dips in temperature here in this house?'

He scratched his head. 'Not that I'm aware of. I mean, there's not much insulation in the walls, but I've never found it freezing cold, and anyway, it's almost summer; there's no need to light the stove yet. Why do you ask?'

'No reason just wondered.'

'Don't worry; I'll light the stove tomorrow if you're cold. Don't want ya coming down sick on me,' he goofed.

'Thanks, really, but I'm sure I'll be fine.'

'Okay, see you tomorrow then.'

Chapter Twenty One

Carrie
1976

Max poked his head out the passenger window as she wound through twisted lanes, splashing through puddles, muddying the rented car. Blue skies promised a good day ahead. Jack should be happy, she mused. Now he'll be able to get his shed painted. A breeze blew strands of hair from her red polka dot head scarf. She turned up her nose at the stink of manure wafting through her open window and rolled it back up.

Halfway there she stopped on the road as hordes of sheep blocked the path, bleating for their owner. Max barking in excitement, jumped from one side of the window to the other, his tail wagging in a frenzy. This succeeded in panicking the sheep even more, and they darted across the road in front of her car. One brushed past the bonnet, hitting the side mirror in desperation to get away.

Carrie was debating whether or not to go back the way she came when the owner in a cap, torn jumper, and mud-caked wellies suddenly emerged out of a field, pulling the gate behind him. Yanking Max back by the collar, she rolled up the window and waited for him to send his flock on their way, anxiously checking her watch. It was after four, and she still had another eight miles to go.

He whistled to his dog, and she was treated to a lesson in sheep herding. The sheepdog stole up behind the flock, snapping at their heels to coax them into the field. After the last sheep was inside, he shut the gate and beckoned her forward with a goofy grin showing a gap in his teeth.

Blowing a sigh of vexation, she started up the engine, but the tyres skidded on the muddy road. There was no traction.

The sheep farmer strode purposefully towards her from across the field. A cigarette jutting from the corner of his mouth.

'You're stuck.'

No kidding!

'Do you want a push?'

'Please.'

'Hold on. Rev the engine as soon as I tell ya, right,' he said, heading around to the rear of the vehicle. 'Now go!'

The car lurched forward out of the slump. She waved at him out the window. 'Thank you.'

'Don't mention it. Come on, Shep, let's go.'

It was gone four thirty when she arrived. She got the smell of burnt meat, and her heart sank. The door opened. Jack had an apron tied around his middle. His hair stood on end, and he looked frazzled. 'What kept you?'

'I got delayed – sheep on the road, then the car got stuck – sorry.'

'Never mind, you're here now. The lamb is overdone though, and the potatoes have turned to mash.'

He looked down at Max. 'The dog stays outside.'

'Of course. Come on, boy, out you go,' Carrie said, pulling him by the collar.

'Tied up.'

'What?! I never tie my dog.'

'I just sowed a row of cabbages this morning. Sorry, Carrie, but I won't have him trampling the new fresh beds.'

Anger flared in her chest; she forced herself to cool down. What was the point in bringing Max at all?

'Come on, darling.' She tapped her side. 'Come with me.' The dog tore around the yard, barking and yapping at birds. He shot in and out of bushes and shrubs, sniffed the ground, then took off again to investigate the sheds before stopping at the back of her car to drink the water she laid out for him. Once he had exerted himself, she brought down the rear seat. He hopped in, and she rolled down the windows. She wouldn't stay long, one hour after dinner, that's it, she vowed.

The meal was delicious, and any earlier misgivings put on the back burner. He told her he had two older siblings, a brother and sister. One was a teacher living in Cork, married with three kids, and the other was an architect, also married, in London. The lamb, although a little burnt, tasted divine, and it went down well. For dessert, he brought out a plate heaped with profiteroles and cheesecake on the side. Then topped it all off with an ice-cold crisp glass of Chardonnay.

'Here's to our first proper date.'

'Cheers,' she said, clinked his glass and took a sip.

Her smile faltered, suddenly unsure of herself. This was unfamiliar territory. It had been three years since her last serious relationship that didn't end well, and she didn't know what way to act around him. She squared her shoulders and sat back, willing herself to relax. Jack put on a record, and a song from the Bee Gees, *How deep is your love,* floated in the air.

'Dance with me.' He folded her into his embrace. Her head touching his shoulder, they swayed to the music, and she had to admit, it felt nice, warm and safe.

'What perfume are you wearing?'

'I'm not wearing any perfume.'

'Oh, must be your hair then.'

The floor was narrow, with little room to manoeuvre, so they danced in the same spot. Cologne wafted off him in waves and another smell – cigarettes. For the first time she noticed slight nicotine stains on his teeth and turned her head away before he caught her staring.

A picture fell from the wall, and one of the forks flew from the table with a clatter, followed in its wake by the plastic salt container. Startled, she glanced up at Jack.

'There's a ghost in this house.'

'You feel it too. I knew I wasn't imagining it.'

He looked down at her serious expression, threw back his head and laughed. 'I was only joking – it's a very old house; there's bound to be creaks and rattles, things falling. You daft girl. There's no such thing as ghosts.'

'Yeah, I know – I was just kidding.' *If only he knew!*

'Hmm…you feel so good,' he said, tightening his arms around her. 'I'm so glad we met.' They were about to kiss when the record got stuck on the first track, repeating the same words over and over. 'Damn, that was my favourite. I'll get another one.'

She heard Max kicking up a fuss outside the window. 'I don't want to leave my dog too long in the car. Leave it for another time.'

'Sure – you're right, I forgot.' He clasped her hand. 'I want to show you the new painting I'm working on, won't take a moment, promise,' he smiled.

He led her to the rear of the house. The room was painted blue; the windows blacked out. Scores upon scores of artwork stood propped up against the walls, some of them stored away in metal trays in filing cabinets. He held up one that was half-finished of a gothic portrait quite unlike any other of his work, and she didn't know what to make of it. But then it was only half-finished. Hard to form an opinion. 'I don't know, is my answer. Show me when it's finished.'

Raking his hands through his hair, he said, 'Truth is, I'm finding it difficult to motivate myself lately. Nothing seems to work, and I'm not getting the buyers.'

'It'll come; just give yourself time. I'm sure every artist worth their salt goes through a mental block now and again.'

He put the painting back. 'You're right; sorry for moaning. Come 'ere and I'll show you my new art room – it's almost done.'

'I will if I can let Max out.'

'Do.'

The dog bounded out of the car, lapped up some more water she had set out for him in a silver bowl and cocked a leg up against one of Jack's tyres. She was impressed by how much work Jack had done in such a short space of time; Diane, his mother helped him sow the garden, he got a contractor in to help restore the house, and next week he informed her he would be tarmacking the drive.

The art room/shed was the biggest of the outhouses, long and rectangular and painted magnolia with just the areas above the door yet to complete.

'I thought, seeing as the weather's so nice, you might fancy giving me a hand to finish this last bit. I know I invited you here for dinner, but I promise not to work you too hard. Besides, it'll be fun working together,' he said, eyes twinkling in earnest.

How can I say no? 'Okay.' She smiled, 'but just for a while.'

'Thanks, Carrie – hold on while I change out of these.'

He disappeared into the house, then came back out moments later with a different shirt and pants spattered in paint stains.

Rolling up his shirt sleeves, he hunkered down to pour paint into a tray.

'What do you want me to do?'

'Could you bring me a bucket of water for the brushes from the tap over there.'

'Sure.'

Leaves rustled in the swaying branches, and the air pulsed with melodious bird chatter. She was filling a galvanized bucket with tap water when suddenly it wasn't water but milk.

The bucket was heavy in her little hands. She felt goosebumps along her arms. It was cold and wet, and she had no coat. Her blue shoes were dirty. Sheets of rain sluiced into her eyes. She lurched across the yard, aching and shivering something fierce. Ginger, Padraig's cat, wound its furry body around her legs, mewling up at her. She stumbled over the cat at the door. The milk slopped and spilled over the side just as the door opened, and she set the bucket down.

'Now look what you've done,' exclaimed a very angry man, cuffing her on the jaw. 'Do you think milk grows on trees?'

Tears clustered at the back of her eyelids. Her chin was red and felt sore.

'Put out the washing.'

'I'll help, Mammy,' piped a little girl in a pink teddy bear pinafore, white stockings, and lilac patent shoes. Her blonde curls were tied back with red ribbons.

'Silly Billy,' the man laughed, 'you can't even reach the clothesline. 'Louisa will do it.'

'Yes, Daddy.'

'Well, go on then.'

She stared after his retreating bulk, a sob catching in her throat and thought, why can't he look at me like that?

'What are you waiting for?' snapped the woman. 'The washing won't do by itself,' she said, thrusting a basket of laundry into her small hands.

The vision faded. Carrie looked down at the water beginning to overflow from the bucket into the yard. *What the hell was going on?* Her hands shook so much that she had to hold on to the wall for support to stop the yard from spinning. She heard a voice; it sounded familiar but muffled as if it was coming from far away. When Jack put his hand on her shoulder, she jumped.

'Are you okay? Did you not hear me calling?'

'I have to go, Jack. I'm sorry. My head is going to burst.'

He palmed her brow. 'You're a bit warm, but that could just be the sun. Will you be all right to drive?'

'Yes, thank you and thanks again for the dinner,' she said, her voice emerging as a croak. She summoned the dog, 'Max, come.'

Chapter Twenty Two

Louisa

1951

I'm inconsolable. Mammy's face is the first face I see every time I close my eyes. Her disappointment. She never loved me, not the way a mother is supposed to. I miss Martha and Padraig so much. Should I have gone home? Did I make a mistake? These questions torture me as I work, and rain lashes the windows, casting shadows along the walls. The hum of the laundry machines is the only sound. Joan glances over at me and mouths are you okay? My mouth trembles, and afraid that I'm going to break down, I turn away and fold sheets into neat squares. The methodical exercise keeps my hands busy and my mind distracted.

Someone shouts from the corridor. A patter of feet. Calls for help. I drop what I'm doing and run out. Reverend Mother Emmanuelle has collapsed. Doors that are locked are pushed open. It's the most activity we've seen in months. Two ambulance men rush inside with a gurney and lift her onto it.

Sister Bernadette elects to travel in the ambulance with her. She sits beside her and holds her hand. Can't say I'm sorry to see her go. She's an evil witch. The doors slam, and the ambulance speeds out of the grounds, siren blaring. Heart attack, I believe. Hope she doesn't live.

'Back inside all of you,' Augusta orders briskly. Her face looks pale, and she is clearly worried.

We are ushered into the sewing room for the evening and, for once, do not have work to do. The nuns whisper by the fire while the rest of us sit around, some doing embroidery and others praying. I'm surprised to see Joan is one of them.

'Who are you praying for?'

'Reverend Mother.'

'To die quickly?'

'Don't say that Louisa. You'll go to hell.'

'I'm already in hell. How can you pray for that evil venomous snake?'

'You wouldn't understand.'

A bell gongs. 'That'll be the post. Will one of you go down?'

'I will, sister.'

She looks at me long and hard before handing over the key to the back door. 'Be back in five minutes.'

'I will.'

I hasten downstairs to unlock the door; the key digs into my palm, the temptation to run is so great I have to remind myself of the consequences should I flee again and the fact that the nuns would never trust me again. I'm almost seventeen. They can't keep me here forever, so I must bide my time.

It's a dull drizzly morning. The postman is taking parcels out of the back of his van. When he turns around my hopes soar. It's Luke. He's got a job. He smiles when he sees me.

'Louisa, so good to see you.'

'Hi, Luke,' I say, blushing shyly.

'Here.' He hands me two packages and six letters.

'How long have you been working as a postman?'

'Only started last week. I'm filling in for the usual fella while he's on holiday.'

'Oh, so you won't be here all the time then.'

'I won't be far away.' He grins. His face reddens. 'Good to see ya,' he repeats.

'I have to go. They'll be wondering where I am.' I'm whispering even though I know the nuns can't hear me.

'Sure. Can't wait.'

I smile then, and he smiles too. He tips his cap and then gets into the van.

Every morning for a week, I get the post, and it's a chance to talk some more with Luke. With Emmanuelle gone, the rules are relaxed a little; they don't watch us as much and the time we spend in each other's company grows and grows. He tells me jokes to cheer me up. Jokes that he memorises from the comics he reads. He has a poodle named Podge with only three legs that he rescued from drowning when it was just a puppy. I like his uniform, it's green and white, and he looks smart. Sometimes he brings me sweets, usually liquorice, but they're my favourite. I love to see him every morning but try not to look too cheerful when I return with the post; otherwise, the nuns will grow suspicious if I'm not careful. My heart sinks at the thought of the other postman coming back, but then Luke tells me he will see me at Church service, and then I know things won't be so bad.

My heart sinks when I hear a new nun has come to take over Reverend Mother Emmanuelle's duties until she returns. All I can think is that she will be hard-faced and cruel, and any liberty that I attained will be whipped from underneath me. Sister Bernadette has called an assembly after breakfast to welcome the new arrival. My shoes are pinching my toes; I need a new pair but daren't say anything. The new girl, Susan, won't talk to anyone and has been like that since she arrived several weeks ago. Since they cut her hair, her cheeks look gaunt, and she has lost tons of weight. She'll never survive if she keeps this up. She folds her arms, pouts, and stares at the square drab grey tiles lost in the cocoon she has erected for herself.

My attention snaps back to the front door as I listen with dread to Augusta, drawing back the bolts and opening it wide, instantly letting sunlight spill out onto the foyer. She stands and looks at each of us in turn. She is smaller than I expected, shorter than Joan's five foot six. Her habit is navy with a white rim around the wimple. Instead of a long robe, she wears a matching skirt below the knees, a cardigan, and flat black shoes. A curly black fringe flops into her eyes, and she has a narrow elfin face. She smiles at each of us, and I swear there's a twinkle when she does it.

'Sister Frances, you're most welcome.' Augusta gushes, pumping her hand vigorously.

'These must be my new charges.'

I like her voice. It's soft and musical, reminds me of my grandmother's, and the way she says charges, not 'penitents.' I glance at Joan to see her reaction, and she smiles back her approval.

'Indeed. Come this way. I will show you to your room.'

Sister Frances follows Augusta up a flight of stairs. I notice that she takes utmost care to avoid certain tiles, and as she ascends, she doesn't touch the handrail but rather covers her hand with her sleeve as if afraid of getting contaminated. I shrug and head to the dining hall for breakfast.

We do Grace before meals, then pull out our chairs to sit down to the usual cold lumpy porridge and burnt toast. I scratch my chin, the itch driving me demented, and there are sores along my arm too. They're breaking out, blood oozing in places from where I had kept scratching. The door opens, and Sister Frances enters the dining hall. We stand immediately to attention as she makes her way to the far table where the other nuns are pigging out on a greasy fry.

Breakfast finishes at eight-thirty on the dot. We are standing up to clear away our bowls when her voice rings out.

'Girls, I would like to speak to you all for a moment, please, before you go about your chores for the day.' Standing in front of us, she rests her palms across her stomach and regards each of us in turn. 'I am concerned that your studies are being neglected,' she begins.

I look at Joan and then the others before reverting to her again. Augusta folds her arms, and Claude scowls her disapproval.

'Girls, help me re-arrange these tables. Our classes will take place here.'

'But, Sister, this is no place for –'

'I'm well aware of that, Sister Augusta, but what choice do we have? The girls need a place to write, to put their books on.' She turns back to us again. 'That's right, place them one in front of the other in two rows. Sister Claude, will you purchase copybooks and pencils for me, please. I believe there's a bookshop in the next block.'

'As you wish.' She mutters to Augusta, 'The Reverend Mother isn't going to like this one bit.'

Claude returns with the order, and I help the others distribute the copybooks and pencils, placing them on each table. We take our seats and look up at the nun expectantly and also a little nervously. Susan twirls at her hair. Hilda burps and rubs her large belly.

'We will start with a roll call. Now give me your names one by one.'

First, she cleans her hands with a cloth, and after that, with a bottle of Dettol disinfectant, then jots down each name onto a sheet. After a moment, she extracts a small Ladybird book on Hansel & Gretel from her bag and asks Joan to read the first page. Joan stammers at first, but then her voice grows stronger and more confident. The book is passed around to everyone until the last page is read out. Sister Frances claps her approval and then gets us to write what we thought of the story.

'Their mum and dad were horrible.'

'The witch was a lot worse, Joan,' remarks another.

'All that candy,' Hilda sighs, 'I wish I could have some.'

'What about you, Louisa? What did you think of it?'

'Hansel and Gretel were foolish and stupid.'

'Susan, I didn't see you writing anything.'

'Because everyone knows that story. Two kids are taken to the woods by their father, the boy throws crumbs along the path so they don't get lost, but a bird eats the food instead, and they are all alone. The girl stumbles upon a magic cottage made of candy; a witch traps them and fattens them up for the oven. The boy becomes free and pushes her inside. The end.'

'Try writing that down.'

Susan sits back, folds her arms and pouts. 'I can't.'

'Can't or won't?'

'Don't know how,' she mutters, rubbing her nose as she stares at the table. 'Ma says it's because I'm thick.'

'I don't believe that for a second. Didn't you know the story off by heart? Give it a go.'

I glance over at her and notice that each letter is turned backwards. It looks strange, and I wonder if maybe she learned to write a different way to everyone else. Sister Frances frowns and chews the end of her pencil contemplatively but doesn't ridicule or shout like all the other nuns, and I like her more and more.

'Has anyone ever told you that you may be dyslexic?'

'No, miss, I mean Sister,' she blushes. 'What's *dishlexic*?'

'It means having difficulty reading or writing. What I don't understand is how you remembered the book so well. Did someone read it to you when you were little?'

She turns red again. 'Hansel & Gretel was my favourite story growing up.' She shrugs, 'Guess I memorised it off by heart.'

'I'm impressed – but we need to work some more on those letters, okay? Come to my office after work, and we'll try it together.'

'Yes, Sister.'

Claude waddles in, puffing, out of breath. 'Come on, girls, there's work to be done. We've a deadline to meet.'

'Go on, go, get back to work. Tomorrow we will begin our poetry lesson.'

Chapter Twenty Three

Louisa

1951

Claude, Augusta and the other nuns grumble and complain about our classwork, and something tells me that this Renaissance of Learning won't last forever. Our laundry work has suffered, we're behind in our deadlines, and they force us to slave until late in the evenings, sometimes as late as ten o'clock. The change in our situation has given us a new lease of life. Something else to occupy our brains other than routine, monotony, and hunger. Sister Frances is strict with homework but doesn't lash out or raise her voice. I wish she could stay forever.

This morning we are studying a poem by Patrick Kavanagh: Inniskeen Road.

Scrubbing her hands vigorously with a cloth, she says, 'Can anyone recite the first verse without looking at your books?'

I love this poem, so I give it a shot.

'The bicycles go by in twos and threes
There's a dance in Billy Brennan's barn tonight…'

'Well done, Louisa. The next verse please, anyone?'

Joan attempts the first two lines but gets stuck after that. She talks to us about imagery, and I'm picturing the dance in my head, going there with Luke and excitement bubbles in my stomach. As we leave to start our chores for the day, she pulls me aside.

'Your English is exemplary, Louisa.'

I feel my face flood red with pride and smile widely. 'Thank you, Sister.'

'How old are you?'

'Sixteen, Sister, I'll be seventeen this August.'

She taps the table with her pencil. Black curls escape from her wimple to coil on her brow. 'You have so much potential; if you keep this up, I believe you will be ready to leave here very soon and maybe even sit the state exam next summer.'

I stare at her dumbfounded. No one has ever said that to me before. I beam up at her, suddenly at a loss for words. Things are finally falling into place; I'm going to get out of here on my own steam and with a qualification. 'Do you really think so?'

'I wouldn't have said it otherwise,' she says, gathering papers from the table and shoving them into her bag. 'But to get better at English, you must practice your writing every day. Have you got a diary?'

I shake my head.

'Come to my study after supper. I have an old one you can use.'

'Thanks so much, Sister.'

My head is bursting with enthusiasm and excitement. For the first time in my life, I believe I'm going to make something of myself, and I can't wait to get started. The steam from the laundry machines doesn't affect me, and neither does the stinging bleached water. I'm on cloud nine; nothing can touch me. Things have changed so much since Sister Frances's arrival. We have extra food at mealtimes and not just lumpy porridge and dripping either. It's mashed potatoes, chicken, beef sometimes and hot tea, not the lukewarm, tepid stuff we've been so used to drinking.

After each class Frances ensures we get adequate exercise and fresh air around the grounds; this could entail an hour's walk, a nature talk, weeding the garden or picking potatoes. And at mass, she teaches us new hymns so we can join in with the choir.

Just before bed, I start my journal. Once I'm alone in the dormitory, I pull out the worn notebook that Frances gave me and begin:

To my sweet baby Carrie,

I want you to know that I haven't abandoned you. I hope you will get to read this and that someday, you will understand and forgive me.

I've been a prisoner at The Sisters of Mercy in Galway for over a year. My mother and stepfather dumped me here just before you were born, Carrie. My love. My beautiful little girl. The nuns took you away from me, but I promise I will find you, and soon we will be mother and daughter again.

I tried to escape from this godforsaken place, but the nuns think I need saving and won't let me go. There are other women and girls here. Some are so innocent, like children really. They don't know why they're here. Just like me. They don't understand why we are prisoners. Or what we have done wrong. You are the light of my life. A precious gift from God. Why should I be punished for bringing you into this world?

This place is evil, Carrie.

I have to get out of here. The nuns are cruel beyond imagining. The world believes that this is a better place for girls like me. We are slaves in this convent. We do not have a voice. The nuns believe we are faceless, base creatures who don't deserve to live. But they are wrong.

Wherever you are my darling baby girl, I hope that you are loved and happy.

Some day we will meet again, and I will hold you in my arms once more.
Your loving mother,
Louisa

Two months have passed. It's Friday morning, I'm alone, polishing the altar, and Luke has stayed behind once again to talk to me.

'I thought we had planned to leave next week,' he grumbles.

His cap is two seats down from the altar. He put it there in case any of the nuns started asking questions. His hair is spiking at the top from when he removed the cap earlier, and this time, a pioneer medal is clipped to his brown turtle neck jumper.

'Sister Frances is expecting my essay next Thursday.'

'Since when do you care about them?'

'Shh, keep your voice down.'

I take his hand, and we sit at the far side of the chapel where no one can see us. 'Sister Frances is counting on me. She thinks I'm a good scholar, Luke. She said so herself. She gave me a journal; I write in it every night – it's almost full already.'

'But I'm counting on you. We've had this planned for ages.'

We had been meeting for several weeks either in the chapel or when he was delivering the mail in the mornings, and sometimes during the day as well. If Emmanuelle had been around there's no way I'd have gotten away with it for so long. Every moment with him is precious. He is my window to the outside world and tells me everything that's going on, including news about his family and the things he gets up to day to day. It's like I'm there with him, and it sustains me while I'm in here.

'I don't want to let her down – can't you see? Let's just wait another few weeks, please.'

'Few weeks! Have you completely lost your mind?'

'I want to get an education; there's nothing wrong with that.'

'Last week, you couldn't wait to leave,' he whines as he paces the floor, running his fingers through his hair. 'I don't understand.'

'Just another few more weeks – I promise.'

I hear the door open and freeze. 'Louisa Hannon, are you in here?'

The steps recede, and I hear a key turn in the lock. I'll have to leave by the side exit and go around to the front of the building. Luke dons his cap, shaking his head in resignation.

'Meet you here tomorrow?' I whisper.

He leans in to peck me on the cheek, not the mouth I notice, and hands in pockets, saunters off down the alleyway. Rubbing my arms to ward off the sudden chill, I scout the building for an open window and find one in the basement.

It's tricky climbing inside as the window is small and narrow. I push the window inward and edge inside, twisting my body to squeeze into the opening. Halfway down the wall, I realise the window is far up from the ground, but it's too late, and I brace myself for the impact as I tumble upon crates, and empty boxes, scraping my hands, arms and elbows against the wall in the process. The clatter alerts a slumbering rat; I watch it scuttle into a hole for safety and think he could have picked a better place to take up residence. I creep out of the basement and tiptoe up the staircase, flattening myself against the wall when I hear Claude and Augusta approach. They pause to talk to one another, their backs to me. My blood turns cold; tomorrow is to be Sister Frances's last day. I grit my teeth at the sound of their relieved chatter.

'Everything will return to normal once Reverend Mother is back.'

'Indeed, and it couldn't happen quick enough,' Claude agrees. 'Did you hear about –'

Her voice trails off as she shuffles down the corridor. It's like a blow to my stomach and my heart. I should have known it was too good to last. Luke was right. I have to get out of here while I have the chance. There's plenty of time for educating myself later.

Class passes in a blur. I can't concentrate and keep getting my words mixed up. Sister Frances passes around a series of quiz questions for us to complete within one hour. Times us on the clock on her desk and sits back. Every now and then I notice her fidgeting with the copybooks making sure they sit as an exact square, that nothing is sticking out, and I wonder at this strange obsession. I'm distracted by thoughts of her leaving and can't concentrate. I hand up my answers at the end, which she looks at in surprise. My cheeks flame. I look to the floor and scuff a speck of dirt with my shoe. I can tell she's disappointed with my answers, and this makes me feel even worse.

After lunch, I'm washing the dishes in the sink, and Joan asks, 'What's up?'

'I got all the questions wrong.'

'So? You're always showing the rest of us up. Brainbox,' she says, slapping me gently with her tea towel.

'Sister Frances looked so disappointed though.'

'I wouldn't worry – she looks like that every time I hand up any work.'

'It's her last day tomorrow. You know what that means?'

Joan blows a long sigh. 'Back to the same 'ole, same 'ole. I'll miss the poetry. Emmanuelle won't let us read anything. It would be nice if we could do something for her before she leaves.'

I hug her. 'Thanks, you're a gem.' Then kiss her cheek.

She stares at me in surprise and touches the spot where I kissed her. 'Don't mention it.'

Up in the dormitory, I take out my journal again and start writing. It's a poem of thanks, and after many, many false attempts, I produce my first poem that goes like this:

You came into our lives and gave us hope
A beacon of light
In a place
Filled with despair
Your kindness and warmth
I'll treasure forever
But best of all
It's just knowing you care

Class begins the next day with a commentary on Yeats and his love for Maud Gonne. Sister Frances keeps wiping her eyes and sighing and doesn't pay much attention to what we're saying. My new purple woollen jumper feels warm and cosy. We all got one each when she started; she said the hall was too cold to concentrate, and the following day handed out woollen jumpers to each of us. After that, we went for a walk in the park to soak up the sunshine and much-needed vitamin D. I could tell by Claude's sour face that she didn't approve, but nobody cared.

Sister Frances fires questions on Shakespeare and gives us tests to complete. She quotes Gaelic and teaches us grammar, spelling, history and even some arithmetic for three hours in the morning. We compare notes, and I can see a change in the girls. They're more talkative, confident and positive. Frances has given us something else to think about. She's given us hope.

So, it's with that thought in mind that I head to her study. It's noon, and class is finished until Monday, and it's struck me that this is the first time I've ever gone to Emmanuelle's room voluntarily. And it feels weird. I knock on the oak-panelled door.

'Come in.'

Beethoven plays softly on the radio. Pencils are arranged in a row on a table alongside a neat stack of copies. The office is spotless, nothing out of place. A bronze crucifix hangs on the wall centre, pictures of Pope John Paul on a desk. Sister Frances sits with her back to me and turns slightly when I approach. She is writing a letter. Her nose is puffy, looks blotchy from crying, and I wonder what she has to cry about.

'What is it? I'm busy.'

Embarrassment floods my face. 'It's nothing; sorry for disturbing you.'

Removing her owl-framed spectacles, she places them on her desk and gives me her full attention. 'Please, shut the door.'

I do as she bids.

'Now,' she smiles, 'what can I do for you?' she asks, fixing a pencil back in place that had rolled when she turned.

I relax and bring out the piece of paper from my pocket. 'I wrote this poem for you as a show of our appreciation.'

She puts the spectacles back on. 'Let me see.'

My ears redden as I hand it to her. What if she doesn't like it? What if she thinks it's silly? I twist from one foot to the other, unable to keep still. Her eyes light up.

'You wrote this?'

I nod.

'Thank you, it's very thoughtful and kind and well-written. Well done.'

She folds up the poem and deposits it in her breast pocket. 'I will treasure it, always. Please, go now; I want to be alone.'

I'm opening the door to leave when a sudden cry stops me mid-stride. I turn to see her shoulders heaving and sobs convulsing her body. I stare at her in shock. I don't know what to do. Should I fetch Augusta or Claude? I go out but then double back.

The only thing I can think of is to place my arm around her in a half-hug. She leans into my shoulder and weeps, great big gulping sobs that cut me in two.

All of a sudden, my hands start to feel numb. I feel an icy draught at my neck like fingers of frost on my skin, and I know what's coming. We're enveloped in cloying vapour; drops of moisture trickle from my nose, forming tracks of tears on my chin. I hear the clanging of metal, feel tremendous heat, then smell smoke and start coughing. Sister Frances on the other hand, doesn't seem to notice anything and is sniffling into her handkerchief. I brace myself, hands clenched together, the knuckles taut in anticipation, then gasp out loud.

There's a man standing behind Sister Frances, one gnarled hand on the back of her chair, the other resting on the top of her head. He is wearing a tweed cap, a red scarf around his neck, dungarees, a white shirt with rolled-up sleeves, and he has a squint in his left eye. The image shimmers and is replaced by another. This time he looks much younger; he is surrounded by pansies, buttercups and wild roses, and a little girl in pigtails sits on his shoulders. The image blurs, and he is the same as before. I can never get used to these apparitions, no matter how many times it happens. But I'm not afraid. This ghost doesn't mean me any harm, so I release the breath I've been holding and wait and see what happens. Sister Frances continues to weep, oblivious to the spectre's presence, whilst also squeezing my hand tight.

'*Look for your watch in the forge.*'

His voice sounds muffled; I don't think he moved his lips. It seems to come from far away, hollow and disjointed.

He bends to kiss her brow and whispers again into her hair. '*Look for your watch in the forge.*'

His eyes meet mine for an instant. Tears glimmer in the brown irises. The apparition flickers, the smell of smoke lifts, and the numbness disappears from my hand.

'Goodness, look at me going all maudlin. My apologies Louisa, dear,' she says, blowing her nose. 'Was there something you wanted?'

My heart is thumping. I'm afraid to tell her about the vision; what if she turns against me?'

But she's been kind and good to us, and this could help her, so I blurt it out, 'I have a message from your father.'

'I beg your pardon?'

'I – I have a message –'

She springs to her feet so suddenly I stumble backwards in fright.

'I didn't put you down as vindictive and cruel! My father is barely cold in his grave.' She pushes me out the door. 'How dare you!'

'He told me to tell you to look for your watch in the forge.' I exclaim breathlessly.

She stares at me, mouth open wide, and slumps back into the chair. 'Close the door.'

I do as she says and wait, head bowed meekly, for the outcome of my revelation.

'How do you know this?'

Her voice sounds small and weak. I look up and gaze for a moment at her flushed cheeks, red from crying. 'I can see visions, always have, ever since I was a kid.' I shrug. 'I don't know why; sometimes they're scary, but other times not so much, and now and again, I can communicate with the spirits. No one believes me. Everyone thinks I'm mad.'

'I have been searching for the gold watch my father gave me for my birthday for weeks.' Her lips tremble, and I think she is going to cry again, but then she sits up straight, sighs and continues. 'I looked everywhere. It was precious and had given up hope of ever finding it until now.'

Fresh tears of joy shine in her eyes.

'Oh, my God.' She puts a hand to her mouth. 'I don't know what to say. What an amazing gift. You're truly remarkable, Louisa.'

'Thank you.'

She paces up and down. 'You should not be here in this desolate terrible place. None of you should.'

'No one wants us.'

To hear it said aloud, I feel my face burn with shame.

'Perhaps there is something I –'

She doesn't get to finish her sentence. The door swings open and Emmanuelle looms at the entrance, fit and healthy as ever before.

'God bless you, Sister, for all your help over the last few months, but as you can see, I am back now and ready to resume my work.'

'Of course. Glad to see that you have fully recovered. I will leave tomorrow.'

'Get out of my study, Hannon.'

I glance at Sister Frances, who bristles visibly at her treatment of me. She mouths the words sorry just before I exit the office.

My heart plummets to my toes, and I flee before the old dragon has a chance to punish me just for being in her presence.

Witch! I can't believe she's back.

I know what's going to happen. Sister Frances and all her good deeds will be thrown aside, and a life of drudgery will return in a vicious swoop.

Joan emerges from the kitchen holding a tea towel. 'What's the matter?'

'She's back – Emmanuelle. You know what this means.'

We file up the stairs together. It's almost nine, and the nuns will soon begin patrolling the convent making sure everyone is in bed. She puts her arm around my shoulders, and as we wash and get ready for bed, I make a decision to tell her about my visions.

Chapter Twenty Four

Carrie
1976

Her hands shook as she turned the key to switch on the engine. She reversed out of the drive and sped back to Clifden, confused, her thoughts in a muddle. *What just happened back there?* She could see everything so clearly. It felt so real. A motorist blared his horn in a warning to keep to her own side of the road. Her heart jolted in fright, and she slowed right down until she got home.

Max jumped out of the backseat, following her into the house, tail wagging, oblivious, and at that moment she wished she was a dog without a care in the world. It had been a long time since she'd experienced visions, so long ago, she'd almost forgotten how creepy they could be. These visions felt more real though, like a window into someone's past. Someone trying to relay a message. None of it made any sense, and there was no one to shed any light on them either.

She had always suspected that there was something different about her ever since she was a kid. Hannah would laugh at her ability and tease her for talking to herself, but she knew the ghosts were real. She stopped laughing the day she was pushed off a bench by Bridie Fogarty, the recently deceased milkman's wife. The bench had been erected in memory of her husband, and Hannah was sitting in his spot. She didn't mock me anymore after that. But when Carrie told her parents about it, they'd clammed up, refusing to discuss it and told her to stop making up stories, that people would think she was crazy, lock her up and throw away the key. Disappointed but scared she repressed her feelings and ignored the visitations until they stopped coming altogether once she started taking the anti-anxiety pills.

And here she was, right back to where she started yet again. But this time her gut told her she couldn't turn her back. She had to face up to what was happening. There was a strong sense of urgency about these visions. This tormented person felt she could communicate through her. And needed her help. But she was in the dark, at a loss as to what to do. If only she knew more.

To cheer herself up, she heated a large slab of apple pie and added a dash of cream on the side. If there was only thing she learned how to do well, that was how to bake. At six years old she would sit on the high stool by the kitchen table and watch her mother bake jam tarts, Christmas cake, soda bread, cakes, and apple pies. The smells rising from the kitchen oven were divine. Carrie smiled at the recollection, feeling the familiar pang of longing and sadness in the pit of her stomach. Her mother's hands white with dough, her apron dusty with flour. And her squeals of delight when she let her lick the end of the bowl. Once Max was fed, she brought the pie over to the couch and, folding her legs underneath her, tucked into the apple pie; but found her appetite wanting and left it on the table for later.

Her thoughts drifted again to earlier that evening. She couldn't get the image of that little girl carrying a bucket of milk out of her head. Someone was trying to reach out to her but why? *What do you want from me?* She removed the locket from her neck and opened the clasp again, stared at the little girl and saw that the girl in the photo was the same as the one she had seen that afternoon. Surely this was no ordinary coincidence. She turned it over and examined the engraving again. *Is this the same Louisa Auntie Tess had called Hannah by mistake?*

Making a decision to call on her after work, she took a quick shower, then laid out her clothes for the morning. Hannah called to cancel the babysitting, something about a fight with Matt. With nothing else to do, she watched a movie half-heartedly until it was time to go to bed.

Work was hectic. She had four viewings in one day, assessment reports to type up, and three letters to compile for the solicitor. All in all, she hadn't had time to dwell on yesterday's events, and for that, she was grateful. Tom was busy mentoring graduate student Jacqueline Casey from Longford, who was doing work experience with the firm. She had a shock of long, blonde curls, a round pasty face, gapped front teeth and talked for Ireland. But it was her laugh that clinched it; it was high-pitched, and she sounded like a dog in pain.

Carrie gave her a lift to her digs after work, then headed back into town to visit her aunt, whom she found outside knee-deep in dirt in the garden. A great wide-brimmed hat covered her head. She wore light blue denim trousers that came up high to her waist and, over that, a grubby pink poloshirt with holes in the armpits. Grey hair hung loosely to her shoulders, and she was tall and bone thin. She wiped her brow with a gnarled freckled hand, turning when she heard someone approach.

'Hi, Auntie Tess,' she said, leaning up to give her a kiss on her dry papery cheek.

'Oh, it's only you, Carrie. I'm planting lettuce, such a dirty job.'

'Here, let me give you a hand,' she offered, reaching to take the spade.

'No, thank you.' She wiped her hands on her pants. 'See, I've a way of doing things.' She stood up, surveyed the work, then, turning to Carrie, said, 'Be a love and make me a cup of coffee.'

Her left eye had dropped slightly, and when she spoke a little saliva gathered on the corner of her mouth, but there were no other indications that she had suffered a stroke in recent weeks. Carrie smiled and headed back into the kitchen. It was a typical county council house; stairs at the entrance, sitting room on the right, a narrow hallway, and a kitchen at the back. There were no fitted units, only a free-standing cooker, fridge, some overhead presses and a Stanley range oven. Brown lino had stained black from scorch marks; a wide window sat above the sink overlooking the garden. She filled the kettle and brought down two black mugs, one of which was chipped had mum written on it. She wondered how she'd bring up the subject of Louisa, then spied the locket in the mirror.

Tess flopped down onto a chair. Carrie made the coffee and took over the mugs to her. They slurped the coffee for a few moments to the peaceful sound of the ticking grandfather clock behind them, a whistling wind blowing through the chimney and the low hum of distant traffic.

'How have you been, Auntie Tess?'

'Not too bad. Doctor put me on a load of pills,' she sighed, 'but I keep forgetting to take them.' She looked at Carrie. 'You've put on weight.'

'Thanks! Just what every girl loves to hear!'

'Suits you. Always thought you were too skinny.'

'Auntie, there's something I've been meaning to ask you.'

Tess took a loud slurp of her coffee, spilling some of it down on her top. She tutted in irritation, grabbed a tea towel from the table and dabbed at the stain. 'What is it?' she asked, glancing at the clock on the wall. 'I want to finish before it gets dark.'

Licking her lips nervously, Carrie dragged her chair over beside her, took off the locket carefully from around her neck and opened it to show her the image of the little girl. 'Would you happen to know who this is?'

Tess put on her glasses and squinted at the photograph. 'No, I'm sorry, can't say that I do.'

She felt a weight of disappointment and frustration in her chest, then suddenly remembered the name underneath. Maybe that will help her memory a bit she thought. 'How about Louisa?'

Tess swallowed visibly and touched her forehead. 'I – I don't know.' Staring at Carrie accusingly, she said, 'Why are you asking me these questions?'

'I'm getting bad dreams, and she keeps propping up. I need to know who she is and why she's plaguing me. Please, Auntie Tess, you know something, Hannah said you mentioned her name not too long ago.'

'I don't know what you're talking about, love.' She hobbled to the door and held it open. 'Nice to see you, Carrie, but it's late, and I've work to do in the garden.'

Carrie could have howled her frustration. *I'm at the end of my tether.* Tess was hiding something; her eyes looked too shifty, and she definitely paled at the mention of the girl's name. *But why? What's the big deal?* The bell tolled for the Angelus, and all of a sudden, she knew what she had to do but hoped and prayed it wasn't too late.

She turned the car around in the direction of west. This time, a woman on a mission. She rolled the window down, her pullover sticking to her skin. A flock of starlings soared into the sky. Cow dung splashed onto the car as she manoeuvred tricky bends and zig-zag corners until the stone two-storey house came into view. There was a light on in one of the rooms downstairs, and smoke unfurled from the chimney. She parked at the front and went up to the front door. Dread and anticipation bloomed in her chest. He won't appreciate another visit; of that, she was sure, but she was also sure she couldn't go on like this either. She needed answers now.

The door opened. 'I thought I said what I had to say last time.'

'Father, please, I apologise for the late hour, but I really need your help. I did what you suggested. I prayed for her soul, but nothing's worked.'

His dog started howling; it was enough to send chills up her spine. On this occasion, the priest wore a navy cardigan over grey trousers, black slippers with a hole in them, the Galway Chronicle in his right hand.

'Come in,' he sighed and closed the door. 'I was just about to make supper.'

'Promise I won't pester you again.'

She immediately got to the point of her visit and showed him the locket. She could smell sausages on the frying pan, and her stomach rumbled. He sat down, took the locket from her hand, and examined the photograph.

'I'm getting visions of this girl and really strange dreams. Nobody seems to know anything about her, and you were the only person that I could think of who was parish priest back then.' *I'm babbling.*

He frowned. 'I know this child.'

Carrie stared at him in shock. Her heart beat faster. She leaned forward. 'You do,' she whispered.

'Yes, if memory serves me right, I believe she was a rather disturbed young girl. Nothing good ever came of that family. Padraig, her brother, became an alcoholic and Martha, the youngest of the family, died giving birth to her first child. As for the mother, she had moved away long before I left the parish. I can't tell you much about the dad – he stopped going to mass a long time ago.'

'But what does all this have to do with me?'

'There's nothing more I can tell you. I think my sausages are burning,' he said, leaping from his seat. 'My advice to you,' he continued with a fork skewered in sausage, 'is to forget about this child and her unfortunate family, and these dreams and visions will fade in time.'

'What was the family's name, Father?'

'I honestly can't recall,' he said, shaking his head, 'it was such a long time ago, you understand. And my memory isn't what it used to be. It could have been O'Hagan or Hanratty – something like that. Sorry, my mind's a blank.'

'But surely their parish church has a register of all marriage and birth documents in its records; maybe I could look there.'

His face reddening with growing impatience he blustered, 'Goodness sake, I've already told you everything that I know. Do your research by all means, but I'm afraid you won't find what you're looking for in that church.'

'Why not?'

'After the fire of 1958, there was significant structural damage to the church, and a new one had to be built in its place. Every last record was destroyed. People forget and move on; after all, you're talking about a very long time ago.'

'Is there anyone else who could tell me who they were?'

'Try the state registry. Now, if you don't mind, I would like to eat my supper in peace,' he said, opening the door.

'Right,' she mumbled, gathering her bag, 'sorry to have troubled you.'

Father O'Dea closed the door, then checked the window to ensure that his visitor had indeed left. He tossed the fry onto his plate, filled a glass of milk and slumped in his chair, casting his mind back to that fateful day when he had sealed Louisa Hannon's fate by sending her to the laundries. He had no inclination to reveal this. It was for the child's own good, and young people today would not understand. What's done is done. However, what he could not fathom for the life of him was the connection between this lady and a young, troubled girl from over twenty years ago…

Chapter Twenty Five

Carrie
1976

C arrie shook hands with the elderly gentleman promising to keep him abreast of how the sale was going. He was moving in with his son and family and had asked her to put his house on the market. It was a beautiful wisteria dormer bungalow with expansive lawns front and back, four large bedrooms and a farmhouse pine kitchen. The area was quiet, two miles from the main road and busy traffic and afforded fabulous views of the Twelve Bens. She had no doubt that it would be snapped up in no time.

Once she got back to Clifden, the first thing she did was contact the archives centre to enquire about the census records of Dunas between 1950 and 1970. She was put on hold for several long minutes.

'Hello, Miss Gillespie?'

'Yes, I'm still here.'

'Are you searching for your family history?'

'Yes, I'm doing my family tree as part of a genealogy project I'm working on.' *She lied.* 'I just found out that some of my ancestors may have originally come from Dunas. Any information at all would be great.'

'Spell the townland.'

'D.U.N.A.S'

'One moment…yes, I see. I have it here. Surprisingly, there was only one home registered in that townland.'

Carrie's heart began to race.

'What was the name?'

'Ah…John and Margaret Armstrong.'

She waited for more information, but when nothing else was forthcoming, she asked, 'Is that it? Didn't they have a family?'

'That's all I have here. Oh, hold on.'

There was a rustling of papers.

'It states on this census form that after Mr and Mrs Armstrong purchased the cottage in 1966, they sold it to a John O'Leary, who resided there until his death last year. Could these be the ancestors you're referring to?'

Carrie paused, then said, 'I'm not sure. I think my ancestors go further back. How about the people who lived there prior to the Armstrongs?'

'To be honest, I'm not entirely certain if our census records go back that far as we only started storing census data in this centre over the last ten years. It's also possible that they may have been misplaced when we moved to a different archive facility last year. Give me your address; if I locate the records, I will send them to you.'

'Thank you, I appreciate it.'

She called out her address.

'Was there anything else?'

'No, thanks again for all your help,' she said, disappointment surging through her as she put the phone down. It could take weeks, maybe even months, to find those records. All she wanted to know was the family name. How hard can it be?

Tom ran into the office; his tie was askew, and he looked frazzled. 'Have you seen my briefcase?'

'It's under your desk.'

'Thank God, thought I left it on the train.'

A thought just occurred to her, surprised that she didn't think of it before. 'Hey, you remember that cottage in Dunas I just sold?'

Grabbing his keys, he replied, 'Yeah, what about it?'

'Who was the previous auctioneer on that house?'

'Murphy-Kavanaghs in Gort.'

Her eyes shone. 'Don't suppose you know their number?'

Briefcase in hand, he turned at the door. 'It'll be no good to you now. They went into liquidation years ago. Sorry, but I've got to run. See you later.'

Christ! She felt like she was being thwarted every direction she took.

She was coming out of a butcher's shop loaded down with lamb chops, a juicy steak, sausages, and bacon when, directly across the street, she saw Jack and his father emerge from the bookies. Hoping to avoid them she reversed back onto the path, then heard her name and groaned inwardly.

'Carrie, over here,' Jack waved.

Nowhere to hide, she dragged her feet over towards them, the bag of meat dangling behind her back. 'Hello, again.' She turned to Jack's father. 'Hello, Mr Hannon.'

'Call me Nathaniel, please.'

Jack slung a possessive arm around her shoulders, hugging her to him. He sniffed her hair. 'Coconut oil, I love it. You look good. Missed you yesterday.'

Her cheeks turned pink.

'Come to dinner this evening,' said Nathaniel. 'I insist. Jack will bring you.'

'Say yes, I haven't shown you the house where I grew up.'

She had been so looking forward to curling up with James Bond for company, soaking up a glass of white wine and making a pig of herself on lamb chops, fried onions and sauteed mushrooms, but there would always be tomorrow; it would be nice to see his home, where he grew up, so she relented.

'Sure, why not…thanks for inviting me.'

'Pick you up at six?'

'Okay.'

Jack arrived promptly at six dressed in maroon pants, a multi-coloured Aran sweater, and gleaming ox blood loafers. 'You look ravishing,' he murmured, leaning in to kiss her cheek.

'Thanks.'

She had spent an hour painstakingly rifling through her wardrobe for something decent to wear, eventually settling on a red print tea dress, a long pale grey fashionable cardigan, black tights, and flat shoes. Her hair was another matter; it refused to behave for the brush and kept spiralling down from the up-style she had agonised over for the last thirty minutes. The locket still hung from her neck, the clasp refusing to open when she tried to remove it. The oval trinket felt cold against her neck and heavy. *I'll take it off later.*

His Land Rover smelled faintly of pine and musk. The upholstery felt rough as she relaxed back, waiting for him to start the engine. Soon, they were speeding through the countryside. They braked at a set of lights; he cursed, lifted his wrist to check his watch, drummed his fingers on the wheel before sighing explosively and hitting the accelerator. Carrie watched him with a frown. *Surely you wouldn't be this rattled going to your parents' house for dinner?*

'What's wrong? You've hardly said a word the entire journey.'

'Nothing, sorry, just a bit distracted,' he said, squeezing her hand.

'Want to offload?'

'No.' He smiled, then turned back to the road. 'Pay no heed to me – almost there.'

A loud gurgling noise broke the silence.

'Good, you're hungry. Here it is.'

After driving around twisted bends, through several cross-roads, and a main road that seemed to stretch to infinity, they'd finally arrived at their destination. Carrie was gobsmacked. The place was huge, opulent, like something from a period drama. Vast manicured lawns swept down to the entrance gates that clicked open as they entered. Two marble lions guarded a series of marble steps supported on either side by enormous pillars. The garden was populated by shrubbery and beautiful roses. She stared up at the house. It resembled a manor house, resplendent in white, long casement windows and intricately carved stone design. Fit for a queen.

Feeling like she should be scuttling around to the servants' quarters, Carrie shadowed Jack into the house. A Chinese butler opened the door. Of course, he would. Like the house, his uniform looked impeccable. Their footsteps echoed across the black and white marble tiles. Directly ahead stood a wide carpeted staircase. Family portraits adorned the walls painted gold and yellow. Lights winked from a massive chandelier that must have cost more than her entire week's wages. There were three oak-panelled rooms, both left and right, a teak cabinet with the white porcelain bust of Oscar Wilde sitting on top, and she could smell furniture polish and cigars.

'This way.'

Her chest tightened. She smoothed down her dress, conscious of her appearance, wishing yet again that she hadn't come. This was no home. This was a museum. Somehow, she couldn't picture a young Jack running up and down the stairs in short pants, making a racket, playing with his toys and mucking the floor. No, this didn't equate to him at all.

A door opened up ahead. Diane. She wore just a hint of makeup, and there was not a strand of hair out of place. 'Carrie, welcome. Lovely to see you again,' she said, kissing her on the cheek.

'Thank you for inviting me.'

'Dinner is through here,' she said, opening the door wide. 'Nate, come and say hello to our guest.'

Nathaniel got up from his armchair and folded his newspaper. 'Hello. Now, let's eat.'

He didn't wait for the others to begin eating. Carrie took a seat next to Diane and waited nervously while she dished out the food. The silverware was shining, and an immaculate lace tablecloth formed a runner down the length of the table. A porcelain gravy jug rested in front of her plate, along with a Waterford crystal glass that Diane promptly filled to the top with wine without even asking her if she drank.

'This is delicious, Diane – thank you.'

'Delighted to have you, Carrie. It's been many months since Jack brought a lady home to meet us.'

Carrie chewed the carrots slowly; they tasted rock hard, almost raw. She took another gulp of the wine and speared a piece of goose with her fork, conscious the entire time of Nathaniel's eyes glued to her face. The door opened, and the same man she met earlier shuffled in with a trolley to collect the dinnerware. She dropped her fork on the floor and was bending to pick it up when Diane tapped her hand and handed her another one from the trolley.

'Jack tells us you're an auctioneer – how marvellous.' As she leaned across the table and clasped her hands, her low neckline displayed a cleavage that would give Dolly Parton a run for her money.

'Yes, I like it.'

Nathaniel hadn't taken his eyes off her since she arrived. Another sip. Head woozy. *Slow down; you're drinking too fast.* She tugged at her neckline, feeling hot and uncomfortable even though there was no heat to speak of and the windows were wide open.

'Are you a full partner?'

Carrie looked over at Nathaniel. 'Junior.'

He grunted, threw down his napkin, then pulled back his chair and stood up.

'Where are you going? We haven't had dessert yet.'

The door swung as he left the room. And for the first time since her arrival, Carrie felt she could breathe again. Diane pursed her lips, downed her wine and shook her head.

'What's up with him?' asked Jack.

'Take no notice. Your father will join us later.'

The butler arrived in with a china teapot, cups and saucers and a tiered stand of cakes, pies, and tarts big enough to do an entire football team.

'Ah, thank you, Whan Soo. That will be all.'

'As you wish, madam,' he said with a bow, closing the door with a soft click behind him.

Carrie tucked into a delectable cheesecake while Diane and Jack regaled her with stories. After a while, she found herself warming to his mother and slowly began to relax until Nathaniel wrenched open the door and stomped into the room.

'Anyone seen my briefcase?'

'Whan Soo put it in your study.' She shot Carrie an apologetic look. 'Please sit and talk properly to our guest.'

'I can't. Not right now.' He glanced at Jack. 'A word, please.'

'Can't it wait? You see I'm with Carrie.'

'Now, Jack.'

'Mum, would you show her around?' he asked, bending to kiss Carrie on the forehead. 'Sorry – this won't take long.'

Jack pulled the livingroom door shut behind him.

'I must apologise for my husband; he's not normally this boorish,' Diane said as she led Carrie into the lobby area. She gave a small laugh. 'Well, not in front of company anyhow. He's been under a little strain with work. You know how it is.'

Carrie said nothing, preferring instead for Diane to take the lead. What could she say after all? That the man was a stiff upper-class jerk?

'Jack tells me you like to read. I think you'll like this room,' Diane murmured, opening a door and ushering her inside.

'Oh, this is fabulous.' Carrie had never seen as many books in one room. The shelves reaching ceiling height spanned the width of two walls. It was vast and airy and felt cold, like it hadn't been used in a long time. There was a gleaming black granite fireplace in the centre, a teak writing desk by the window, an armchair and a round table. The room was gloomy, and dust motes circled in the air. Her hands itched to browse through the books. 'May I take a look?'

'Of course. Take your time. I need to make a phone call anyway.'

Diane closed the door on the way out, and Carrie was alone at last. *Which book to look at first?* There were so many. If she had a library like this, she'd never leave the house. The books were all hardback, all in different colours, each volume arranged according to their genres and alphabetical order.

There were books on agriculture, astronomy, biology, botany, horticulture, and science, and on the second row, a section of mystery novels by Agatha Christie and more fiction.

I wonder if Jack would let me borrow this one. Taking the book *Uncle Tom's Cabin* over to the table, she dragged over the armchair, settled into the upholstery and started to read the blurb on the back to the sound of the clock ticking and an eerie wind whistling down the chimney. The vision, when it manifested, came swift and sudden. She gave a cry of alarm, and the book slid from her grasp to the floor.

It was like the last time when she felt she was a voyeur looking in. The room was different, a bedroom with fewer paintings, and there was an old-fashioned light fitting. She stood transfixed by the image before her, unable to participate or utter a word, helplessly watching on in horror as the two people grappled on a bed. The vision was hazy, but what was happening in front of her eyes was not. Her tongue stuck to her throat, and hot tears coursed down her cheeks, trapped between worlds unable to stop the violence. The girl whipped her head from side to side, crying out, pummelling his chest with her fists, and twisting her body in vain to escape. The vision morphed again, and this time the man turned.

Carrie gasped in recognition. Her hand flew to her mouth in shock. 'You bastard! Leave her alone. I'm calling the guards.'

Running footsteps. The door swung open. Nathaniel burst inside, followed by Jack and his mother. He stared around the room seeking out the culprit, then frowned in confusion. 'Who are you yelling at?'

Carrie's face flamed in mortification. There was nothing there. *How will I explain this?* 'Must have fallen asleep while waiting for Jack.'

Nathaniel's eyes narrowed.

Turning to Diane she said, 'Thank you for the dinner, but I'd better get home.'

'What's your rush all of a sudden?'

'Carrie has work in the morning, Nate.'

'A coffee won't hurt,' he said, draping his arm around Carrie's shoulder, 'give me a chance to get to know you.'

'Just a coffee then.'

'Splendid.'

They sat in a small cosy sitting room branching off the dining area. Flames licked from an open brick fireplace. A portable television occupied a corner alcove. Dark green leather furniture took up one section of the sitting room. A stuffed pheasant peered out from a glass case on the mantle shelf. Beech leaf wallpaper gave the room a quaint homely feeling. Diane wheeled in a table with a teapot, cups and saucers, a silver spoon, jug and sugar bowl.

Carrie sat next to Jack. A chill of foreboding in her bones, aware of his father staring at her from the armchair opposite. Tucking a strand of hair behind her ear, she took a big gulp of coffee burning her tongue in the process and managed to spill some of it onto the saucer. She looked at the family photos on the cabinet. Several were of Jack's older sister's graduation, her wedding and some of her children who lived in Cork. Two photos Diane explained were of her son, Aidan, who lived in London but planned to return home for good before Christmas. He might have been Jack's twin they looked so alike.

They ate Mikado biscuits which she barely tasted. Wishing she was at home with Max by the fire.

'How are your parents?' Nathaniel asked suddenly.

She swallowed a stab of pain in her chest. 'My parents died just under two years ago.'

Jack dropped his cup on the saucer with a clatter. 'How come you never told me?'

'It never came up,' she whispered.

'How did they die?' Diane asked.

'In a boat accident.' Carrie was feeling hot now under their scrutiny and undisguised sympathy.

Jack touched her knee. 'God, I'm so sorry, Carrie. You must have been devastated.'

Her face was red from the fire. It was too hot in here.

Nathaniel leaned forward. 'What were their names? I might have known them.'

'Eleanor and William Gillespie.'

Something unreadable flitted across his face. He turned white and stood up.

'Now, where are you going?' asked Diane grumpily.

'Out.'

'I must go too. Thanks again for the lovely dinner.'

Diane clasped her hands and gave her a warm hug. 'It was my pleasure, love. So delighted to meet you, do please come again, won't you?'

She nodded and all but fled to the front door. Jack apologised for his father's rude behaviour and drove her home, both of them brooding in silence. Relieved to be alone at last and away from Nathaniel's hostile scrutiny, her thoughts returned to the disturbing vision, the sickening sensation in her gut when she stared at the face that looked so much like Nathaniel, only younger, the girl's cries that went unheard, the brutal act of rape and she shuddered. Another vision from the past. *I can't take much more of this.* Jack's parents must think she's mental. How could this be happening? They slowed down for a funeral cortege, a large crowd following a black hearse on foot into Saint Michael's church, and she was jolted suddenly by a memory from her past.

She was just gone six and had accompanied her mother and father to a funeral in her grandmother's house, where her uncle Patrick was being laid out. It was late August, a warm balmy day, and the scent from the flower arrangements made her sneeze. The air felt claustrophobic with the constant barrage of people in black arriving to pay their respects. She spotted what looked like her uncle standing by his coffin, staring in and weeping.

'Get up, get up,' he repeated.

Carrie thought this was most peculiar, having figured that he had been in the coffin already, and maybe he wasn't dead after all. He looked the same and sounded the same. How could there be two of the same people? She slid off the chair in her pretty navy pinafore and black patent shoes and went over to him. 'Uncle Pat, what are you doing?'

Patrick jumped with fright and staggered backwards. 'You can see me! How can you see me?'

'Sure, everybody can see you,' Carrie giggled, a frown on her tiny face, just as her mother walked right through his body and took her by the hand to lead her away from the coffin.

The funeral party trudged into the church and the street cleared once again. As they drove off in the direction of home, she was convinced now more than ever that all the visions centred around one person. Louisa. And they were connected somehow. There had to be a way of getting to the bottom of it. Finding out the truth, but she was stumped. Nothing made sense. Because it had been such a long time since she had experienced any kind of visions or crazy dreams, she was finding it difficult to come to terms with the knowledge that they were back with a vengeance and that Jack's father had something to do with it. She had to do some more digging before things got out of hand. Just when she was starting a new relationship too.

Jack pulled into the yard, turned off the engine and drew her towards him into his embrace. For once, she refused to think and gave herself up to the enjoyment of the moment. The passion of his kisses. It was only when he began fumbling with the zip of her coat the memory of Nathaniel's brutal assault hit her full force, and she pushed him away.

'What is it?' he exclaimed, hitting the steering wheel with the heel of his hand. 'Every time I try to get close, you push me away.' He stared out the window. 'You're messing with my head, Carrie.'

'I'm…I'm sorry. I've got to go,' she stammered, wrenching the door open.

A hand on her arm. She looked back at him.

'No, I should be apologising, not you. I guess I'm not used to women blowing hot and cold on me,' he said with a grin. 'Look, we'll take it slow; I promise.'

'Look, Jack, I really appreciate your patience with me. Take care.'

Chapter Twenty Six

Louisa

1951

We're in the dorm, lights out, neither of us able to sleep despite the long day we've had. I'd resolved to tell her about my strange ability, but now I'm not so sure. What if she judges me? I couldn't bear her disapproval.

'Susan went home today,' Joan whispers from her bed. 'Did you know?'

'No, I didn't. Are you sure? It's not some yarn the nuns told you?'

'Saw her go with my own two eyes. She left with some woman.'

'That leaves fifty of us in total. I wish someone would come and take me away.'

'I wish someone would come and take you away too. Shut up and go to sleep.'

'Sorry, Hilda,' sighs Joan. She looks across at me. 'Don't say that – you're the only friend I've got here.' After what seems like an age has passed, she glances across at the other girls, at their sleeping forms and patting the mattress says in a hushed voice, 'You were going to tell me what happened before?'

I tiptoe over to her bed and perch on the edge of her mattress, waiting to hear their snores.

'This stays between us – promise?'

'Cross my heart and hope to die.'

'You're going to think I've a screw loose.'

'No, I won't.'

'Right,' I say, glancing at the sleeping forms as I stall for time. My chest tightening as I wonder for the umpteenth time if I'm doing the right thing, then recall Sister Frances's reaction. She didn't mock me and call me a charlatan or, worse, a liar, so I take a deep breath and begin.

Joan stretches out on the bed, hands cupped under her chin, listening to my story. I tell her about the different visions beginning with the ones that got me into trouble at school and ending with the ones of strange spirits I encountered in various locations. All lonely, wanting to reach out for comfort. Her eyes widen in shock, she doesn't look away, but instead, her expression takes on a dreamy appearance.

'Wish I could have visions. Sounds so exciting.'

'No, it isn't. It's frightening not knowing when you're going to get one. They're so sudden and unexpected they'd scare Jesus himself down from the cross.'

She sits up, eyes shining and grabs my hands. 'Don't you see, it's a gift from God. You're blessed. Wish you had told me sooner.'

I sit cross-legged on the bed. 'Do you really think it's a gift from God? Never thought of it that way.'

'Yes, I do. I pray every day, and nothing like that ever happens to me. Tell me about the last vision again.'

'I saw Sister Frances's father. She told me he'd just died only a few weeks ago. He wanted her to know that he was okay, and that was it.'

They hear the patter of footsteps and scramble into bed, fully clothed. The sound dies away, and I sit up again, and so does Joan. The other girls are turned on their sides, snuffling in their sleep, but I'm wide awake and want to keep talking, so I go over to her again.

'You never did tell me why you're in here?'

She looks away for a moment as if deciding whether she'll confide in me or not. I observe her in dismay; her once long, gorgeous blonde hair has been cut up short, and there are sores on her mouth.

'You don't have to tell me if you don't want to.'

Her lower lip wobbles, and tears spring to her eyes. 'I had an affair with a married man. I'm a sinner, a wicked girl. I deserve to be here.'

'No, you don't! Don't say that. No one deserves to be here. So, you made a mistake, doesn't mean you have to pay for it for the rest of your life.'

'I had a baby, his baby, and they wouldn't let me keep him.'

I cover her hand with mine and squeeze gently. 'You'll have another. It wasn't your fault.'

Joan hangs her head. 'It was my fault, Lou. You see, I knew he was married, and still, I pursued him. Emmanuelle's right; I am a shameful hussy.'

'What about him? He could have said no.'

'I only thought of myself, no one else.'

'Please, Joan, don't think that. They want us to feel shame. That nobody loves us, and nobody wants us. You have to be strong for when you get out of here. Have courage.'

'Oh, Lou, what about your own baby?'

'She's out there somewhere, and when I get out of this place, I'm going to find her and bring her home.'

'What if you can't find her? What then?'

'Don't say that. I will find her! I shan't rest until I get her back. She's got to know the truth. I won't have my Carrie believing that I abandoned her – no way.'

Joan slumps against the pillow and yawns. 'Oh, if only it was that simple.' Turning on her side she mutters, 'Go to sleep, early start in the morning.'

We've just had breakfast, the usual cold porridge, dry bread and warm water. Sister Claude is herding us into the laundry room when a raucous kicks up in the corridor. I glance over my shoulder and catch a glimpse of the new arrival kicking and screaming, being propelled by a nun at either side, lifting her bodily off the ground.

'You little minx, wait 'til the Reverend Mother gets a hold of you,' Augusta sputters, hauling her along the floor.

Her face is cut from scratch marks. The girl looks about my age, maybe older; her beige pinafore has dirty streaks down the front, she wears two different colour knee socks, her mousey-brown hair is dishevelled. She looks strong, her high cheekbones are flushed red, and rage glitters in her brown eyes.

'What are you gawking at?' she hurls at me. 'I'll give you something to gawk at.' She twists out of their grip. 'Let me go!'

I step inside and shut the door to screeches of outrage and the loud slap of Emmanuelle's backhand amid shrill screams of abuse. As today is Friday, we're busy folding sheets, towels, shirts and linen ready to send off to the various clients scattered around the Galway region. Today is the only day we don't have to steam, wash, or iron the laundry, and it's less taxing on the hands. I look down at my knuckles, usually skinned from bleach and scrubbing floors, and note that they're beginning to heal at long last.

In recent weeks two of the girls came down sick and were confined to bed. The doctor recommended that we get fresh air into our lungs and vitamin C to avoid an epidemic from spreading like wildfire throughout the convent. Emmanuelle fearing what that could mean for the laundry reluctantly agreed, and our first proper outing will take place this afternoon for one hour.

At approximately two o'clock, we are escorted to the park, supervised by the nuns taking up the front and rear of our party. The sun is shining in all its glory, birds chat and sing in the trees, and the air caresses my cheeks. It feels so good to be out in the open, feeling the breeze, smell freshly mowed grass, see life away from the stifling heat of the laundry. Passers-by ogle, us but I don't care. We walk in single file through the park to the sounds of ducks, a spotty kid kicking a ball with his father.

Emmanuelle makes us recite three decades of the rosary, once again ruining the moment. I don't see the new girl among us and can only conclude that she is locked away in the *dungeon* until the nuns see fit to let her out. All too soon, the time is up, and we're scuttled back across the bridge to drudgery once again. Augusta pushing us on, stick in hand like we're a herd of cattle.

Just as we're about to cross the street, Hilda whimpers in pain. I run back to her to see if she's all right. Her face is pale. She clutches her belly and staggers, water pooling at her feet.

'Sister, something's wrong with Hilda.'

Augusta pushes me aside, and sighs. 'Her waters have broken.'

Claude flaps over, and together we help Hilda into a taxi. She grabs my arm. 'Lou, stay with me. I'm frightened.'

'Out of the question,' Augusta snaps, leaning over to shut the rear door of the cab.

'Please.'

I look from one to the other, and it is Sister Claude who eventually gives in. She sits in the front, and I'm in the back, wedged between Augusta and Hilda, holding her hand. She gasps in pain at the contractions. I hold back her hair and squeeze her clammy hand as the memories of my own delivery return in full force. At the hospital, the nurses take over, and only I am allowed to remain by her side.

Hilda looks so small and thin in the bed it's hard to believe that she'd be able to push the baby out. Her labour intensifies, and her gasps of pain become screams. The mid-wife coaxes her to relax while I dab her brow with a wet sponge and use my other hand to rub her back.

'I can't do this anymore.'

'Course you can. A stór. Deep breath and push,' the mid-wife, a buxom, stout ginger-haired woman, commands gently.

'We could do with a few more like you,' remarks the mid-wife to me with a broad smile. 'You working here long?'

She has me confused with someone else, then I look down at my clothes and understanding dawns. When Hilda got sick all over me in the car, I was in a right state. One of the assistants lent me her uniform; she said I would need something clean and sterile before I could set foot in the maternity ward.

A rush of heat flushes my face as I flounder for a reply. She's so open and kind, and even though I know I'll never see her again, I don't want to tell her the truth. 'My last day, today,' I mumble, conscious of Hilda hearing every word and knowing what a liar I am.

'We're short-staffed at Saint Luke's maternity and could do with an extra helping hand if you're interested?'

'That would be great, thank you,' I say, darting glances to the door, hoping and praying that none of the nuns will turn up and blow my cover, but so far so good, it's just the three of us.

'Excellent. My name is Margaret Hayes. Deep breaths love.' She turns back to me. 'I'm filling in today while the usual mid-wife is on maternity leave. Here's my card. Give me a call in about four weeks' time.'

My chest flutters with excitement. A job, a real job, working in a hospital helping people. I can do this. I know I can.

I'm brought back to earth when Hilda squeezes my hand. I can't believe I'm going to witness the birth of a newborn baby. It's truly amazing, a magical, wonderful feeling.

'Hilda, I can see a head. Wow!'

The baby slithers out at approximately half past two in the morning, bloody and bawling at the top of its lungs. It's a girl. She's the size of a doll and has the most beautiful blue eyes. One of the nurses pulls across the curtain while they bathe Hilda and check her over. She looks very tired and pale, and there are red circles around her eyes. I give her some privacy and step outside until the curtain is opened again. I watch spellbound as the midwife wraps the baby in a blanket, then hands her gently over to Hilda, a tiny bottle of baby milk at the ready. Hilda stares down in wonder at the infant in her arms.

'Isn't she an angel,' she coos, kissing the infant's forehead.

'She's beautiful. What are you going to call her?'

'Her name's Sarah,' she beams up at me, 'after my aunt.'

A lump in my throat, green with envy.

'I will come back and check on you later,' says Margaret. 'Rest for now.

Hilda grabs my arm. 'Stay with me, please.'

I'm about to reply when the familiar scent of incense mixed with chamomile wafts through the air.

'You did well,' says Emmanuelle bustling into the ward, all elbows and rosary beads swinging. She observes Hilda with the baby and purses her lips. 'Give me the child – I will feed her; you need your rest.' Hilda looks as if she's about to protest but, too tired to argue, flops back against the pillow.

How dare she tell her what to do. God, I hate her.

'Go back to the laundry, Hannon and take that ridiculous uniform off.'

I kiss Hilda on the forehead and whisper, 'Treasure this moment.'

The baby's cries echo in the ward as I'm leaving, and I return with leaden footsteps to the institute. That night I cry into my pillow, for myself and for Hilda, at what would surely await her. My stomach is in a knot, and though I know the baby will be taken away from her soon, I can't help feeling envious and wishing it was me rocking my baby in my arms. Unable to sleep, I take out my journal and pencil, worn down from use, and compose a poem.

Carrie my angel
My love so sweet
Without you beside me
I am not complete
When you are sad
Smile and be glad
When you feel fear
Trust me I'm near.
I'll always protect you
Night or day
And Love you always
No matter what they say

Chapter Twenty Seven

Louisa

1951

We march to morning mass, Claude leading the group. I'm thinking about Luke and wondering if he'll show when the new girl waddles side to side, mimicking the nuns and making funny faces. I smother a giggle and turn my head away.

'Miss, I've got to go to the loo,' she says suddenly.

'It's Sister. Hold on to it!'

She makes a show of clutching her stomach. 'But I've got unmerciful cramps, Sis. Oh, God, I think it's the runs this time!'

'Will you keep your voice down!' Augusta snarls, her face all red. 'You're excused from mass this morning. Go on before I change my mind.'

I'm surprised to see Joan in the chapel already, rearranging orchids on the altar. Mass is the usual barrel of laughs, and I'm itching to escape from the incense-cloying atmosphere of the foyer and all its inhabitants. The priest stutters his way through the sermon, and Joan does a reading. I shiver from the cold and wish I had my warm purple jumper that Emmanuelle confiscated on her return to duties, claiming that it looked too garish for humble penitents. The choir drone the same old hymns and I see no sign of Luke today, only his parents.

Once the congregation have vacated the chapel, instead of rushing us out back to work, Emmanuelle holds us back and goes up to the altar accompanied by the portly priest. I glance at the others and wonder what's happening.

'Now that I have you all here,' he begins, 'I would very much like you to represent the Sisters of Mercy for the St. Patrick's Day event. The Reverend Mother has told me time and time again how hard you work and what excellent seamstresses you all are. And I thought wouldn't it be wonderful if we could make costumes for our new float to celebrate St. Patrick and the good work that you all do here, day in, day out. As a reward for your contribution, you can all attend the parade.'

Emmanuelle's head jerks up at this last comment. 'I don't think that is such a good idea. The girls may become overexcited and get lost in the crowds.'

'Not if you and the other sisters go with them.'

She scowls and, after a moment, nods her head in assent.

'Wonderful,' he exclaims, clapping his hands. 'Now, here is what I propose.'

Half of us are sent to the laundry, and the other half put to work in the sewing room, making up costumes for the parade. I'm paired with Joan, and together, we get started on a robe fit for Saint Patrick. It's quiet in here; the only sound is the fire crackling in the hearth. Claude hands us an old sheet which I make short work of with my scissors. I tear off a large fragment and shape it into a robe. My stitches are jagged and clumsy, and I keep pricking my fingers. It's then I notice the rosary beads around Joan's neck.

She sees me looking and whispers, 'Sister Bernadette gave them to me.'

'Why?'

Joan turns red and mutters, 'You wouldn't understand.'

She's right there; I wouldn't, jabbing the collar with my needle. What's going on with her? I've divided the material into different sections, and by afternoon, the collar and one sleeve are on. I think about the parade. I could lose myself in the crowd, and nobody would notice. If I got to the port, I could stow away at the back of a ferry, get out of Galway altogether.

Sister Bernadette relieves Claude and inspects our handiwork, pausing now and then to make suggestions. When she comes to me, she eyes my stitching dubiously, shakes her head and moves on. I'm not that bad. My fingers ache, and I feel a headache coming on. Joan, on the other hand, is flying it and is almost finished one garment. The gong sounds for lunch. My legs are stiff as I follow the procession to the dining hall. We assemble outside Emmanuelle's office and shadow the nuns. My stomach growls, and my throat is parched. I sit opposite the new girl who picks at her food with disinterest and scowls her disgust.

'This slop is not fit for a pig.'

'Shut up.'

'Who are you?' she rounds on Joan. 'My mother!'

The eggs are soggy, and the bacon is burnt to a crisp. I chew, not tasting it. The girl pushes the plate aside, folds her arms and stares ahead. Everyone else gobbles back the food, no matter how revolting it is.

'You should eat, just to keep your strength up,' I tell her.

She turns her head, and I think she's going to tell me to get lost when she says quietly, 'Is the food always like this here?'

'Pretty much.'

'Stop talking, girls.' Emmanuelle's voice booms from behind me.

She picks up her fork, spears a rasher and chews noisily with her mouth open. Joan glances over and frowns her disgust.

'What's your name?'

'Louisa,' I whisper. 'What's yours?'

'Carmel.'

'Where are you from?'

'The moon.' Carmel throws down her fork, making a racket. Sister Augusta marches over and grabs her by the ear.

'You're on kitchen duties. You too, Hannon. Hop it, now!'

I wheel out the trolley and start collecting the dirty dishes from the tables while Carmel fires the cutlery into a plastic container. She doesn't care who hears her and saunters around like she owns the place, hands in her pockets, whistling to herself. In the kitchen she tosses plates into the sudsy water with a loud splash and crows at the top of her lungs.

If you can't beat 'em, join 'em. It feels so good to sing even if we are out of tune and slaving in a kitchen, one ear cocked for pounding footsteps. No one came running to lecture us, and that's because there is more insulation here than anywhere else in the entire convent.

I put away the plates on the shelves. Carmel dries her hands. 'I like you. You're different to the others.'

'Thanks,' I smile. 'Not so bad yourself.'

'Whadda you make of these penguins?'

'Soulless.'

'Ha, good one,' she says, splashing water onto the floor. She looks down at the spreading pool. Hand to mouth. 'Oops. Hope they slip on it.'

She opens the fridge and peers in. 'Look what I've found.'

I can smell it. My mouth waters.

'Come on.' She pulls my hand, and together we race up the stairs out of sight. Emmanuelle can smell trouble a mile off and will surely know we're missing, but I don't care. We enter a small disused storage room and feast on the chicken. Oh, it never tasted so good. The meat is delicious. I pull off a leg while Carmel gorges on the breast. My hands are sticky with grease. I would have liked some salt, but what the hell it tastes divine and soon, only the skeleton remains.

Carmel wipes her hands on her dress. It's too small for her, reaching way above her knees. She catches me staring at her bruises; they're everywhere, brown and yellow marks on her arms, legs, and I bet on her torso as well. I feel my face flush and look away.

'What are you gawking at?'

'How come you've got so many bruises?'

'None of your business.'

Shouts downstairs. Our names being called.

'Where you going – stay put.'

Dread blooms in my chest. If they find us in here, we're doomed. I won't be able to sit for a week if Emmanuelle has anything to do with it. 'Come on; we can't stay here.'

'You go. I don't care what they say.'

'I've had enough beatings to last a lifetime.'

She folds her arms. 'Piss off, then, chicken.'

Hysterics bubble up inside me, and I run to the dormitory, throw myself on the bed and curl up in a foetal position.

Within seconds, I feel a hand roughly pull me out off the bed. Augusta pinches my arm and waggles her finger in my face. 'What are you doing up here?'

'Period cramps.'

She grunts. 'Get down to the laundry. Now!'

'Hannon?'

'Yes, sister?'

'Have you seen the new girl?'

'No, sister.'

'Get to work, then.'

I'm no sooner down the stairs when I hear screams, cursing, and doors being slammed. Carmel is hauled across the landing by Emmanuelle on one side and Sister Claude on the other. My heart sinks. All I can think about is myself. What if she tells them I was in on it?

'Let me go, bitches. Let me go, I said!'

Her voice is drowned out by the loud noise from the washing machine, and for that, I am thankful. Shame floods me, but I've gone through too much abuse in this horrific place already to take anymore.

Joan watches me load the laundry, and once I'm in earshot, hisses, 'She's going to get you into trouble.'

'Her name's Carmel.'

'I don't care what her name is. Do you know she doesn't believe in God?'

'So, what. He hasn't done us much favours.'

Her mouth drops open; you could pick her jaw up from the floor. 'How could you –'

'Problem, girls?'

I jump, didn't hear her behind me. 'No, Sister Claude.'

'Get on with it, then and no talking.'

Grinding my teeth, I glance back at Joan and feel an overwhelming urge to shake her. What's got into her? So damn pious all of a sudden. She's starting to get on my nerves. I stretch. My back aching again, my fingers sore, the skin peeling from using too much detergent. The door opens. I turn slowly and stare in shock at the butchered head of Carmel as she pretends to stroll into the laundry with not a care in the world. My face must register my shock as she looks up and pins me with her scrutiny. The colour drains from my face as I picture what the nuns have done to her. Her face is bloodied where the scissors dug into her scalp and some of the blood ran freely. Her lovely hair is in ruins, but the defiant glint in her eyes is still there.

Though it's my turn to iron the laundry, I let Carmel do it instead. She looks like she could break in two, and this is the easier workload. She is quiet, and her face is pale, too pale. Claude steps outside, and I rush over to Carmel, sheets draped over my arm, ready to be folded. 'Are you okay?'

'What do you think?' she snaps without looking up at me.

My eyes dart to the door expecting Emmanuelle to call me out, but no one comes. 'They found out about the chicken?'

She nods. Slams the iron down. 'You'd swear it was the crown jewels or something,' she says through gritted teeth. 'Don't fret, I'll live. But I guess that's not what's really bothering you, is it?'

Guilt floods my face with colour as I scramble for a reply.

'I'm not a snitch, so shove your concern somewhere else.'

'Sorry,' I mumble.

'This style is becoming all the rage, you know.'

I grin.

'Lou, help me fold these sheets,' says Joan glancing warily from me to Carmel.

When I look back, Carmel is pinning what's left of her hair back with wooden clothes pegs. I giggle, and she smirks, pointing with her index fingers to her new hairstyle as if to say, Check it out. I give her the thumbs up and discover that I actually like her. She's brave and kind, and I admire her tenacity and the speed with which she bounces back no matter what happens to her.

Saint Patrick's Day comes and goes, lashing rain preventing us from attending. Typical, after all the work we put in.

Shamrock pinned to our uniforms, the only concession for our hard efforts. Next year I will go and see the parade, stay as long as I want, just me and baby Carrie, and no one, no one will stop me.

Chapter Twenty Eight

Carrie

1976

There was no milk in the house. Again. Pulling in at the nearest Esso petrol station, Carrie rummaged in her pockets for loose change when she suddenly realised she'd left her purse back at Jack's parents' place. Reversing out of the forecourt, she headed in the direction of their house, hoping and praying that Nathaniel had gone out and she wouldn't have to face him again. Parking the car at an angle, she raced up to the door and was about to knock when she noticed it was already open.

Angry voices erupted from the dining room. Carrie froze mid-step on the porch.

'That girl is unhinged, I'm telling you.'

'Something startled her, that's all.'

'Stay out of this, Diane!'

'How dare you talk about her like that. I'm leaving.' Jack's voice reached her ears.

'Listen, I knew her father, that family are no good, he used to work for me, it was so long ago I'd forgotten. You don't remember the construction business I owned; you were too young – well, he stole a whole month's supply of timber.'

Carrie gasped at this. Jack must have heard. When he saw her at the door, his face turned white.

Heart galloping, she spied her purse on the telephone table just within reach of the porch. Knees knocking together in shock, she grabbed it, ran back to the car, gunned the engine, and tore out the driveway back to the petrol store. Not pausing to consider Nathaniel's cruel lies, she filled up the Beetle with fuel, her hand shaking so much, petrol spilled onto the ground. She paid the attendant, then drove home in a daze of bewilderment, vowing never to set foot in that house ever again.

Max started barking when the doorbell rang. She peeped through the window and cringed. The last person she wanted to see stood outside looking shifty and disgruntled, rain plastering his hair to his forehead.

'Carrie, please, let me in.'

She opened the door, folded her arms and stepped back.

'What do you want?'

'Dad shouldn't have said that. I'm so sorry.'

'Sorry that I heard what he said, or are you apologising for him?'

'I don't know what's got into him, he's always been a grumpy old bastard, but this is way below the belt.'

'He called my father a thief. He's a liar; Dad never worked for a building contractor.'

Jack lowered his gaze to the floor, then back to her again. 'Maybe, when you were very young, you wouldn't remember.'

'Just go home and leave me alone.'

'I can't leave it like this. Please, Carrie, don't take it out on me. I didn't say those things. He's a jerk, and I'm going to have it out with him.'

'My dad is gone. You still have yours,' Carrie said, tears glimmering. 'I won't have his memory tarnished by a bully.' She covered her face, and her shoulders jerked from sobs.

Jack enveloped her in his arms. She stiffened at first, then huddled closer, loving the warmth, the smell of paint mixed with Cologne. *Oh God, what am I doing?* She tried to pull away, but he resisted and stroked her hair. 'Think I'm falling for you,' he whispered huskily.

Her eyes widened in surprise. She twisted to look up at him, and then he bent to kiss her tentatively. It was so sweet she longed for more, but all of a sudden, the telephone shrilled, and the moment was gone.

'Let it ring,' he grunted.

'Could be work.'

Her head was reeling as she went to answer the phone, but there was no one at the other end, and now the moment had gone, and she just felt foolish for letting her guard down.

'Wrong number.'

He made a move to take her in his arms again, but she stopped him. 'It's late. I've work in the morning.'

'Right,' he said, looking wounded. 'Of course. So have I. Ring you during the week?'

'Okay. Bye, Jack.'

She leaned against the closed door and sighed. *Am I doing the right thing? I don't know what is happening to me.* She recalled the feel of his arms around her, the warmth, the longing, and the tingling in her nether regions and knew without a shadow of a doubt she wanted to feel it again and a lot more. *To hell with his father. I just won't have anything to do with him.*

The next few weeks passed in a blur. Tom had been preoccupied with his dad in hospital and was out of the office most of the time. Then, one Wednesday, he announced that they had to move premises before the end of the month because the owner wanted to sell up. Together they scoured the property section and finally settled on a ground floor office two buildings down. Files were boxed and stored away, and builders helped to move the furniture. The place was stripped bare within days, and with a little help from the furniture movers, they finally moved in.

She looked around her and smiled. Her office wasn't as big as Tom's, but at least she had privacy, with great views of the Connemara mountains in the distance. And it was centrally heated too, no more huddling up to a mangy gas fire. She hung a photo frame of her credentials and one of her parents on the wall, then tidied a bouquet of pink chrysanthemums in a vase on her desk before grabbing her bag and heading out to meet Jack, who stood waiting for her outside. Time had hurtled by, with Jack avoiding his father completely. Six weeks ago, he'd shown her how to paint. At first, she was nervous, but she gradually got the hang of it. Daffodils were the easiest, and she even managed to paint their proper shape. It had been messy but colourful, and after a while, she began to enjoy herself. She got more paint on herself than on the palette. During the month that followed, they caught several movies, went out to dinner, to dances, and yesterday had a romantic picnic by the sea. She wondered where he was taking her this evening, hoping they would get some alone time together.

'Hey you,' he grinned, leaning in to kiss her.

He smelled of musk, soap and leather. They linked arms. 'Where are we going?'

'You'll see,' he said, opening the door of his Land Rover.

At that moment, Nathaniel barged out of the chemist, stopping short as soon as he saw them. His expression darkening, he marched towards them, but not before Jack hissed at her to get in, slammed the door and drove off in a squeal of tyres.

Miles of silence stretched between them, Jack's knuckles white, taut with tension on the wheel. Carrie fiddled with the buttons on the radio. Debussy notes floated into the air.

They arrived at the National Park. The sun, a great orb of yellow, was setting over the horizon. He took her hand, tugging her towards the lake where a blue and yellow canoe bobbed in the water. Stepping into the canoe, Jack held out his hand for her to take it.

She froze. Then stepped back. 'Sorry, I can't. Please, take me home.'

'What? It's just a small boat – come on.'

Spinning on her heel, she marched back to the car.

'Wait! Carrie!' he called, sprinting after her.

She was standing against the bonnet, arms folded. 'My parents died while out in a boat.'

'It's just a canoe. You'll be safe with me.'

'Take me home, Jack, now!'

The drive back was long and interminable. Carrie stared out the window, lips pursed, blinking back tears. He stopped outside her house, pulled in but didn't make any move to get out. As she opened the passenger door, he touched her arm.

'I get it, okay. I didn't think. Please don't be angry. You're the only good thing in my life right now. I just wanted to make you happy – take away that sadness.'

Turning to look at him, she whispered, 'You can't take it away; no one can. I need time, that's all.'

'I love you.'

Carrie stared at him, mouth agape. 'But you hardly know me.'

His ears reddened. 'I know enough. How do you feel?'

Warmth flooded her body head to toe, and she couldn't stop smiling. She grabbed him by the lapel of his jacket. 'Come inside, and I'll show you.'

When he pulled back, she frowned, flushing with embarrassment.

'God, you don't know how much I want to, but I won't take advantage of you when you're vulnerable. That's not the kind of guy I am.'

Relief flooded through her, and smiling, she said in a husky voice, 'Next time then,' opening the passenger door, a dreamy expression on her face.

'Hey, what are you doing with my cousin's pendant?'

Carrie turned and picked up the locket. 'This belonged to your cousin?' She said in surprise. 'I found it in your house – I don't remember putting it in my pocket, sorry. Pretty little thing, isn't it?'

'Can I see it?' he said softly.

She removed it from her neck and handed it to him. 'It's yours now.'

He opened it and stared at the photo.

'Who is the little girl?' Carrie asked.

'My cousin, Louisa. I never met her, but I remember Mum showing me a photo of her once, and she had that locket around her neck. It stuck in my head 'cos it was the oddest piece of jewellery I'd ever seen.'

Her pulse quickened. 'How come you never met?'

He shrugged, 'Don't know. She was a lot older than me, almost sixteen years I think, could be that she moved abroad.'

'Can you tell me anything else about her?' Carrie asked, trying not to sound too desperate.

'Um…she used to help my mum around the house when she was younger – she liked to dress up in her clothes. That's all I know. It's funny, but they never really talked about her. Keep the locket; it looks better on you,' he quipped.

'If I'm going to keep this locket, I'd really love to know more about this lady.'

'I could ask Mum about her if you like –'

'Really? I'd appreciate that, thanks.'

'Let me put it on for you.'

She held up her hair out of the way so he could clasp it around her neck. His warm fingers tingled her skin, and a hot flush of desire swept through her. They kissed passionately, and after a while, he released her with a disgruntled sigh.

'Hold that thought,' his eyes twinkled. 'I'll see you during the week?'

She nodded, breathless. Watched him drive away.

That night she lay in bed, one arm cupping her head, staring up at the ceiling, rehashing the whirlwind of events that had taken place over the last few months. Happy in the knowledge that she might finally get some answers about Louisa.

Excitement in her belly, she pictured Jack, their legs entwined, tangled up in the sheets and gave a long sigh of contentment. The only fly in the ointment was his dad's disapproval which she still couldn't understand, and neither could Jack. It'll be her birthday next month; she'll ask him to stay over. Her eyelids drooped, and with one hand resting on the dog, she fell into a deep sleep.

Carrie awoke with a startle to the faint cold brush of lips on her forehead and to an icy room. The curtain billowing in the wind. A mist in her bedroom and a hint of jasmine. Stunned to see the shadowy figure of a girl watching her intently. Her heart began to palpitate.

'Louisa?' she croaked.

The apparition shimmered for a moment, began to fade, then slowly disappeared from view.

Chapter Twenty Nine

Carrie
1976

She lay wide awake until five the following morning, turning and twisting before falling into a restless sleep. The alarm awoke her. Groggily, she hit the off button. She flipped over onto her back, dredging through the cavern that was her mind, the strange dream that had felt so real of the woman looking down at her. Carrie decided to take the day off to sort through her muddled brain once and for all. Hannah's words, 'You don't look a bit like your mother,' spurred her to go through the most recent photos taken of her parents. She flicked through the albums splayed out on the carpet, concentrating on similarities between them and obvious differences. She loved her parents to bits, and questioning the truth of her upbringing felt like the ultimate betrayal that cut her to the core. By midday, her eyes started to feel gritty from tiredness. The only obvious differences between them were her parents' heights and, of course, her dark eyes. Her mother was short with blue eyes. Her father too, but then that didn't really mean anything as sometimes height and eye colour could pass from grandparents too.

After a mug of coffee and an egg sandwich, she decided to visit Tess again. If she didn't do something she'd go barmy, and these visions and dreams were bound to plague her until she got to the bottom of it one way or another.

'Come on, Max, let's go.'

The dog's ears pricked to attention, and he gave a small bark of excitement. After her car got damaged, she'd purchased a red Mini. Only three years old. And it moved like a dream. She was driving out of the yard when a jeep braked suddenly, almost colliding with the Mini.

Adam rolled down his window. His face scarlet. 'Sorry, Carrie, I was miles away.'

'No harm done. Where are you off to in such a hurry?'

'To my new place in Roundstone,' he replied, ruffling Max's head through the window. 'The sale finally went through yesterday. I'm sixty acres richer.'

'Wow, congratulations! Bet Nuala will be glad to get you out from under her feet!'

'Oh, God, don't talk to me; I'd even considered kipping on your sofa. Mam can be such a fuss pot. Mothers, eh?'

She lowered her eyes.

He thumped the wheel. 'Put my foot in it again, haven't I? Sorry, Carrie.'

'It's all right, really – can't tiptoe around me all the time, so don't worry about it.'

A horse stomped its feet in the box behind, blew noisily through its nostrils.

She got out of her car and went over to have a look. Adam joined her.

'Oh, Adam,' she exclaimed, touching his arm, 'she's a beauty.'

'Cost me a quare penny too.'

A sleek black car slowed to a crawl to overtake Adam's jeep on the narrow road, its wheels skidding on the verge before it sped by so fast it almost whipped away Adam's side mirror.

'Maniac!' Adam shouted, bending to examine his jeep for scrapes and dents.

She stroked the mare's face while the Irish Draught nuzzled her jacket, searching for a carrot or an apple.

'You should come over sometime and check out the stables.'

'Thanks, I'd love to,' Carrie said, rubbing the sleep out of her eyes.

'Are you okay? You look a bit distracted.'

'I'm fine, just a little tired, that's all.'

'Your parents' anniversary is coming up soon.'

'Yeah,' she said, scuffing the ground, 'next month.'

'I'm just a call away if you fancy some company.'

She smiled. 'Thank you, I appreciate it.'

'Anyway, best be off. This horse will break the door down if I don't get going soon. Bye.'

Tess was at her favourite hobby, plucking weeds when Carrie pulled up. Sunlight dappled the surrounding meadows, and the trees were in full bloom, the branches alive with scurrying creatures big and small. She made her way over, a knot in her chest, wondering how she was going to bring the subject up yet again.

'Hello, love.'

There was a streak of dirt across her brow. Her long green garden gloves were caked in mud. She got up, brushed dirt from her faded blue pants, reaching out to hug her warmly. 'What brings you to this neck of the woods?'

Carrie only lived five miles away and smiled at this. 'Do I need a reason to see my favourite aunt?'

'Get away or that.' Holding her at arm's length, she clucked. 'You've lost weight; your mother isn't feeding you enough – tell her I said so.'

Carrie stared at her, aghast. Christ! *She has dementia. I'd forgotten all about it. She looks so well.*

'Bob, how many times have I told you not to trample in my garden. Be a good girl and make us some tea. There are fresh scones in the oven that I made this morning.'

As soon as she headed towards the house, Max bounded up, tail wagging. 'Chasing rabbits again, Max?'

Tess still believed her beloved Bobby was still alive, and not wanting to have to explain that it was a different dog, she caught Max by the collar and locked him into the back of the Mini with the window down halfway.

'Don't look at me like that. I won't be long.'

A long green raincoat hung from a hook on the back door. An umbrella stood in the corner. The kitchen presses were painted dark brown. Carrie filled the kettle, then peeked through the pile of papers that covered the worn tablecloth like an eiderdown quilt. Nothing here but unpaid telephone and electric bills. The drawers yielded the same result. The kettle hissed to the boil. She glanced upstairs, then back to the window where Tess was still digging.

All I need is five minutes.

She sprang for the stairs. Because the radio was blaring, she failed to hear a car pull up. Carrie counted four doors, the left was locked, one room so full of clutter she couldn't even open the door, another was the door to the bathroom. Tess's room was the last. She hurried inside, her heart hammering in her chest, listening out for the kettle's whistle. *Where would I hide a secret?*

Carrie pulled out drawers, tipping makeup, handbags, underwear and socks onto the frayed grey carpet, rifling through the wardrobe bursting with outdated clothes. She sifted through the mouldy items one by one, clothes scented with mothballs, single earrings, jewellery that would have been fashionable twenty years ago, old photos of Hannah as a baby just stuffed in amongst the rubble. After several long moments of searching through vintage items, she sat back on her haunches, begging her brain to think.

There had to be something here. Then she saw it. Carrie dragged over a chair, stood on it, and brought down a shoebox from the top of the wardrobe. She blew away the dust, sat on the bed and then took off the lid.

Inside lay a bundle of envelopes secured by elastic. She took them out, removing the elastic band. They looked like official documents relating to the house and other legal jargon she didn't understand. At the bottom was a white envelope.

Her head jerked up at the sound of running footsteps on the stairs. With trembling fingers, she stuffed the envelope into her back pocket and crammed everything back into the box just as the door was flung open.

'Mum, did you not hear -?'

Her eyes bugged.

Heat flooded Carrie's face. 'Hannah, I can explain.'

'What the hell are you doing in here? How dare you plunder my mother's things! What kind of person does that?'

'It's not what it looks like – please, you know me,' said Carrie jumping up from the bed.

'Get out before I call the guards!' Shooting her a look of loathing, Hannah pushed her out the door.

Carrie ran downstairs to the sound of the kettle yelling at the top of its lungs outside to where her Mini was parked around the side and fumbled with her keys.

Tess stooped to pick them up. Handed them to her. 'You leaving already?'

'Sorry, Auntie Tess, I have to go,' she said, opening the car door with jerky movements.

There was a tightness in her chest as she blinked back hot tears. She felt sick with self-disgust and couldn't bear to look at herself in the mirror. Max rested his head on her lap all the way home. *What have I done? Hannah is never going to trust me now.* All that frenzied searching just for crazy old dreams. I need my head examined, she thought. Once she got home, she was debating whether or not she should bite the bullet, call over and have it out with Hannah when there was a loud, angry knock on the front door.

Max started to growl, raising the hackles on the nape of his neck. Pulling the curtain aside, Carrie peeped out and frowned. *What's Jack's father doing here?* Perplexed, she paced up and down, bit her nails, then jumped when he banged the door again.

'I know you're in there. I want to talk to you; come on, open up; it's important.'

I'll get no peace until he leaves. Closing the kitchen door to shut the dog in, she took a deep breath and opened the door a crack. He pushed past her in a long navy overcoat, his grey-black hair askew. 'Don't worry, I'm not staying.'

'What's this about Mr Hannon?' she demanded, folding her arms.

'What do you want from my son?' he spat viciously. 'Stay the hell away from Jack.'

Carrie baulked as if she'd just been slapped. 'W…why? I don't understand.'

'Just do as I say – it's for your own good,' he barked, spinning on his heel to leave.

Standing in front of the door barring his exit, she retorted, 'Not until you give me a good reason.'

'Okay…his fiancée wants him back.'

Fiancée. What?

She stared at him stunned, looked away, then back to him again. At his self-assured smug manner and knowing calculated expression. *He thinks I'm not good enough and means to frighten me off, that's all. How come Diane didn't mention it? I don't believe him.*

'That good enough reason for you?'

Lifting her chin, she said, 'If what you say is true, then Jack can tell me himself.'

His face darkened, 'Don't be a fool.'

She swung the door open. 'GET OUT!' Her chest heaved up and down as rage burned like wildfire through every fibre of her being. Her hands were trembling. She'd never felt so livid in all her life. The gall of the man!

His mouth twisting into a sneer, he advanced towards her. Placing a hand either side of her head, he pressed her back against the wall and, eyes glinting dangerously, leaned in.

'Wha…what are you doing?' The words were dry and ratchety in her throat. He stood so close she could smell the tang of his body odour. Max squealed from the kitchen, scraped at the wood to be let out. Her breathing accelerating, she raised her knee to kick him in the crotch when he suddenly stood back. She could breathe again. His tongue flickered out like a snake to wet his lips. She fought the urge to run for the shower.

'You had hay in your hair,' he chuckled, tossing the sprig to the floor.

'Jack will hear of this – get out now!'

His gaze locked to hers, and for a moment, she was deathly afraid. He shook his head, muttering under his breath, 'Stupid bitch. Don't say I didn't warn you.'

As soon as he was gone, she slammed the door with enough force to bring the roof down and ran the bolt through. Shaking from the shock, she stayed rooted to the spot and didn't move for a long time until Max's frenzied barking broke her paralysis.

Chapter Thirty

Louisa

1951

Weeks tumble into months, and I'm still here but not for long more. Life is a little bearable, what with Emmanuelle taking leave to spend time with her sick mother. New girls are dumped in the convent, more nuns arrive, and soon we're overcrowded. Beds are pushed together to create more space in the cold unforgiving dormitory, and we are worked to the bone.

'What are you doing?' Joan asks.

'Counting the days to my escape,' I say, letting the calendar drop.

We're working the dinner shift this evening. My back is aching and I long to sit down. Steam rises from the boiling water in the sink, unfurling into the air. Joan packs away the last plates onto the shelf and slides the aluminium door across. A crucifix dangles from her neck, and when she thinks I'm not looking, she tucks it inside her uniform out of view. I finish mopping the floor, wipe the sweat from my forehead and lean against the counter, hardly able to stand up.

The banging noises from the laundry machines reverberate around my tired brain.

Augusta pokes her head in, glances around, purses her lips then closes the door again. As soon as she's gone, I leap onto the counter and sigh with relief.

'Don't let her catch you sitting there.'

'Oh, who cares!'

Joan stands before me. 'I care. I don't want you to get into any more trouble.'

'Why do you wear that cross?'

'It comforts me.'

'I don't understand you – God doesn't care about us.'

'She told you that – don't listen to her.'

The door opens; I breathe a sigh of relief to see that it is only Carmel. She pulls me by the hand. 'Where are we going?'

'You'll see.'

'You haven't finished helping me polish the glasses,' Joan complains.

'Who is she? Your keeper?'

I'm about to say something in her defence, then remembering the crucifix around her neck instantly harden my resolve. Anyone who follows the church after everything that has happened deserves what's coming to them.

Carmel leads me down to the basement. It's cold in here. There are more empty cardboard boxes than ever before, but nothing's changed since that time I tried to escape. I rattle the door handle. It's locked. It's getting dark.

'Over here,' she hisses.

She's behind the biggest stack of boxes, sitting cross-legged on the concrete floor. I hear the plaintive cry, and my mouth curves into a smile. A tabby kitten plays with a runaway thread from her sleeve. She is gorgeous and cute.

'I call her Whisper. Isn't she beautiful?'

Crouching down, I sit next to her and stroke the delicate fur. She purrs and rubs her head against my arm, bouncing from Carmel back to me, tail curled in the air, full of mischief.

Carmel takes out a small plastic box. Lifts the lid and tosses her tiny pieces of chicken.

'So that's why you took it?'

Whisper finishes the food. Carmel stands abruptly, catches the kitten, and puts her out through a tiny window, then stands to watch her run off into the trees. 'She'll be back. She always comes back.'

A gong sounds for night prayers, so we trudge back to rejoin the procession to the chapel. Sister Claude holds a lamp aloft, counting the heads as we enter one by one. She leads the prayer group off with eight decades of the rosary. I'm freezing, and I'm sure there are blisters on my knees from kneeling in the same spot for almost two hours. A familiar voice makes me jerk my head up. It's Joan standing at the pulpit; her face is in shadow as she sings the Alleluia hymn. I'd never heard her sing before. She sounds like a nightingale, and I could listen to her all evening. So sweet, pure, and innocent. Sister Augusta claps when she finishes. Carmel's face is creased with dislike, and she can't keep her eyes off her.

On the way up the stairs after vespers, Carmel sticks out her leg on the step tripping Joan up. I'm three people behind and don't see it happening until she topples backwards, creating a domino effect on everyone else taking up the rear. I clutch the handrail to stop myself from falling. The damage is minimal, and nobody is seriously hurt. Joan, however, has turned white and there are grazes across her knuckles. Instead of reporting the incident, she heads straight to bed, pulling the blankets up over her head.

I cross to my side of the room. The lights go out.

'Louisa, come here,' says Carmel.

'No talking,' says Sister Bernadette before she closes the door.

'What do you want?' I'm tired and cold, and I need my bed. She clicks on a torch under the blanket.

'Where did you get that?' I ask, glancing at the door.

'From the kitchen – where else?' She shuffles to the side. 'Scoot in; I can't see you in the dark.'

Fully clothed, I join Carmel under the bedclothes. The torch light is weak but sufficient to see one another. We start to giggle. Then she grabs my hand. Her skin is rough, and her huge palm dwarfs my hand.

Suddenly out of nowhere, she starts to cry, great big gulping sobs that shake her shoulders. I try to pry away my fingers, but they are held steadfast in an iron grip, so I wait for the cries to subside and for her to tell me what is wrong. The clock ticks the hour. Snores rise from the beds, and my eyelids begin to close.

She speaks softly, jolting me awake. I rub my eyes with my free hand wishing she'd get on with it and let me sleep.

'I feel like two different people – one minute I'm full of energy, and the next I want to throw myself out that window. My parents couldn't make head or tail of me. The doctor said it was some kind of chemical imbalance.'

'What's a chemical imbalance?'

'Damned, if I know.'

'We shouldn't be in this place. Is that why you're here – your parents had enough of you?'

'The local shopkeeper caught me with my hand in the till, nosey old Biddy; I shoulda knocked her out when I had the chance. That was the third time. It was either here or a correctional facility, so my parents chose here.'

I didn't know what to say, so I kept quiet. My eyelids drooping, fighting to stay awake.

'Hey, you've gone silent on me. Shocked ya, did I?'

'I'm just tired,' I said with a yawn.

A mattress creaked on the bed across the dormitory. Joan covers her head with the grey pillow. 'Shut up and go to sleep.'

'Go back to your praying, Joan.' Carmel jeers.

I move to get out of the bed.

'No, don't go just yet. I like having someone to talk to.'

'I'm exhausted. Tomorrow, okay?'

The following morning, I look for Luke in the choir but don't see him. It's been weeks now, and I can't help feeling he's given up on me. Three more dragons have joined the order, each worse than the other. They make us scrub the floors on our hands and knees with just a wire brush and bucket of water. Then supervise us in the laundry and later in the sewing room. There's no time to talk. The dogs on the street are treated better.

Augusta drills us each evening on our Catechisms before going to bed. Fit to drop, I stumble over the prayers and get a stick across the knuckles for my trouble. Carmel answers back at every opportunity; she's black and blue from canings; I don't know how she does it. They even watch us undress, making sure we get into bed. I'm so sick of this place. Every day feels like a decade, and my hair is starting to fall out from the stress. I've lost so much weight I don't recognise myself anymore. Carmel keeps me sane with her quirky comments and unbelievable resilience. I think I would be beating my head against the wall by now if it weren't for her.

Having said that, she disturbs me too. Her moods change all the time. One never knows what she's going to do or say next, whether she's deep in depression or high as a kite. I look down at my fingers, red and sore. Mass drones on, and again I look to the aisle where Luke usually stands. His parents stand stiff and rigid, staring into hymn books. His brother, Steven, I think he said his name was, glances around before picking his nose, then wiping his finger on his short pants.

I'm seventeen soon. I'd vowed to be out of this dungeon by then, but the future is bleak, and I'm afraid. There's nowhere for me to hide, but another year in this place will kill me; I know that for sure. I'm weak with the hunger and malnourished. My periods have stopped, and I get terrible pain in my lower back. No one can help me, I think, as the priest gives out Holy Communion.

After breakfast, we trudge to the laundry room to find it is locked. Sister Marguerite is flapping about in consternation over the missing key. It is decided that we will paint the outside walls of the convent instead in anticipation of Brother Benedict's visit from Glenstal Monastery. I welcome the fresh air and equipped with buckets of white paint, paint brushes and water we head outside.

It's a warm sunny day, and I feel my spirits lift bit by bit. Carmel and I are instructed to begin on the rear of the convent while Joan, Hilda and the others commence on the sides. Hilda has barely said a word about her baby. I wonder how she's feeling, but she won't open up and refuses to talk about it like it had never happened.

I'd never painted before, and I found the action of brush strokes soothing. Birdsong filtered through sun-choked canopies overhead. I could hear the sound of traffic on the main street outside the entrance gate and the patter of footsteps on the pavement. I welcomed the heat on my pale cheeks and wished the laundry room would never be unlocked. Then it occurred to me. I turned and looked at Carmel whistling to herself, firing paint on the wall two windows down from me. 'It was you, wasn't it?'

'Don't know what you mean,' she sang.

'You took the key.'

'Keep your voice down. I locked it this morning before mass.'

I laughed then, a real belly laugh.

She flicked white paint at me, I returned the favour, and soon we were both covered in it, but I didn't care. We sat on the grass.

'Let's run for the trees.'

'You first.'

She jumps to her feet, pulling me up with her. 'Come on, then.'

'Aw, be serious, Carm, how far do you think we'd get?'

'When then?' she asks, hands on her hips glaring at me.

'Not now, okay. We need to get supplies and clothes, find somewhere to live. Where would we go?'

Sister Marguerite shuffles around the corner, takes one look at us and grabs our arms. She hauls us into the convent, up the stairs to the bathroom and orders us to strip. Augusta comes in while we're in the cubicles, arms full of clean uniforms, which she tosses over the doors, narrowly missing the toilet bowls.

'Once you're dressed, I want you to wash the dormitory windows. I want to be able to see my face in them when I return. Understood? Make no mistake, girls, this behaviour will not be tolerated, and to ensure you heed this warning, there will be no dinner for either of you today. Sister Augusta will supervise you.'

After we drag a ladder from the shed, we set to work cleaning and polishing the windows using grimy cloths and newspaper.

Augusta makes me do the same window three times, pursing her lips and shaking her head. The glass is thick with green algae and grime, and my elbows are starting to tire from scrubbing so much. Augusta paces up and down the dorm, pointing out bits we missed, her nasally voice driving me cracked. Twice I nearly slipped from the ladder. Voices sound below; it must be time for dinner. My stomach rumbles as I glare over at Carmel. This is all her fault. If she hadn't been messing to begin with…

I'm about to ask Augusta if I can take a break when a clattering noise makes me glance over at Carmel. Augusta runs to her side as she falls off the ladder, pulling it down on top of her.

'Oh, dear heavens, child, are you hurt?'

Carmel blinks up at us in a daze. She's grazed her knee, and her left ankle is sticking out at a horrible angle. Her face contorts in pain when Augusta tries to help her sit up.

'Stay with her, Hannon, while I get some help.'

'What happened? Are you okay?'

'It's my ankle; think I twisted it. I misjudged the rung and slipped.'

She rises from the floor, hopping on one leg.

'Does it hurt?'

'Nah, just a sprain. But did you see the look on that old bat's face? Priceless.'

I stare at her in shock. 'You did it on purpose!'

'Course,' she grinned, 'got you off work, didn't I?'

I don't know what to say. She's crazy. 'But you could have been seriously hurt – you're insane.'

We hear footsteps hurrying towards the dormitory. Carmel promptly sits back down on the floor, one leg drawn up to her as she groans. I put my arm around her pretending to offer support.

Chapter Thirty One

Louisa

1951

'Leave us, Hannon.'

'Yes, Sister.'

I'm relieved to get away and not miss dinner after all bad and all as it is. On the way down to the hall, I reflect on what has just happened. Carmel takes a lot of chances. She's unpredictable, but to injure herself on purpose just to get off cleaning the windows seems a step too far, and I can't help wondering what else she is capable of. And if I should be keeping my distance.

Later in the afternoon, I'm down on my hands and knees, scrubbing the concrete floor. Joan has the easier task of dusting the skirting boards. Now and then I look up and see her glance at the huge round clock on the wall, then resume dusting. She's wearing a navy pinafore today, and her hair has been cut short.

'What's eating you? That's the fourth time you've looked at that clock since we started.'

She walks over towards me. 'Take a break. I'll scrub this paint off.'

I sit on the step and flex my fingers as she works, breathing life back into them again.

'I don't like her.'

'Who?'

'Carmel – who else,' she says, tossing the brush into the water.

'Why – because she stands up for herself?'

Joan pushes her fringe back from her forehead and stands up. 'She's trouble, and you know it, Lou.'

It's another four days before I see Carmel. Her ankle has healed, and she's back in the laundry with the rest of us. There are blotches on her face as if she's been crying and she won't speak to anyone.

'What's wrong with her?' Hilda whispers to me.

'I don't know.'

Just as we're filing out the door, I pull her aside. She looks desperate; the scabs on her scalp are bleeding, the face scars more prominent, there's a mile of dirt under her fingernails, and she reeks. Tugging her arm free, she follows the others, eyes vacant.

It's now Friday. Carmel's been on my mind all morning. I didn't see her when I was getting dressed, and she wasn't at mass either. I hope she's okay. Life in the convent is unbearable without her.

The sun is splitting the rocks as we head outside to work in the garden. It feels great to get out of the oppressive mouldy air and into nature. The nuns own an allotment to the rear of the building. It's long, stretching to about an acre. Besides vegetables, it also contains roses, marigolds, tulips, pansies, and crocuses. Our job is to pick the weeds. They've given us rubber gloves so we don't get stung by the mountain of nettles springing up all over the place, and there are thistles too. I stoop to pluck stray dock leaves and toss them into a black galvanized wheelbarrow. The birds are singing on the branches as I hum to myself. Sister Gardenia, a short, stout nun newly ordained to the order, piles bulbs into crates.

Behind her is Maude, who's come out of her shell a little bit since her sister left and is starting to put on weight again. Joan is at the front, bedding down compost. Now and then I hear her talking to Gardenia and laughing. I feel a pang of betrayal, shake my head in bafflement and pretend not to notice.

Sweat pools under my armpits. I pause to stretch my back when a familiar sight comes into view. Carmel jogs over to Gardenia, who instructs her where to begin. She gives me a thumbs up, then tears into the job at hand, yanking thistles up from their roots. She fires them into a box and then proceeds to the next row. Gardenia, unlike the other nuns, praises us for our work, distributing glasses of ice-cold lemonade to everyone in the group. Then, at noon, we head back inside to wash our hands. The gong announces lunch. I'm famished and wolf down every morsel.

There's no time to speak to Carmel as we're split into groups, one half to finish the laundry and the other half to peel and chop the carrots and parsnips we picked from the garden two days ago. The sun has gone in, and it's turned cold. I rub my arms to ward off the chill as we traipse back inside to prepare the vegetables for sale in the town market.

I feel hot all over, and my body aches, but then this is nothing new, so I don't pay any heed. My teeth begin to chatter, and I can't keep warm. I feel sick and wonder if I'm coming down with the flu. I start to cough. Tears blur my eyes, and I drop the knife. It falls with a clatter to the tiles alerting Sister Assumpta, who'd returned to the hall to get her pamphlet she'd left on the table.

'Goodness, gracious, child,' she says, hand to my brow, 'you're burning up. Off to bed with you. I will get one of the girls to bring you some broth.'

Coughing and sneezing, I undress and climb into bed. Assumpta throws a cover over me and places a cold compress on my forehead. I've never felt as sick in all my life. Maybe this is what it feels like before you die. My throat hurts. One minute I'm hot, and the next minute I'm freezing. I just can't get comfortable. I hear footsteps approach outside the door. My eyelids grow heavy, and I drift off. When I wake again, it's to feel the warmth of skin against mine.

My eyes fly open in shock. I struggle to get up, but I'm weak, and every movement takes effort.

'Go to sleep.'

Carmel strokes my hair, her hot breath fanning my ear. She's so close, it feels claustrophobic, but exhausted I tumble back into a deep sleep, not waking until some hour the following morning and to an empty space beside me.

The chills are gone, but I ache all over. Joan appears by my bedside with a tray. The smell of soggy egg makes me heave, and I turn on my side drifting off to sleep once more. When I open my eyes, it's getting dark outside. I can't believe I slept the entire day. I sit up, swing my legs out of the bed and get dressed. Driven by hunger, I go down to the hall where Joan, Hilda and Carmel are collecting the plates to take them to the kitchen.

'You're better again,' Joan cries, throwing her arms around me .

'I'm starving – please say there's some leftovers.'

'I saved some for you,' says Carmel, 'it's in the fridge.'

'So did I,' Joan says.

A flash of irritation crosses Carmel's face as they both lead me to a table, sit and watch me eat a potato, pork dripping and toast, gobbling them so fast like it's the last supper.

Footsteps approach. The swish of a robe. Our heads turn in unison as Sister Claude waddles into the hall, lips pursed, taking in the three of us.

'This is not a doss house. Get back to work. Now!'

The chair makes a scraping sound across the tiles as we scuttle to our various tedious tasks. Something is niggling me, but for the life of me, I can't put a finger on it. The beast that is the enormous washing machine breaks down, and we have to wash the remaining linen by hand with only one hour left before bedtime. Carmel helps me fold a sheet, and it's then I remember the way she was only a few days ago.

'Are you okay, now?'

'Why wouldn't I be?'

'It's just that,' I whisper, 'you looked sick the last time I saw you.'

She glances around her, then says in a low voice, 'It's swings and roundabouts, you know – one minute I'm up, the next I'm down.'

'Stop talking, O'Brien.'

'I'm not talking, Sister.'

Sister Claude marches up to us with a cane. 'What did you say?'

'That I'm sorry for talking, sister.'

Everyone knows Claude is hard of hearing. Carmel flinches when she strikes the table. 'The rest of you, go to bed. O'Brien can finish here.'

Not completely deaf then!

The baskets are spilling over with sheets, shirts, and other dirty linen. It would take her all night to complete the work.

'But, Sister –'

'Don't but Sister me – that'll teach you to give back cheek.'

I glance sympathetically over at Carmel, then trudge after the others back to the dormitory. After prayers, I brush my teeth and eye myself in the mirror. It's not a pretty sight. My lips are sore and bloodless, and there's not enough weight on my cheeks. I look haggard, like a woman three times my age. Replacing the lid on the almost empty tube, I plod back to the dormitory and stare up at the ceiling where I count the tiles, beginning with the row on the left and working my way across.

Gentle snores drift through the room. I wish I could nod off as easily. The mattress is lumpy, springs poking my back, and I really could do with another blanket. A full moon emerges from behind the clouds, a great big shiny orb blasting its brightness through the windows overhead. I turn over on my side and rummage under my mattress for my journal but can't find it. Must be further down than I thought, so I get out of bed and lift it up to search underneath. Panic engulfs me. It's not there. What if one of the nuns discovered it? Surely not; they would have said something by now. I check under the bed. Nothing but cobwebs and dirt.

That journal meant the world to me, and now it's gone. Could I have left it down somewhere? It's possible. I force myself to remain calm and climb back under the covers, my feet frozen from the concrete floor. Huddling under the single blanket, I'm trying to jog my memory when my eyelids grow heavy. I can't keep them open any longer, and soon I drift off to sleep.

The smell wakes me. Someone's farted. I can't move. A heavy arm is draped across my chest. Hot breath in my ear. Bile bubbles up my throat as I scramble out of bed. Carmel falls flat on her face. Her nightdress ridden up above her thighs. She's wearing no knickers. Disgusted, I draw the blanket over her and rush to the bathroom, where I lean over the sink and puke.

How long has she been there? What would the others say if they knew? The clock chimes five am. I hurry into my clothes and head down to the laundry room to start on the new order before the others get up. As if I didn't have enough to deal with in this godforsaken place. The room is eerily silent after the day's activities. I unfold the ironing board, then get to work on a basket of washing. The iron hisses out steam, and soon, the methodical action begins to soothe my nerves.

I have to get out of here. I turn seventeen in less than three months. I have to convince the sisters that I am reformed, somehow. Hail stones rattle the windowpanes making me jump. At least there's heat from the iron, and my fingers are beginning to thaw. With nothing else to distract me, my thoughts soon return to last night and how long Carmel was lying beside me. I feel sick. There's a burning smell. I glance down at the shirt in horror to see a round scorch mark beside the collar. Remembering what happened last time, I scrub at it frantically and toss it back into the washing machine again.

At six, the door opens. My heart sinks to see Carmel. She sashays up to me like I'm her date or something. What am I going to do?

'Missed you this morning.'

Her voice is husky, just as I feared. How am I going to wriggle out of this one? I take a deep breath. Have to tread carefully here. 'Was there something wrong with your bed last night?'

She tosses her head back and laughs out loud.

'Shh, the others – they'll hear you!'

'I heard you mumbling in your sleep. You said, "God, it's freezing" so I thought we could warm each other up.'

'Are you out of your mind? If any of the sisters caught you –'

The door opened. 'Thought I heard voices. My, aren't we enthusiastic this morning, girls.' Carmel is folding a sheet while Augusta inspects the work. 'That's not ironed right – do it again.'

By the time we sit down for breakfast, I could eat a horse. I deliberately choose a seat as far from Carmel as possible and dive into the porridge. Whenever I look up, she's watching me, and I can't stand it. Emmanuelle is back and assigns us the tasks for the morning. We're divided into groups and set to work in the kitchen, laundry, and garden. My job is to sweep and tidy the glasshouse and pull weeds, and I'm relieved that Carmel is made work elsewhere.

Weak sunshine filters through the roof. Broken pots are strewn all over the interior. Green algae blocks out much of the light, and there is dirt everywhere I look, but it's warm and peaceful in here. I'm alone for the first time and don't have to contend with the nuns for once. I clear a bench to make room and place scores upon scores of pots, vases, and buckets in a row on top. Any debris I throw into a wheelbarrow, then commence organising the flowers at the other side. They are a mix of pansies and primroses, pretty, all different colours, shapes, and sizes. Blue, yellow, pink, red, so many I'd never seen before, some in full bloom, others just plants. I place vegetable seeds in trays, then hang tomato vines from hooks on the ceiling. The work is tedious, but at least it gets me away from the laundry for a while. I pack freshly cut carrots, onions, and lettuce into crates underneath the bench, along with radishes, turnips and potatoes. The sweat is pouring off me by the time I get around to sweeping the floor.

Sister Augusta pops in and smiles her approval. 'This is the most work that has been done in years. Well done, Hannon.'

I wish she'd call me by my first name, but it's great to get any praise at all in this place.

'Finish up here; you're needed in the laundry.'

'Yes, Sister.'

She pauses at the door and turns. 'You know, I must admit, you have changed considerably since we brought you here. This place has done you the world of good.'

'Thank you, Sister,' I say, staring at her, daring to hope.

'I'm going to recommend to Reverend Mother that you stay on here for another couple of years. We need more girls like you.'

As soon as she's gone, I hurl a potted plant at the door.

That night I lie in bed staring up at the ceiling, Augusta's words repeating in my mind. It doesn't matter what you do here, good or bad, they've no intention of letting you go. Sometime during the night, the mattress dips as Carmel climbs in beside me. Her cold leg wraps around mine. I stiffen and jerk upright to a sitting position.

'What are you doing? Get out.'

I can't see her in the dark. She giggles but doesn't move. 'You're hot when you're angry.'

Bile gushes up my throat. Pushing back the blanket, I leap out of the bed, shivering in my thin night dress. She touches my shoulder. I shrug away her hand.

'I'm only messing. Come on, come back to bed; you'll freeze.'

Everything about her stinks. Joan was right. How could I ever have liked her?

'Leave me alone, Carmel, fuck off back to your own bed.'

She grabs my arm, her fingers like talons, pinching my skin and hisses in my ear. 'I have your journal.'

'Bitch! Give it back!'

'Bet Emmanuelle would love to know what's in it.'

The other girls are awake now, sitting up in bed.

'You wouldn't dare!' I despise the way my voice squeaks.

'We'll keep our nightly arrangement and say nothing to no one. Deal?' She digs her nails in, impatient for an answer.

I nod, and she releases me so fast I stumble. With a big smile on her face, she tucks my precious journal inside her nightdress.

Light floods the room as a switch is flicked on. Emmanuelle fills the doorway. 'I heard voices. Why are you out of bed?'

'I was just going to the toilet.'

I lock the cubicle door. My heart is pounding. As if things couldn't get any worse, now, I have Carmel to contend with. The lights go out. I'm afraid to go back to bed. Maybe I'll never sleep again. I bury my face in my hands and groan. I have to get that journal back. But how?

My head starts to nod. I curl up in a foetal position on the floor and give into tiredness until daybreak.

Chapter Thirty Two

Carrie
1976

J ack had been calling for days, but Carrie refused to answer. She saw him arrive from the upstairs window. Her stomach felt sick after what happened with his father. Forearmed with the knowledge of where this conversation would inevitably lead, she wiped her sweaty hands on her grey slacks and went down to let him in. 'Hi.'

His hair was dishevelled. He looked pale, and there were rings under his eyes, but her heart still did somersaults at the sight of him, which only succeeded in twisting the knife further.

'I called, but there was no answer, several times in fact,' he said, looking at her with a wounded expression.

She closed the front door and went into the kitchen, Jack at her heels.

He didn't sit.

'What's going on, Carrie?'

Folding her arms, she sat back against the chair and eyed him levelly.

'You tell me – your father was here last week, barged into my home and warned me to stay away from you.'

'He did what? I'll fucking kill him!' he said, spinning on his heel toward the door.

'Is it true about your fiancée?'

He stopped mid-stride and turned. 'No – yes, he told you about Brigitta – I don't believe it. Look, we were engaged once, but that was a long time ago.'

'He said that she's back in Galway, wants to mend bridges.'

'God, Carrie, Dad shouldn't have said that – he'd no right.' He ran a hand through his hair. 'I didn't know she was in Ireland, let alone Galway.' He hunkered down and folded her hand in his. 'I'm so sorry about this – what he put you through, but any feelings I had for her are long gone.'

Carrie believed him but wasn't sure if it was enough. She extricated her hand and stood. 'Still doesn't explain why your father hates me so much. He scared me, Jack.' She paused. 'I don't think this is going to work, sorry.'

'Please, I really like you. I'll beg if I have to. Don't give up on us just yet. Let me have a word with him, sort this shit out. Carrie, you're like a breath of fresh air, the best thing that's ever happened to me. I won't let you go.'

He looked like he was going to cry, so she gave him a bear hug but then stepped back. She didn't want to give up on them either, but there was only so much she was willing to put up with too, and after that, it just wouldn't be worth the hassle. She hardly knew Jack, after all. 'Give me some time to think about it, okay.'

'Take all the time you need – no pressure. I'll talk to Dad, beat some sense into him.'

'Did you ask your mother about Louisa?'

'I didn't get a chance – she and Dad had a huge fight – it's been unbearable at home,' he said, dragging his hand through his hair again. 'She's gone to stay with a friend for a few days. Look, I promise I'll say it to her when she gets back.'

'Yeah, okay,' she replied in a disgruntled voice, cheesed off at the way the universe seemed to be forever conspiring against her.

He put on his coat and went to the door. Kissed her briefly on the lips, then, turning up his hood, dashed to the car.

Carrie needed a holiday. Things were getting way too intense. First, Han fell out with her, and then she was almost assaulted by Jack's father. She wondered what would happen next. She called Tom.

'Tom, it's me, Carrie. Can you hold the fort for a few days?'

'Is everything okay?'

'Yeah, just fancied a break away to clear my head. My parents' anniversary is coming up this week.'

'Christ, I'd totally forgotten, sorry.'

'I'm all right, honest, don't worry.'

'Any place in mind?'

'No – not yet. I'm working on it though.'

'A mate of mine has a lovely cottage to rent, he'd do a special deal if I asked him, but it might be too close to home though.'

'Where is it?'

'Near Ballysteen by the coast.'

'Sounds perfect. All I want is two or three nights.'

'I'll give him a ring, see if it's available.'

The following morning Carrie was packed and ready to go. She wasn't completely telling the truth about her parents' anniversary as it had been last month. Luckily, Tom had the memory of a fish and didn't question it. His friend, Owen from college, owned the cottage and refused to charge her a cent, nor did he mind her bringing Max for company. A dog lover himself, he and his wife Sarah and their two kids had moved to Cahersiveen, where they ran kennels on six acres.

On the way to the rental, dark grey thoughts mulled through her brain. Hannah had refused to talk to her despite several phonecall attempts and calling to her house. She wouldn't even listen to her explanation and shut her out. But what was more pressing on her mind was Jack's father and his bizarre attitude towards her. She honestly couldn't see a future for them if his parents were dead set against it. She didn't want that hassle in her life. She'd been through enough already. The man was aggressive, maybe even dangerous. Who knew what he'd be capable of? She couldn't risk that.

I can't keep dwelling on this.

At the traffic lights she inserted a tape of Abba's latest hits and started singing along to *Super Trouper*. Max whined and covered his ears. The songs reminded her of the last night she was out with Hannah and the fun they had. She smiled to herself at the memory of the lad with the cowboy hat and spurs, how they had drunkenly tottered home together.

Lost in the past, she missed the signpost for Ballysteen and ended up travelling five miles out of her way. She stopped at a petrol station and bought a sandwich and a bottle of coke to take over to a bench at the rear. She let out Max for a pee, then poured water into a plastic bowl and laid it on the grass. He took a couple of gulps, but he was more interested in the sandwich she was eating.

Carrie broke off a piece of ham and some crusts and tossed it to him. Taking the map out of the glovebox, she spread it out on the bench and marked her destination. A breeze ruffled her hair. An elderly man filled up his Volkswagen and walked into the shop. A crow flew down, ignoring Max's barking, scooped up the remaining bits of bread in its beak and flapped away. Stretching her legs for another five minutes, she gathered up the map and, calling Max, headed back to the car. She was hoping to arrive before noon and make up for lost time.

The roads were slick with rain, but the sunshine was doing its best to scatter the glum grey clouds. Max snored beside her, lying on his back, four legs up in the air, with not a worry in the world. How she envied him. She bit into a Granny Smith, manoeuvring sharp bends as she drove, trying to focus on the journey and free her frazzled mind. She was almost there. Traffic was beginning to build up at the junction to the town. Looked like she wasn't the only one taking a break. This was her second time in this pretty seaside village, but it was such a long time ago she'd completely forgotten the route.

She drove past the woods on the right. The cottage stood close to Kylemore Dominican Abbey, which might be worth having a look at later. First, she had to pick up the keys from the local shop and buy a few groceries.

Job done; Carrie arrived at the cottage at approximately half past twelve. It was like something out of a movie. The little house was whitewashed, thatched with two red half doors and tiny red windows and there was smoke coming from the chimney. Set on one acre of land, it was shielded from view by overhanging oaks framing either side. A blue and yellow painted gnome guarded the door. There was a little garden with a swing seat to the side and a wooden hut to house tools.

She let Max out, then gathered her stuff from the car. A lit stove stood in a quaint, cosy sitting room on the right. A bookshelf of books. Flagstones in the hall, a tiny beech kitchen, and lovely colourful landscape paintings on all the walls. The dark interior was offset by a Velux window. A peach floral bedspread covered a cast iron double bed and there was even a large cushion on the floor for Max. A bottle of unopened red wine welcomed her from the top of a round table in the kitchen. Tucked away in a corner was the narrowest bathroom she'd ever seen, so small only one person could squeeze in there at any one time, which suited her needs perfectly.

Carrie fried up a few sausages and waffles. There was no television, so she switched on the radio. It felt very peaceful, and she was glad she came. If Jack called, he wouldn't be able to get her, and she needed that space. The only sound was the scrape of branches against the windowpane and the rustle of leaves in the breeze. Max sniffed the ground and ran from one room to another. Tongue out, panting and yapping in excitement. He didn't care where he was as long as they were together.

Tired from travelling and the stress of the last few days, she decided to lie down with the intention of just resting for a few minutes. Her eyelids closed after a while. She was awoken by a wet tongue licking her face. For a moment, she didn't know where she was as the room blurred into focus. Owen's cottage.

Max began to whine and paw her knee.

'I'm coming.'

She stretched, unlocking the kinks in her neck and threw on her walking boots. Fastening his lead, they headed towards the wood at a jog. Not many people were about, Painted Lady butterflies flitted in abundance, landing on daisies and buttercups then flew off again. Blue tits hovered around a bird feeder suspended from a birdhouse. A gurgling, giggling stream cut through the wood, offering a melodious backdrop to the multitude of pines, firs, and beeches. Tomorrow, she planned to visit the Abbey, then take a tour around the area.

By the time she ran five miles she felt wiped out and could run no further, but at least she felt better. She spied a seat overlooking the sea. As she sat down, she felt something soft and flat in her back pocket. It was a white envelope. The one she took from Auntie Tess.

Heat flooded her face again at the memory. The envelope looked worn, creased, and yellowing at the edges. The window in the centre had an address on it. It was addressed to her mother, which was what prompted Carrie to grab it that fateful day when Hannah threatened her with the gardai. Guilt had forbidden her from opening it until now. Ignoring her rumbling stomach, she ripped it open.

Time stood still.

Chapter Thirty Three

Carrie

1976

Her hand shook. She stared in disbelief at the yellowed paper. It had begun to drizzle, but she barely noticed. Max tugged at the leash, impatient to get going, and once free, wandered off, dragging the lead behind him.

A cold sweat broke out on her forehead as Hannah's innocent remark blasted her once again. *You know you don't look a bit like your mother.* Maybe she knew all along. All those years, Mum never said a word. And Dad too. Why didn't they tell me? Why all the secrecy? I would have understood - in time.

On hearing footsteps approach, she looked up. Her eyes widening in surprise.

'Look who I found.'

'Adam. What are you doing here?'

She dried her eyes, scooting over on the bench so he could sit down.

'I have a place here. Didn't I tell you? This wood is my local haunt. I come here every evening.'

'It's beautiful, you're lucky,' she said, blowing her nose.

'Are you okay?'

There was no point keeping it a secret, and she had to talk to someone. Thank God it was Adam. She passed him her birth cert.

'Found this while rummaging through Aunt –' She was going to say Auntie Tess, then stopped herself.

He looked at her curiously, then scanned the contents. His gaze flew to her in shock. 'You're adopted! How long have you known about this?'

'About two minutes.'

'God, this is huge, Carrie – I don't know what to say.'

'Neither do I. They never said a word all those years. They should have told me.'

'Come on, you're getting wet – where are you staying?'

'I have a loan of a cottage for a few days.'

'Is it nearby?'

'Within walking distance.'

'Come on then.'

They linked arms and, on the way, bought a pizza and a bottle of wine. Adam shoved the pizza into the oven while Carrie went to fetch two glasses. He looked good. His hair had been recently cut. He was clean-shaven and dressed casually in grey slacks, a beige sweater, and walking boots.

The rain had come down in earnest, blasting the window-pane like thousands of nails. She heard Max scraping at the door and let him in, towel-dried him and set a bowl of dog food on the floor. The pizza smelled divine, mozzarella cheese and pepperoni. Adam cut out the slices, and they ate in companionable silence.

Afterwards, sitting by the fire, they broached the subject again.

'Do you know who your father is?'

'No, it just mentions a woman called Louisa on the birth certificate. I can't make out the surname. Can you?'

'No, sorry – it's very faded.'

'I suppose you could contact the Births, Marriages & Deaths registration centre in Dublin, they might be able to shed some light on it. Don't forget your Aunt Tess – she owes you the truth, and I wouldn't leave until I get it.'

'Yes, that's what I will have to do. I can't believe there's a woman out there, and she is my mother. She gave me up. I don't know how I feel about her. What if Louisa doesn't want to see me? What then?'

He leaned forward and touched her knee. 'If you would like me to go with you – I will.'

'Thanks,' she smiled. 'That's such a relief – I don't think I could do this by myself, but are you sure? You must have other things on. I don't want to be a pest; you've been so good to me already.'

'Come on, that's what good neighbours are for.'

'Except, you're not my neighbour anymore – you live here now.'

'I wouldn't offer if I didn't mean it – we've known one another for years. You need support – this has come as an awful shock to you.'

'I know, but…'

'Tell you what. Buy me a drink, and we'll call it quits. How's that?'

She smiled. 'Deal.'

Carrie looked away, pulled absently at a loose thread on her jumper. 'This is going to sound crazy, but I've been having dreams about her, my birth mother, maybe even visions. They feel so real; it's like she's been trying to communicate with me or something – I don't know.' Her face reddened. 'Sounds daft.'

'I remember you telling me about the girl you thought you saw at the time your car went off the road, and don't forget you've had visions in the past too. Do you remember that day when you came running into class and told Mrs Fogarty that the reason you were late was because a man tried to stop you going in the gate?'

'Oh, God, yeah, I was only ten. It was just after Easter break. He kept pushing me back, said it wasn't safe.'

'And the wall collapsed shortly afterwards, and nobody mocked you again.' He was thoughtful for a moment. 'Everyone was afraid of you after,' he chuckled, 'including me for a while.' Looked at his watch. 'I have to go. Horses to feed, and so on. You should call by while you're here.'

'Maybe another time, sorry.'

He looked disappointed, but she didn't want to make her life any more complicated than it was already. They seemed to connect a lot better than before, and they were more relaxed around each other. Maybe it was because he wasn't her trainer anymore, but she still had feelings for Jack. And besides, Adam just thought of her as a friend; he'd never implied anything else.

She stood and gave him a hug. 'Thanks so much, Adam. I really needed that.'

'You're going to be all right – you know.'

'I know. Hey Adam?'

He turned at the door. 'Yeah?'

'We keep this between ourselves, okay.'

'Of course. Talk soon. Bye.'

Chapter Thirty Four

Louisa

1951

I try to avoid Carmel like the plague, but she seems to be sticking to me like glue everywhere I go, and there's no getting away from her. At breakfast I plead a sick stomach and I'm excused from kitchen duties, where I know Carmel is plonked for the morning, crowing at the top of her voice. How could I ever have liked her? I should have paid heed to Joan, my friend, right from the beginning.

Just before mass, I nip back to the dormitory, taking the steps two at a time. Another five minutes and Carmel will be joining the others in the chapel. They'll be expecting me and wondering where I am. I have to be quick. It's strange finding myself in the dorm during the day. Normally, we don't have a second to spare, and this is the last place we come to every night. All the beds are made up neatly. Identical prayer books sit on lockers in exact same positions. I bend down and peer under her bed. Nothing there. Toss the pillow and search under the threadbare blanket, feeling around for lumps but find nothing. Same under the mattress. The bell tolls for mass. Frustrated, I bite my lip. Anxiety charges through my body. My heart is thumping. I'm going to get a panic attack. Where the hell could she have hidden it? An awful thought begins to form. What if she's stuffed it inside her blouse? I'll never get it back if that's the case, and I'll be beholden to her forever. I shudder at the thought of her revolting sweaty limbs entwined with mine every night.

No! No way. I can't let that happen. It has to be here. The journal would be too bulky under her clothes. Once again, I'm on my hands and knees, searching for loose floorboards, but the floor is smooth, and I'm running out of time. The bell tolls again. As I'm standing up, I lose my balance and fling my arm out to grasp the edge of the locker. The locker wobbles. The bible slides to one side. I gasp in disbelief. There it is underneath the bible. I grab my journal, kiss the cover, and then shove it deep inside my skirt. I'm never letting it out of my sight again.

Carmel looks behind her and winks when she sees me floundering in the door. She smiles and turns back to the altar. I sneak up behind the girls and into my seat just before the priest comes out. The nuns rise in unison with the choir and sing the first hymn. Out of habit, I glance over. My heart leaps out of my chest. Luke is here. I can hardly contain my excitement. He looks over at me for a moment and smiles.

There's a collective shuffle as everyone kneels, then Joan goes up to give the first reading, and we sit back down. Mass passes in a blur. We stand to recite the *Our Father* and soon file up to the altar to receive Holy Communion. As I walk up, hands joined demurely in silent contemplation, Luke passes me on the way to his seat and slips me a piece of paper which I hastily shove up my sleeve.

There's no time to talk to him. Sister Marguerite hunts us out back to work. At least I have Luke's note to look forward to. I ask Marguerite if I can go to the toilet.

'Make it quick.'

'Yes, Sister.'

Sensing Carmel's eyes boring into the back of my head, I hasten down the dimly lit corridor to the two cubicles and shut the door, locking myself inside. For a moment, I panic; the paper is gone then I feel something at my elbow. Sighing with relief, I sit on the toilet bowl and read.

My dear Louisa. So sorry that I haven't been in touch. Got a new job doing deliveries. Our own place! Meet me in the morning when the van comes in. Love you.

Tears spring to my eyes. I can't believe it. I'm actually going to be leaving this hell hole. Finally. I feel giddy with excitement. One more night in this dump, that's all. I flush the toilet. Open the cubicle door and return to the laundry for the last time. A spring in my step. Flushed and beaming from ear to ear.

The floors of the laundry room are slick, and I almost skid on the floating dirty water. Sister Claude is droning the rosary, to which the girls answer in dull, flat monotone voices. My shoulders sag after a moment as guilt washes over me at the thought of leaving them here in this hot, suffocating environment day in day out. But maybe once I get away, I can advocate for them, help them somehow.

Weak sunlight seeps through the barred windows, failing miserably to brighten the room. I look down at my skinned hands, red raw from washing stinking sheets in hot water. The nuns never got their hands dirty and never gave us gloves either. Joan glances over at me curiously, then returns to her ironing. I want to tell her but can't right now with the nuns watching, supervising our work.

My back is breaking. I long to sit, take the weight off. I have to pinch myself now and then. I still can't believe I'm leaving, then once again look at all the pale faces and wish that they were all leaving too. The bell tolls twelve for the Angelus. We bow and mumble the required prayers before being herded to the main hall for lunch.

Carmel walks with me. I feel like shoving her against the wall for the anxiety she put me through but don't want to end up in solitary confinement and not able to meet Luke tomorrow, so I grit my teeth and try to keep two metres apart.

'You're looking smug,' she taunts in my ear.

There's a smell off her breath, so I move further away, hitting my elbow off the wall as a result. Wincing at the pain, I take my seat at the long centre table. Carmel sits opposite, staring me down. My journal is wedged inside the elastic of my knickers and pokes into me every time I move. We babble the usual *Grace Before Meals*, then eye the scraps on our plates with resignation.

Hilda and Carmel are on kitchen duty, much to my relief, while Joan and I are pegged to scrub the corridor. Now is my chance while there is no one watching us. A clock ticks on the wall. I drag over the bucket with industrial chemicals. My nose twitching from the strong odours, eyes watering. Joan's back is to me, on hands and knees scrubbing the floor. Her lips moving to some silent inner prayer. She looks up upon hearing me approach, sits back on her haunches and wipes her brow. 'I can't get these stains off.' Her eyes suddenly become alert. 'What is it?'

'Great news,' I whisper, 'I'm leaving with Luke tomorrow.'

'What? Are you sure?'

I show her the note. She surprises me by throwing her arms around me. 'That's fantastic news. Oh, Louisa, I'm thrilled for you.'

'Come with me.'

She shakes her head. 'I can't.'

'Please, Joan. I couldn't bear the thought of you being here when I'm gone.'

Her face flushes. 'I won't be.'

'Fantastic, so you will come with me then.'

'Don't get mad okay – I'm going to be an auxiliary.'

'What's that?'

'A novice nun.'

I stare at her incredulously. 'Are you out of your mind? That's the dumbest idea I've ever heard.'

'It's not dumb.' She mumbles and stands up.

'*They're* making you do this.'

'No, they're not, Lou,' she says, tilting her chin up stubbornly. 'This is what I want.' She's absently fingering the cross around her neck. 'Please be happy for me.'

'When does this happen?'

'I start training next week.'

A door opens. Footsteps recede, then silence once again.

Blinking back tears, Joan whispers, 'I'm going to miss you. Please write to me.'

We hug again, and I nod. My throat feels dry. My heart is saddened. Of all people, I shall miss her the most. We talk then about the future and meeting up again in different circumstances. 'Have you said anything to Hilda or the others?'

'No, and you mustn't either.'

'My lips are sealed.'

'I'm so excited to be going and a little nervous too. Thought I'd never get out of this dump. Are you sure you want to be a nun?'

'Certain. Don't worry about me.'

Later that night, we're kneeling at our beds, mumbling the rosary. I'm thinking of my new home, living with Luke and the prospect of a whole life together in comfort. Being able to go where I want and when I want. I could ring that midwife I had met during the year and take up a position in her hospital. I'm so thrilled I could burst. But I'd be lying if I said I wasn't nervous too. My first time out in the real world as an adult. This will be my biggest test yet, and once I start working, I plan to find my daughter and bring her home. With me, where she belongs.

The rap of a cane makes me jump. It's Augusta with nothing better to do as usual. 'Your lips aren't moving!'

'Sorry, Sister, won't happen again.'

Lights are out at nine. I'm brushing my teeth when someone taps me on the shoulder. Without turning, I know who it is. I keep brushing. Cold tiles beneath my feet. The lavatory is freezing.

'It's cold, but we'll warm up soon.'

'Get lost, Carmel. If you come near me, I'll scream at the top of my lungs.'

'No, you won't, remember I –'

I spin so fast she startles in surprise. I wave my journal in her face. She scowls and backs off. The shutters come down. And turning on her heel, she walks out. I've won. I just hope she'll leave the others alone when I'm gone.

The last night in this godforsaken hole. I turn over on my side with a mix of feelings. Relief, trepidation, and a little sorrow for the other poor souls trapped here and what they have yet to face. I can't save the world, that's what I tell myself as I plump my gawdy pillow that's almost as flat as the sheet I'm lying on. Over at the far side, Carmel's light is on, her eyes squinting at something.

It's only then that I realize the note from Luke is missing. In my gleeful victory dance in the lavatory, it must have fallen out of my pocket. My eyes bug in horror. How could I have been so stupid?

Is that what she's reading?

Her light goes out. I exhale in relief and then lie awake for hours until daylight. The morning bell wakes me up, bleary-eyed with aches and pains all over from a restless sleep. I wash in a hurry, pull on the uniform and join the others for prayers, then breakfast. My stomach is sick with nerves. I can't eat. What if something goes wrong? What if Carmel squeals?

Joan squeezes my hand. 'It'll be all right,' she whispers.

Hilda is first into the laundry, followed by me, Joan, some of the new girls then Carmel. I look up at the clock. An hour to go before the first van arrives. I'm sorting out massive, soiled sheets and holding my nose when Carmel sidles over. I stiffen, pay no heed, and I'm surprised when she starts piling the sheets into a basket ready for transport. She's humming. 'No hard feelings, eh.'

I nod and don't reply, conscious of the ticking clock and the power she could hold over me if she was the one who found my note. Sister Claude leaves the room briefly. My hands start to sweat, and my heart is thumping so fast I fear I'll pass out from the stress.

'I shouldn't have taken liberties,' she says, 'guess I was lonely. Can we put it behind us?'

I stare at her in surprise and nod. There are no words.

Claude returns. 'Delivery van is here; he's early for a change.'

This is it. I've almost forgotten to breathe.

'Hannon, take out the basket to him. Make sure it's labelled.'

'I'll bring the other one, Sister,' Joan interjects hurriedly.

'Right. Move along then.'

We wheel the heavy baskets out of the laundry, down the corridor to the back door. Every vein taut with tension, I unlatch the lock and step outside. Luke is standing by the van, a worried look on his face.

'Oh, Louisa, please don't forget me,' Joan sobs crushing me in a bear embrace.

'I won't. I'll miss you.'

'Lou, come on,' Luke urges.

A rain shower drenches me as I run to the open van door.

'Louisa, wait.'

I freeze. It's Carmel. One foot in the van, the other is on the asphalt. I want to ignore her but fear if I do, she'll raise the alarm out of spite, so I turn slowly. Arms outstretched, she envelopes me in an equally crushing hug.

'Carmel. No!'

Sounds like Joan. Too late, I register the danger as the knife plunges into my spine.

Chapter Thirty Five

Carrie

1976

It's been two days since she discovered the birth certificate. At home once again, she awoke to birdsong outside her window, having spent the night twisting and turning, unable to sleep until some ungodly hour of the morning. It hit her instantly as everything came flooding to the surface. And for a moment, she found it difficult to get out of bed. To face the day with this new revelation, armed with the knowledge that life as she knew it will never be the same again.

Staring up at the ceiling she recalled all those years she had been kept in the dark. *Why wasn't I told?* Lots of people get adopted. She trusted her parents and believed them when they said she took after her grandparents in appearance. She'd loved them, worshipped the ground they walked on. Tears tracked down her cheeks unheeded. Her whole life was a lie, and they knew it.

Stroking Max's silky head absently, she ran through her options. She would visit her aunt to find out the truth. A grimace. Only she wasn't her aunt at all. Sadness bloomed in her chest, threatening to overwhelm her. She didn't know who she was anymore. It was like her entire identity had been wiped out in one fell swoop. Everything she had ever known and everyone she had ever loved no longer seemed real. She could feel the walls hemming her in. Her chest tightening.

The familiar onslaught of another panic attack, so she forced herself to take deep breaths, inhale and exhale slowly until the feeling subsided.

Her hand closed around the locket, and she opened it. She would have to confront Louisa. A shudder. Rising panic. She didn't know if she wanted to. *I need to process everything first before meeting her. Come to terms with what she has done then I'll make a decision.*

'Right, Max, rise and shine.'

The dog took a few more digs before getting down off the bed. Wishing she didn't have to go to work, she half-heartedly tucked into a bowl of cornflakes. Remnants of a coffee stewed on the table. There were butterflies in her belly, and the cereal was tasteless. Back in the room she selected a black knee-length skirt and baby pink blouse. It was the best she could do, and she was not in the mood for dressing up. Hopefully there wouldn't be much on, and she could slip away early.

Her black patent heels clicked on the tiles. She shrugged on her grey coat, set a bowl of pedigree munchies on the ground, and departed just before eight. Traffic had built up at the junction to Clifden, but when she let herself into the office, she was the only one there. The property list sat on her desk. She sifted through them one by one, scheduled appointments and showings and then made some telephone calls. A hollowness in her chest, feeling numb, close to tears.

Tom opened the door, hung up his suede jacket and switched on the kettle. He'd shaved off his beard. Bits of paper sticking to his chin from where he nicked it that morning shaving.

'Hey you, how was your break?'

'Fine,' she replied, not looking up.

Lorraine O'Byrne (née Barry) was an Irish author of children's stories and adult fiction. Inspired by her childhood in rural Ireland, Lorraine distilled her interest in fairies, pixies and other supernatural creatures into her children's stories such as The Hippity, Dippity Witch.

Lorraine's first adult fiction was The Wrath of Voodoo in 2004, about a young Irish woman who went on an adventure to Kenya. Despite an interest in the supernatural, Lorraine always brought her trademark humour to her writing, as 2015's Escaping the Prince testifies.

Lorraine graduated from the University of Limerick with a BA in European Studies, before obtaining a diploma in freelance journalism and an MA in Creative Writing, also from UL, where her tutor was bestselling Irish author Donal Ryan.

Like so many Irish writers before her, from WB Yeats to Edna O'Brien, Lorraine was inspired by Ireland's natural landscapes and succeeded in seeing the ordinary in the extraordinary.

Lorraine spent her final years working as a carer for the elderly in her community while she lived on a farm in Co Limerick, with her beloved husband Donal, and their cherished family pets. Lorraine enjoyed many outdoor pursuits such as hill walking and horse riding. The rural chimes of farm life proved stimulating for her imagination, as it was here, she completed her final novel, I Will Find You, a story of a long-buried secret seen through a supernatural prism.

To find Lorraine's books - Scan QR Codes below
(Full List overleaf)

Facebook

Linktr.ee

Books by Lorraine O'Byrne

ADULT FICTION

I Will Find You
(new release)

amazon.co.uk
buythebook.ie
The Crescent Bookshop
O'Mahony's Booksellers
Talking Leaves Bookstore
- Castletroy

The Wrath of Voodoo
Written under Lorraine Barry

feedaread.com
amazon.co.uk

CHILDREN'S BOOKS

The Hippity Dippity Witch

feedaread.com
buythebook.ie

Lucy Pebble's Miracle

amazon.com
barnesandnoble.com
feedaread.com

Escaping the Prince

feedaread.com
amazon.co.uk
buythebook.ie

Poppy the Cygnet

feedaread.com
amazon.co.uk

CHILDREN'S SHORT STORIES

Watch out Bobby

Feedaread.com

The Bull that Longed to Be a Horse

amazon.co.uk
feedaread.com

The Intruder

amazon.co.uk
feedaread.com

He studied her for a moment, then said. 'New client this morning – would you deal with her? I've a meeting in Athlone at two.'

Carrie covered her face with her hands, shoulders shaking.

'Hey, what's wrong?' he asked, hunkering down by her chair in concern.

'I'm so sorry, Tom, you must think I'm a right basket case.'

'You're the most solid, together person I know. Do you want to talk about it?'

She couldn't keep a lid on her emotions if she tried. Tom was so understanding and patient. It wouldn't be fair to hold back on him now when he trusted her implicitly and was so accommodating. So, she told him about the birth cert and the shock of finding out about her real mother.

He gave a low whistle. 'Jesus, no wonder you're upset.'

She dried her eyes, blew her nose and nodded.

'I'll reschedule this lady's appointment. You go and talk to your aunt. You can't have all this bottling up inside you and work at the same time.'

'Are you sure? I feel like I'm taking liberties all the time.'

Tom held her hands in his. 'You didn't ask for this, Carrie. Other people would have fallen apart at this news but not you. Take as much time as you need. You're a valuable asset to this company, don't ever doubt it. I'll be here when you get back.'

She threw her arms around his neck, grabbed her coat and left.

Carrie was sitting on the toilet after another bad dose of the runs. The thought of visiting Tess had turned her insides into mush. She flushed the toilet, washed her hands in soapy water and went out. Market day this morning. The square was crammed with stalls of every description, some selling vegetables and fruit, others plying customers with chips, hot dogs, books, flowers, and the sweet scents of cheap perfume. There were a lot of people milling about, some old, some new. The laughter of children. It was a warm, sunny day, and everyone was making the most of it. She rolled up her sleeves. Bag slung over her right shoulder, she crossed the street to the car park. A glance in a shop window made her blood run cold. That couldn't be Nathaniel. He was standing on the street corner in conversation with John Roche, the local butcher. Nothing sinister. Perfectly normal. Berating herself for being paranoid, she turned down to William Street, where her car was located, unlocked the door, and sat in.

The drive to Tess's house was short, and she got there within minutes. Carrie stared dully at Hannah's car parked outside. Damn. The last thing she wanted was another confrontation. But she had to be strong and take no crap. *God! She's not even my real cousin*. Her shoulders slumped again at this reminder. She touched her head to the cold steering wheel and briefly closed her eyes before getting out of the car.

As she walked up to the door she couldn't help feeling like an intruder, and hoped and prayed that Tess was okay and lucid, capable of having this conversation. She was bringing her fist up to knock when the door swung open. Hannah stood stony-faced, arms folded, radiating hostility, but she was prepared for this reception and refused to be cowed.

'I'd like to come in, please.'

'Mum is not good at the moment.'

Her heart sank at this; just what she feared.

Then.

'Hannah, is that Carrie? Don't leave her standing out there in the cold!'

'Come in, then,' she said grudgingly.

Hannah's little boy Noel peeked around her shyly. He had beautiful brown curly hair and bright blue eyes, and this morning wore short pants and a stripey t-shirt. His knees were red and skinned like he'd just fallen.

Carrie stooped to his eye level. 'Hello, little man.'

'Go and play,' Hannah ordered.

He ran off up the stairs, a fire truck in his hand, she could hear him making vroom noises on the wooden steps.

The kitchen area was cluttered as usual, and there was nowhere to sit. Hannah didn't offer to clear a space, so she moved papers from a chair and sat down by the table. She caught a whiff of onions and leftover cabbage from a pot on the stove. Tess was sipping tea from a china cup; she was wearing bright red lipstick today, and her shoulder-length hair was parted to the side, taking years off her. An album lay open on the flowery tablecloth; she'd been sorting through photographs.

'Want tea?'

'No, thanks.' Carrie swallowed. Raised her chin a fraction. 'There's something I need to talk to you about.'

'If it's an apology…' said Hannah.

'I didn't come here to apologise.'

'What then?'

She took out the crumpled envelope from her back pocket and extricated the birth cert, noticing that Hannah had turned white as a sheet.

'How come no one told me that I'm adopted?'

Tess dropped the photo she was just about to place in the plastic pocket of the album, emitting a sharp cry like an animal in pain. Her hand flew to her mouth as she sat staring at Carrie, stunned.

'It was for your own good, that's why,' said Hannah. 'We were trying to protect you.'

'You knew!' Carrie leapt to her feet. 'You knew all along, and neither of you bothered to tell me!'

Tess started shuffling the photographs. Her hands were trembling. 'What is she talking about, Hannah?'

'I'm talking about Louisa, my real mother.'

'Stop shouting!' she cried, hands up to her ears.

'Sorry, Tess, but I've got to know.'

Hannah went over and dropped to her haunches beside her mother. She covered her mum's hand. 'Mum, it's okay, finish your sorting. Carrie and I are going to take a little walk. We'll be back soon.'

She kissed her on the forehead and stood up, beckoning Carrie to follow her outside to the garden, where they sat miles apart on a bench.

'I don't know where to begin,' Hannah said at last. 'Should have told you the truth ages ago, but I didn't know how. Guess I was afraid it would create a rift between us – after all, we wouldn't be cousins anymore. What I'm trying to say is, I didn't want to lose that bond that we had.'

'When did you find out?'

Hannah reddened. 'We were kids – do you remember when we used to play hide and seek?'

Carrie nodded.

'I was hiding in Mum's wardrobe, and it was there I discovered the shoebox containing your birth details. I was shocked. Mum gave me a hiding for going through her stuff and made me swear not to tell anyone, least of all you.'

'But why all the secrecy? I'm sure I wasn't the only one to be adopted in Ireland. I don't understand.'

'Louisa was disturbed; your mum said she wasn't fit to be a parent and that's why they had to take you away from her and why I couldn't say anything in case –'

'Who's they?'

'Louisa was taken to a convent in Galway. The Sisters of Mercy. A place for troubled young girls. She was making up stories and behaving like a lunatic. They had to do something. You were adopted shortly afterwards, and that's all I know – and...'

Carrie drowned out the rest of the conversation in the struggle to absorb everything she'd been told. She wasn't rejected by her biological mother, and that gave her some small comfort. But all those years of not knowing, they should have told her. She had a right to know. Hannah lied. So did Tess. But so too did her parents. They kept her in the dark, treating her like a child. Protecting her from the truth so they could live happy trouble-free lives.

'Who is my father? His name wasn't mentioned on the birth cert.'

'I don't know, that's the truth, I swear.'

'What do you know about truth?'

'Where are you going?'

'To visit The Sisters of Mercy and to see my mother.'

'Louisa is - dead.'

Carrie went white and stared at her, flabbergasted with shock. 'No. I… I don't believe you.'

'It's the truth, Car. I'm so sorry.'

The blow was swift and brutal. She sank to the cold ground. Wrapped her arms around her knees and wailed, rocking to and fro. Hannah dropped down beside her and hugged her tight. They stayed like that for a long time until Noel bounded out the door, calling her name.

'Please, I know I don't deserve to ask this but don't go yet. I'm sorry for getting so mad at you before, but I didn't want you finding out the truth – and hating me for keeping it from you.'

A fresh wave of grief washed over Carrie, the words going over her head. How could she lose a parent twice? She would never get to see her birth mother. Hold her. Embrace her. Brush away all those cobwebs from years upon years of deceit and withheld information. *How could life be so cruel?*

Conscious of the coldness of the ground seeping up through her body, she slowly staggered to her feet. Feeling drained and empty.

A tap on her elbow. She looked down.

'Don't cry.'

Little Noel. She ruffled his hair, too choked up to say anything.

Hannah went into the house, re-emerging minutes later carrying something in her left hand. 'I thought you should have this. She had it with her when she died. Luke, the lad she was going to run away with, found out who adopted you and posted it to your address. Your mum didn't want the journal, she was going to burn it, but my mother decided to keep it for you.'

Carrie looked at her, then at the journal. She opened it. The paper was yellow and dog –eared, but it was the name overhead that struck a chord. Louisa in big, bold letters scrawled across the top. The only link to her mother. Without another word, she got in her car and drove away, tears rolling down her cheeks.

She came to a fork in the road but, instead of heading home ,pulled into a car park and took out the journal. She traced her mother's words with her fingers. Held the journal up to her cheek and sniffed the paper as if to absorb Louisa's essence, make it a part of her somehow.

The writing was barely legible, some of it scratched out in places. Her heart lurched painfully to see her name etched on the paper, imagining what Louisa must have been going through at the time she wrote it. She read the poem over and over. Her mother's love poured onto the paper, outlining the desperation that she felt over her agonising loss and how the nuns continued to torment her even after she was bullied into giving her up. It was all there, everything in black and white. There could be no doubt. Louisa did not want to let her go, and this was proof. She read on. The cottage where her mother grew up was in Connemara. That's why she was getting the visions.

Carrie turned the page and froze in shock. Louisa gave a horrifying account of the rape and the man that did it. The images were stark and frightening of a young girl being pushed onto a bed in a large house, how her attacker was bulky, staunching of whiskey as he forced himself upon her.

Her legs wobbled. She felt like she was going to get sick.

I need some air.

Carrie stumbled out of the car. Threw up on the tarmac-adam. Suddenly everything fit together. The house, her mother was born in that Connemara cottage. And it was most probable that she was also confined to that horrible attic room. The picture in the locket was her, had to be. Oh, God, Jack. She got sick again as the thought of what could have happened between them blasted her full force. She was shaking. Her heart was racing. Unable to face home alone with her demons, she drove around the block until *The Crow* came into view.

The bar was almost empty. A fire crackled in the hearth. Six men and a woman propped up the counter and turned when she came in. One of them she recognized as Father Finnan nursing a pint of Guinness, the last person she wanted to talk to, and she hoped he'd stay away. The bartender asked her what she was having, a white apron circling his waist.

'Just a sherry, thanks.'

She took the drink over beside the fire, sat down and stared into its flames, the sherry working its magic down her throat. The men turned back to the bar and talked in low undertones, some of them guffawing and some staring morosely into space.

Carrie's fingers slipped from the glass, and it crashed to the flagstones in bits.

She was bending to pick up the shards when a voice said abruptly, 'Leave it, you'll cut yourself.'

'So sorry, don't know what came over me.'

Out of the corner of her eye, she noted the curate walking over, hands clasped. So, she grabbed her bag, thanked the bartender, and left.

Dusk had fallen in the meantime. Feeling guilty about leaving Max alone, she bought some pedigree dog food and went home. The house was freezing. She quickly lit the stove and dished out food for him, but she couldn't stomach a bite. Her mind was a whirl. Jack didn't know what was going on. She had to tell him but how? She didn't want to go through it all over again, which was what she would have to do in order to explain what was going on.

She paced the floor, needing someone to talk to. Tom wasn't at home. That only left Adam. It wouldn't be fair to throw all this on him. Not when they'd just become friends again.

She knew she had to tell Jack; he had a right to know, but the thought of it made her feel sick. She didn't know if she could do it. She was about to blow his world apart. However, the sooner she did it, the quicker she could move on.

Chapter Thirty Six

Carrie

1976

Carrie took a deep breath then dialled Jack's number. The phone rang four times before the answering machine picked it up.

'Sorry, can't come to the phone right now. Please leave a message.'

Feeling a mix of relief as well as frustration, she was about to hang up but then decided to leave him a message. No point putting off the inevitable. It was time he knew the truth.

Someone was knocking at the door. Jack put the razor back in the cabinet, glanced at his reflection in the bathroom mirror before throwing on a t-shirt over his jeans, and padded barefoot out to the porch. There was red paint on his ear as if he'd been scratching it with his paintbrush, more holes in his jeans than fabric.

He peered through the spy hole and grimaced, opening the door a fraction.

'It's you. What do you want?'

'That's no way to greet your father. Mum and I have been trying to reach you for days. What's going on?'

His hair, usually immaculate, was dishevelled, and his face was an ugly red.

'I'll tell you what's going on – you spouting all those lies to Carrie about me and Brigitta when you know full well there's no truth in them. What's the matter? Cat got your tongue, Dad?'

'Don't speak to me like that. I'm still your father. Show some respect.'

'Let go of my arm!'

Nathaniel sighed and stepped back. 'Look, maybe it's for the best that it didn't work out. Brigitta is back now and –'

'What are you on about? I didn't say anything about it not working out.'

Nathaniel recoiled like he'd just been slapped.

'Oh, just go, Dad, will you. Shut the door when you leave.'

Jack marched up to his room to get dressed for work, fuming at his father. The telephone rang downstairs in the hall.

'Let the machine get it,' he muttered angrily to himself, in no mood for talking to anyone.

Carrie dialled the number for the Sisters of Mercy Convent, wanting to know everything about her mother and got through on the third ring. The nun sounded eager to talk about Louisa. She introduced herself as Sister Joan Franklin and offered to meet her in person, so they scheduled an appointment for the following Thursday.

It was the first step in the right direction. A chance to know who her mother really was and why she was incarcerated in the convent. The nun had said if there was anything else she could do to help, she just had to ask.

Feeling a little better, she made some coffee in a mug, sat by the table, stirring the liquid and staring contemplatively into space. A half-eaten shepherd's pie lay congealing on a plate. Max's nose touched her thigh. He had smelled the food. She set it down on the floor for him, then got up and fetched her mother's journal from her room. Her mother's locket was tangled up amid the blankets. Must have fallen off during the night, she mused. Hanging it around her neck, she picked up the journal and brought it with her to the living room.

Tears fell to the page as she read her mother's harrowing account of life in the laundries. A lump formed in her throat. She must have been so scared. Three months were blank where she'd written nothing at all. The tone picked up slightly from the month of November 1950. There was a boy called Luke. Louisa was planning to run away with him. Everything was arranged. She lifted her mug to take a sip. Her coffee had gone cold. Her brow furrowed. What could have happened to Luke? How did Louisa die? Maybe this nun, Joan will give her some answers. Her hand closed around the locket.

'Oh, Mum, I wish I could have met you.' She whispered. 'Now, I have no one.'

Buttercups, daisies, pink and yellow wild primroses danced in the breeze. It was warm, and the grass was soft and springy beneath her feet. She was running through a hilltop meadow. Her dress was white with a blue sash across the middle. Her waist-length brown hair lifted in the wind. She was laughing because Louisa was chasing her through the meadow. She was barefoot, wearing a short blue dress, a white ribbon in her hair and around her neck hung the locket, a gift from her grandmother, glinting as it caught the sunlight.

All of a sudden, it grew dark. The air felt thick and cloying, and she found it difficult to breathe. Thick black angry clouds scudded across the sky. A rumbling of thunder.

Louisa shouted, 'Watch out, Carrie!'

She jolted awake. Looked around, momentarily disorientated. Blinked the sleep out of her eyes. The living room slowly blurred into focus. It was just a dream, but a wonderful dream, nonetheless. Swinging her legs out over the couch, she tried to grasp its significance, but the details were already fading from memory. She trudged to the bathroom to throw water in her face.

A pale reflection stared back at her. There were rings around her eyes, puffy from lack of sleep. She undressed, stepped into the shower, and let the spray blast her back to life. Towelling herself dry, she threw on a blouse, cardigan, and grey pants and laced up her boots. It was another hour before Jack's visit, assuming he got her message, so she decided to grab some fresh air. This time there was no sign of Nuala, and for that, she felt grateful. The woman was shrewd and didn't miss a thing.

Max was busy rooting around in the ditch for a rabbit. The air felt crisp on her cheeks but mild. She set off at a jog down the road to calm herself down. Her mind reverted once again to the dream and the buoyancy that came with feeling she had spent time with her mother. The locket bounced as she ran, so she tucked it inside her top. On the way back, she spied Nuala returning home with Davey after doing their weekly shopping.

Nuala rolled down the window. 'Hello, haven't seen you around in a while.'

'Hi, Nuala, been busy, you know how it is.'

'Do you see that van over there?'

Carrie glanced back to the grey transit pulled to one side in off the road. 'Yeah, what about it?'

'I'm sure it's been there since we left over an hour ago.' She turned to Davey for confirmation. 'Hasn't it?'

'Same one, aye.'

'Maybe they broke down. Look, I've got to go. Hello, Davey.'

He nodded a greeting. Hair tufts stuck out from inside his cabbage ears. Between that and his perpetual red nose, he always reminded her of a garden gnome.

A jeep drove into their yard as they parked up.

Carrie glanced over as Adam got out of the jeep, a tall redhead in tow. Must be serious if he's brought her home to meet the parents she thought, surprised to feel a pang in her stomach. Later she would dismiss it as just being lonely, a product of feeling vulnerable and turned to go back into the house.

Her stomach was in a knot at the thought of having to give Jack the news. Six o'clock approached. Her fingernails were worn to the quick as she wondered how she was going to broach the subject. Time raced on with still no sign of him coming. She was about to call him, thinking that he hadn't heard her telephone message, when there was a loud knock that made her jump. At last, almost an hour late too.

The phone rang just at that moment.

'Come in. It's open.'

Turning her back to the door, she picked it up. 'Hello.'

'GET OUT NOW.'

There was no time to react to the strange voice. A hand clamped over her mouth and dragged her backwards onto the floor. One arm under her neck, the other wrenching her hair. Max kicked up a racket outside, barking and howling. She couldn't breathe. Smelled his sweat and smoke. With her free arm, she elbowed him into the ribs, but her movements were jerky, growing weaker by the minute.

'You stupid little bitch, couldn't leave well enough alone. Could you?'

Nathaniel!

He had gotten her in a vice grip, arm around her neck, cutting off her air supply. He hauled her onto the couch. Pushed her down. She coughed and rubbed her neck. Out of the corner of her eye, she spied the shape of a piece of wood under the chair that Max took from the log basket. Fear galvanised her into action. With her outstretched foot, she drew in the wood, reached down for it and flung it aiming for his head. The blow barely made contact, only grazing his temple, but it was enough to startle him for a second and enough time for her to make a run for the door.

Nathaniel lunged for her ankle. She screamed, toppled to the floor, banging her knee off the leg of the armchair. Pain shot up her leg as she cried out, face contorting in agony. She was beaten. There was no way out of this. *I don't want to die this way here alone with him.*

She looked up at him with raw hatred, imagining how Louisa must have felt when he brutally attacked her. Convinced now without doubt that it was him in the vision assaulting her mother. Louisa had been trying to send her a message; that's what those visions and dreams were about; they were warnings. If only she'd understood before now.

She clenched her hands as red, hot anger swooped through her body. Her knee hurt so much she thought she had broken something. She hung on to the pain; it was the only thing keeping her alert so she could be ready for his next strike. Rain struck the windows, the sound like rattling stones hammering to get in, but all she could think about was poor Max. Soaking wet, wondering why she wasn't letting him in.

He was sitting astride the chair, shirt open, appraising her with amusement. Cocky, so self-assured, in no hurry.

'You're a pretty little thing when you're angry – just like your mother.' Her eyes bulged with horror as he started to unzip his pants. 'We're going to have a bit of fun before I kill you.'

She gave a low moan, eyes wide with fear. Terror electrifying her into action, she scrabbled to the side, but he was on her in a second. Pinning her arms over her head, he straddled her body and regarded her.

'Jack will be here in a minute. I've already phoned him.'

'Will he indeed? Too bad I wiped out your message.'

The colour drained from her cheeks. *Oh, Jesus, no!*

Her breathing coming in shallow gasps, she yelled, 'You won't get away with this – everyone will discover the truth, the beast that you are.'

He laughed. 'I've told Diane that I'll be away on business this evening 'til tomorrow. No one knows I'm here except you.'

She had to think and think fast. If she could just move her leg. He was so heavy, making any escape impossible. *Got to keep him talking. Please let Adam think something's wrong when he sees Max is left out in the rain.*

'Nothing happened between me and Jack. Let me go.'

'Shut your mouth, or I'll shut it for you! My life was perfect 'til you came along. No one knew any wiser. I had it all worked out. Jack would marry his fiancée; I would get my promotion, then retire to Spain with Diane. See, I had my suspicions, particularly when you got that vision. Only one other person had visions. Your bitch of a mother, Louisa. I had my suspicions the first time I clapped eyes on you. The resemblance was uncanny. It couldn't have been just coincidence. I knew then who you were when good old Father O'Dea confirmed it – after a few pints. You had to go; there was to be no question of letting you live.'

He regarded her with a cold, calculated expression of contempt that sent shivers of fear down her spine. 'This ends now.'

Nathaniel snapped open the buttons on her blouse when mercifully, something or someone seemed to knock him off balance. Carrie saw her chance, and jumping to her feet, lunged for a poker. Chest thudding, she hobbled for the door to open it, only to discover that he had locked them in. The key was gone. She could hear him lumbering to his feet, swearing. She'd have to get around him to get to the back door. The kitchen window was low; it was her only shot.

Nathaniel clutched his side where the missile poker hit him out of nowhere, wincing at the pain.

Just as Carrie was climbing on to the sink, he grabbed her around the waist and pulled her off. She dropped the poker and kicked out at him hitting his shin. He roared in pain but didn't release his grip. Yanking her up by the hair, he dragged her upstairs to the bedroom. Carrie cried out in pain, her scalp burning like he was about to pull her hair out from the roots. Breathing heavily, he pushed her back onto the bed, rolled up his sleeves, drew out orange twine from his pocket and, with one swift movement, bound her wrists together, then her feet.

Carrie stared up at him. Refusing to give him the satisfaction of showing how scared she was. Swallowing her fear, she spat, 'Is this how you treat all your children, Daddy?'

He flinched. Then leaned over her. 'No, just you.' He clamped duct tape over her mouth, then grabbed her by the throat and squeezed.

Stars swam as he began to cut off her air supply.

I can't breathe.

She was starting to lose consciousness, a black veil descending, when he let go abruptly. Carrie spluttered against the plastic tape, sucked in huge gulps of air. Tremors of fear ran up her back, every inch of her body throbbing from being trussed up like a pig over a spit. Her eyes, like saucers, dreading what he's going to do next. He watched her watching him and gloated. Loving his empowerment. Bile surged in her throat, but if she got sick, she'd suffocate. Slowly opening her blouse, button by button, he watched for her reaction, taking pleasure in her torment. Nathaniel yanked off the duct tape, then lowered himself to kiss her. She whipped her head side to side to avoid his wet revolting slobbery tongue.

His breath was foul. Please, oh God, no, this can't be happening. She screamed and struggled against the restraints. Before his lips touched hers, a sudden gust of wind shook the foundations of the house. The curtains billowed inwards. In the seconds that followed, Carrie registered a scent of decay and heard pounding on the walls like they were going to cave in at any moment now. A strange mist seeped up from the floorboards.

Nathaniel glanced around him, at the door, up at the ceiling, then looked down at Carrie.

A disembodied voice identical to the telephone message warning her to get out of the house ricocheted from the walls. EVIL. WICKED. Over and over. He clapped his hands to his ears to drown out the chanting and whipped around.

'What is this witchcraft?' he bellowed. Eyes darting left and right, he released his grip on her upper arms and stood in front of the bed. Head to one side. He glanced down at her shaking form. The doors banged shut. First the bedroom door, then the wardrobes, one after the other. The chair began to rock back and forth. The overhead light started swinging. A sudden coldness so bitter she could see his smoky breath form-ing clouds in the air. Nathaniel's head jerked to the left, and he was knocked off balance. Carrie suddenly felt the bonds loosen on her wrists, one by one. Heart pounding, she pulled the cord free from her ankles, scrambled off the bed, and leapt for the door. He lunged for the hem of her blouse to pull her back. With one wrench, she was able to break free from his grasp and, half-stumbling, half –sobbing, pelted down the stairs to get help.

Nathaniel lurched to follow her. The door slammed shut in his face with a loud, ominous bang.

He sprang towards it, tugged on the handle, but it wouldn't open. He glanced over his shoulder. Eyes wide, mirroring pools of fear, he jumped to the window, sweat pooling under his arms, his shirt sticking to his back.

'Whatever you are. Get away from me!'

A dense swirling black fog seeped from the crevices, slow at first, then gathering momentum, it loomed above him, dissolving all at once into hundreds of squawking crows with beady eyes that flapped around his head. He cried out. Hands flung in front of his face to block the onslaught. The birds descended upon him. Pecked his clothes, arms, skin, and face. Blood spurted from his wounds down along his hands. His eyes bulging in terror, he tried to knock them off, but the birds kept coming. Stinging him with their talons and nev-er-ending sharp questing beaks. There was nowhere to go. His breathing became laboured, each breath swift, intense. Immense pain rocketed through his chest, so great his breath emerged in shallow gasps, in such excruciating agony it could have cleaved him in two. He staggered, hand clutching his chest, didn't realise the window was wide open and tumbled to his death.

The door burst open as Adam and Carrie charged inside. They stared around them in stunned disbelief and bewilderment. The room was empty. They looked at one another in shock. At the hundreds of black feathers floating to the floor. The strong scent of rot. The closed window.

'Adam!' Carrie cried, pointing out the window, 'look.'

Nathaniel's body was face down on the concrete. She raced down the stairs out into the yard. Checked for a pulse and found nothing. He was dead. But how did it happen? It was as if someone had pushed him. She glanced up at her bedroom window and gasped.

A figure stood at the window, smiling down at her. Her heart lurched as her hand flew to her mouth, tears tracking down her face.

Somehow, she'd known it was Louisa all along, deep down. 'You saved me,' she whispered.

She felt a hand on her elbow. 'You, okay?'

She nodded, smiled, and wiped away the tears. She clutched her locket in her fist and looked up to the window again. She'd gone. May she rest in peace.

'Bastard got what he deserved.' Adam shook his head. 'But what I can't work out is how he fell.' He glanced up at the closed window in bafflement.

The guards were notified and informed that Nathaniel suffered a massive heart attack and fell off a roof while fixing an aerial to the chimney. Carrie ended her relationship immediately with Jack but didn't tell him the truth about his father. She lied that his father had called to make amends and, in so doing, had offered to fix her aerial and went up onto the roof. There was no way to explain the truth. It was enough that he had died. Diane was aloof, keeping her distance as if she knew something had happened but couldn't pin what it was down to exactly, and she didn't see either of them again. In later months she would discover an article in the *Connacht Tribune* announcing Jack's engagement to his fiancée Brigitta.

Soon after, in response to her ordeal, she put her house up for sale, unable to continue living there again after everything that had happened.

Chapter Thirty Seven

Carrie

1976

Carrie planted daffodil bulbs on her mother's grave just on the outskirts of Galway city, the only good deed Louisa's mother had done for her. The cemetery overlooked the harbour. She knelt in front of her headstone, touched the cold marble, and wept deep wracking sobs for what might have been.

A touch on her shoulder.

She looked up to see a wizened old woman in a headscarf, long brown coat, and a bunch of carnations in her left hand.

'So good of you to come to my daughter's grave.'

She flinched like she'd just been slapped. This woman had to be her grandmother. The same grandmother that abandoned Louisa to her fate all those years ago. She couldn't look at her. She wanted nothing to do with her. So, she nodded in response, averted her eyes, and hurried out of the cemetery, hands shoved in her coat pockets, head bent against the rising November winds.

It was Sister Joan who told her where she was buried when they met at a coffee shop three weeks previous. She'd been nervous at first, not knowing what to expect but was soon put at ease by Joan's easy-going charm, wit, and kindness.

The nun wore a navy jumper and black skirt, a crucifix around her neck. For meeting Carrie, she didn't bother with the wimple and habit. They shook hands and embraced.

'You were going to tell me how my mother died?' Carrie said, setting her cup on the saucer.

'Yes, it was another girl, a troubled soul called Carmel Shinnors, who killed her. Louisa was about to leave for a new life and go and search for her daughter. You.' She smiled. 'She was so happy to finally leave the institute. I should have seen it coming.'

'What happened to her?'

'Carmel?'

'Yes.'

'Truth is, we don't know. After that tragedy, she was never seen again.'

Carrie's eyebrows drew together sharply. 'You mean she's still out there, somewhere?'

'Afraid so.'

'But how? I don't understand –'

Sister Joan reached over and patted her hand. 'Wherever Carmel is, she's long gone.'

'What, what did Carmel look like?'

Sister Joan sighed, 'It's been such a long time I can scarcely remember. She had long hair at one stage, dark, I think. Her eyes were like flint, black almost. She became unrecognizable after a while.' Her neck flushed red. 'The other sisters punished Carmel for being a wild cat for flouting the rules over and over. The marks they inflicted were stains that will never fade. Interior and exterior permanent smears. Scars on her face and across her head. You see, she was not like the others. But like the others, her parents did not want her. Carmel was strong, resourceful. Nothing got in her way. Louisa made the mistake of trusting her and – well, you know the rest. I was devastated when it happened. We all were. But Louisa would want you to get on with your life, of that I am certain.' She looked at her hand. 'You are not married.'

Carrie blushed. 'No.'

'What will you do now?'

'Haven't decided. I can't go back to my home anymore, not since…'

'You don't have to talk about it. I fully understand, it's been a terrible ordeal.' She stood up and shrugged on her coat, which was also navy. 'I am so pleased to have met you.' Her eyes moistened. 'Your mother would have been so proud.'

'Thank you.'

They embraced again and walked out to the car park.

'You look so much like her. She was my best friend, you know.'

'Have things changed for the better at *The Sisters of Mercy*?'

'We still have twenty-five girls in our care. I am fighting for them, Carrie, every minute of every day, but I am just one nun. Most don't stay with us for any longer than a few months. Once we see that they are rehabilitated, they are released back to their families.'

'And the laundries,' Carrie prompted, 'have they been reformed?'

She hesitated before answering. 'I cannot truthfully say yes.'

'But surely, you've been through it, you know what it was like slaving every day on those massive machines?'

She pursed her lips. 'I must go. God bless you.'

Carrie watched her get into a green Mini and drive off. Grimacing in disgust. Nothing had changed.

It was almost Christmas. Carrie was packing her suitcase, ready to leave on the next flight to London. Tom was dismayed and bitter about her leaving so suddenly, constantly complaining about having to find someone else to fill her shoes and on such short notice too. She hated leaving him in the lurch but could stay there no longer. Too many memories, it was time to put the past behind her.

Hammering sounds from next door. Davey was erecting a long-awaited gazebo for Nuala. He probably wouldn't even notice she'd gone. Her eyes travelled around the yard and landed on a dog's bowl. She rubbed her nose as a fresh wave of grief threatened to drown her. Poor Max. She never knew what happened to him after being locked out in that terrible storm. Dogs reacted in different ways. Max was so well looked after; he probably took fright in the wind and rain and ran away. What she'd give to hold him again, keep him close. She sniffed, blew her nose, drew herself upright, and gave herself a mental shake. Time to move on. Let go.

The new owners were moving in at the weekend. Hauling her cases down the stairs, she took one look around at the home she lived in almost all her life. The memories of her adoptive parents. The scorched stains from the ashes of her father's pipe when they missed the fire and dropped onto the lino instead. The embroidered ivory net curtains her mother made, the frayed carpet on the stairs. Patches on the walls where photographs should have hung. The big orange bath where her mother used to wash her, that sat in the centre of the kitchen floor in front of the gas fire to keep her warm. She looked out the window. Vacant paddocks, training with Adam. Oh, God. She was going to miss him most of all. He really came through for her over the last few months. If it hadn't been for him, she would have buckled for sure and ended up in hospital. If only things were different. If only she hadn't waited so long to tell him how she felt. She'd marry him in a heartbeat. Now, he was with someone else. She was too late. The story of her life.

With a sigh, she trudged out to her car. Her flight was leaving in just over three hours. There wasn't much time. Slamming down the boot, she ran next door to say her goodbyes.

'Come in, Carrie.'

Nuala's plump cheeks were smudged with flour. The same blue rollers in her permed hair. She ushered her into the kitchen, where the stove was lighting, exuding waves of heat. Davey smoking his pipe, got up when he saw her, pumped her hand, a tool belt suspended from his waist.

'We'll miss you, love.'

'The place won't be the same without you,' said Nuala.

A lump formed in her throat, her eyes misting over. 'I promise to visit you both.'

'You'll be too busy living the high life in London, so you will.'

'Stick on the kettle, Davey.'

Carrie glanced at her watch. 'I don't have a lot of time; my plane leaves in less than three hours.'

'Sure, you'll have time for a cup of tea and a scone.'

Carrie nodded and smiled. She was going to miss these two. She sat down at the farmhouse table while Nuala set china cups on saucers and Davey buttered some scones, adding jam and a dash of cream to the mix. There were strong scents of cinnamon coming from the oven and an equally strong whiff of dog. Rover, their ageing cream Labrador was snoozing under the table, his paws jerking every few seconds indicating that he was dreaming, probably chasing a rabbit.

'I went to the post office today; the price of a stamp is gone up, can you believe it? Who did I meet, only Mary Jones? You remember Mary; she's the one who married Kevin Kiely, the fella that owns that huge farm – although it's about time for him to be marrying, and he well over fifty or was it forty-five –'

The phone rang. Nuala erupted out of her seat. 'I'll get it. Pour out the tea, Davey.'

Carrie's teeth sank into the scone. She licked her lips. 'Delicious, thank you.'

Nuala was only gone a minute when the cuckoo sprang open. Nearly time to go. But she felt so at home she didn't want to leave. Davey poured another cup and exchanged a glance with Nuala coming back in.

'Thanks so much, Nuala,' Carrie gushed, giving her a hug. 'I'm going to miss this.'

She didn't catch the panicked look Nuala shot her husband as she stood up to take her coat.

'Just before you go, I must show you some photos of you and Adam together when you were training. They're in a drawer here somewhere.' Nuala pulled out a compartment from the hall table and shuffled around until her hands closed over the photos. She handed them to Carrie one by one.

'Yeah, I remember these. Gosh, I was a lot younger then.'

'And did you see this one?'

Carrie glanced at her watch, then down at the photo and frowned. It was taken not too long ago when she was out walking with Max. A beautiful picture. The wind in her hair, standing by the marina, staring thoughtfully out to sea.

'Who took this?'

'Adam, of course, sure, I wouldn't know one end of a camera to the other.'

'Thanks for showing me,' Carrie said, handing her back the photograph, 'but I really do have to go now, sorry.'

A screech of brakes wailed to a stop outside. The door was wrenched open. A patter of footsteps.

'Oh, thank God, you're still here.' Adam's hair was standing on end. He was wearing a short sleeveless jacket, a pullover buttoned up to his neck and dirty jeans.

Nuala and Davey closed the door, leaving them alone.

'Thought I'd missed you,' he gasped, clearly out of breath.

'Good to see you, Adam, but I'm going to miss my flight.'

'Don't go, please.'

Her expression faltered. 'What do you mean? I have to; there's nothing for me here. I can't stay after everything that has happened.'

'Nothing? Are you sure?'

She looked at him. Her throat suddenly dry. 'What are you trying to say?'

'I don't want you to go.'

She shot him an exasperated look. 'For goodness sake, why not? Spill it out.'

'Haven't you guessed, you blind, stubborn fool? I'm in love with you.'

She stared at him, speechless. Stunned. 'What did you say?'

Clasping her hands in his, he repeated, 'I'm in love with you.'

'But you can't be – what about that woman, that redhead I saw you with?'

He threw back his head and laughed. 'Alice? She works for me, that's all.'

A slow smile curved her lips. With one leap, she threw herself at him, wrapped her arms around his neck. 'I love you, Adam.'

They kissed, locked in each other's embrace.

'Does this mean you're staying?'

She nodded and laughed. 'I'm staying. Oh, Adam, I'm so happy!'

They embraced again.

'Mum, Dad, you can come in now.'

Nuala's eyes lit up when she saw them together, hands entwined, pure joy on their faces. They hugged and kissed and hugged again.

'There's someone here that wants to see you.'

She looked a question at him.

'Close your eyes. Put out your hand.'

She couldn't believe it. 'Oh, my God, Max.' Crouching to the dog's eye level, she gushed, 'Come here, boy.'

The dog looked none the worse for wear. Wagging his tail, Max bounded over to her, showering her from head to toe with licks. She threw her arms around his neck, hugging him tight, crying with joy. She couldn't believe it. She was full sure she'd never see him again. Max barked his excitement, brushing his head off her knees, jumping up to lick her on the face. Pure Magic.

'I can't believe it. Where did you find him?'

'Someone had picked him up then must have let him go again. I found him rooting through a neighbour's rubbish tip. Fed him a good meal, washed and groomed him until I could bring him to you.'

'Adam, I don't know how to thank you. This is the best day of my life.'

'This is the best day of my life,' he affirmed with smiling eyes. 'Come and meet my crew. See what I'm planning to do with the place.'

'First, I've to sort out a place to live.'

'Don't worry about that; you can stay with us until you find somewhere,' Nuala said.

'Really, Nuala, it's too much. I couldn't impose.'

'You are family now; it's no trouble,' said Davey with a conspiratorial wink at Adam.

'Maybe just for this weekend,' Carrie smiled, 'thank you both so much.'

Carrie travelled with Adam in his jeep, snuggled up to his side, Max on her lap. They agreed to date for a while, get to know one another properly as a couple. The drive to Roundstone was bliss, laughing and joking and cuddling, discussing plans for the future, their life together.

'I just have one question.'

'Just one?' he teased, ruffling her hair.

'How come you didn't tell me how you felt all those years we spent together training?'

He paused to gather his thoughts, then replied, 'We were both in relationships. The timing wasn't right, I guess.'

He turned off the engine, leaned over and kissed her hungrily on the lips, and it was another twenty minutes before she finally came up for air.

Chapter Thirty Eight

Carrie

1976

It was almost five when they pulled into the yard. She could see horses in the fields, a large training arena, office suite, a set of multi-coloured jumps and stables to the rear. It looked magnificent, like a huge American ranch: at least sixty acres or more. Up to about forty cattle grazed in a fenced-off field on one side and on the other stood a modest unfinished cream bungalow, red brick corner coins, complete with its own flower garden and separate driveway.

'This is amazing, Adam,' she breathed. 'Aren't you a *dark horse*,' she grinned. 'I'm blown away.'

Clutching her waist, he bent to kiss her neck and inhaled the scent of strawberry shampoo from her hair. 'Glad you like it.' He took her hand. 'Come on, there's someone I want you to meet.'

They went to the stables, where a woman was busy mucking out. Muscles bulged on her forearms, and her long red curly hair was tied back. Khaki dungarees stained with grass. Her back was to them, scooping horse dung into a wheelbarrow. She turned upon hearing their approach. The smile died on her face.

'Hey, Alice, how's it going?'

'Good, yeah.'

She looked at Carrie. 'Do I know you?'

Carrie was taken aback at the woman's directness. 'Don't think so; I've never met you before.'

'This is Carrie, my girlfriend. Alice is a wonder with the horses.' He smiled. 'Don't know what I'd do without her. She can turn her hand to anything. You'll be seeing more of her from now on, so I'd better let ye get acquainted while I check on the mares.' He started to walk out, then turned, 'Maybe you'd show Carrie the ropes?'

'Sure, Adam.' She said to Carrie curtly, 'Come with me. We have thirty stables in total. Twenty in this section and another ten to the rear of the building. Most of the horses are out in the paddocks, but there's always work to be done – some get sick and have to be stabled. And then there's the herd – they have to be dosed, treated for worms, moved around from field to field.'

'How long have you been working here?'

'Not long, eight months, give or take.'

'Are there many others working here?'

'You'll see soon enough. This way.'

Carrie noticed she had crow's feet, so she couldn't be that young. Scars crisscrossed her temple, and another one ran the length of her nose. Her skin looked red, flaky, and sore.

'Where you from?'

'Clifden. You?'

'Con – Kerry,' Alice corrected herself. 'Carrie is an unusual name. I've only ever heard it mentioned once.'

'What can I say? I'm unique.' Carrie grinned.

Alice didn't reciprocate. They started walking through drizzly rain towards the office when Alice stopped short and stared at her locket. 'B…Beautiful jewel,' she stammered. 'I saw one like that – before.' Her voice trailed off. 'Where did you get it, if you don't mind me asking?'

'It belonged to my mother. Do you want to see what's inside?'

Alice nodded. 'Sure, I'd like that. Don't want Adam to think I'm being nosy, though.'

Carrie smiled. 'I won't say anything. Besides, it's just a locket,' she said, taking it off and handing it to Alice. She wanted to get on with her. Maybe even become friends. She obviously knew a lot about the work.

Alice pried open the locket with her fingernail while Carrie browsed through the files on the bookcase, familiarizing herself with his work. The office wasn't big, but it was practical, and everything was organised in alphabetical order. There was one walnut desk and matching chair, with photos of his parents on the shelf. A scent of rose air freshener lingered in the air. The steady drip of rain on the roof.

'So, are you staying nearby – Alice?' Carrie asked, turning to look behind her.

She was gone. The opened locket discarded on the chair.

Another three weeks had gone by, and she still hadn't found a place to live. Carrie was going for a ride with Adam. It was a mild, breezy afternoon, a good day for a gallop. He wanted to show her a lake on the other side of the estate where they could have a picnic sometime. Alice got their horses ready, and together, they set off at a trot across the wide vast expansive fields.

'Race ya.'

'You're on,' she squealed in delight, kicking her horse's flank.

He was a big brute. Chestnut, strong and powerful. It felt great to feel the wind in her hair as they galloped. She'd forgotten how good it was. Adam sped past her.

'Come on, slow coach,' he yelled.

She laughed, kicked the horse on faster, gaining on him until he disappeared behind a clump of bushes. Carrie slowed to a canter as the lake came into view. Just then, she felt herself sliding off the saddle. She looked down in fright. It had come loose. She fell off, landing on her rump.

Adam stopped his horse and ran towards her. 'Are you all right? What happened?'

She got up, dusted the grass from her pants, and tested her ankle. Nothing was broken.

'I'm okay – the saddle came loose, wasn't tightened properly I guess.'

'Alice should have known better; I'll have a word.'

She put her hand on his arm. 'No, don't, I'm okay. These things can happen, sometimes.'

'You're a good person, Gillespie.' Placing his arm around her shoulders, they walked back, pulling the horses ,behind them and nothing further was said on the subject.

Carrie was in the office sorting out a proper filing system when Alice walked in looking for Adam. 'He's not here. Is there anything I can help you with?'

'No, it's Adam I wanted.'

Alice started to walk out when Carrie said, 'We're going for a drink later if you'd like to come? You could ask Evan, and we'll make it a foursome. What do you think?'

Evan was a farm labourer on the estate that had taken a shine to Alice. He was quiet and reserved and had lots of tattoos.

'I'll pass. Tell Adam I was looking for him,' Alice said, swinging the door shut behind her.

Carrie spent another blissful night with Adam, albeit in a cramped single bed. They talked the whole night, in between passionate lovemaking, giggles and more passion. Sunshine streamed through the window, waking her up. There were no curtains, just a sheer voile, and only for the fact that the room was situated to the rear of the house anyone could see in.

The brush of fingertips. 'Good morning, sleepy head.' He said, leaning down to kiss her.

She looked up at him, pulling the blanket over her shyly. 'Hi.'

'Ready for a day of pure laziness?'

'Bring it on,' she smirked.

'Hey, I meant to ask. How are you getting on with Alice?' he was lying on his side, looking down at her.

'I don't know; she's a bit distant, curt. She was looking for you yesterday.'

'She wanted an advance in her wages, said it was urgent, so I didn't question it.'

'Where does she live?'

'Nearby, in town. Right, madam, time for breakfast.'

'Any chance you'll put some curtains on the window? I don't want to wake up every morning to Evan gawking in at me.'

He laughed and turned scarlet. 'Jesus, sorry, I should have had this place furnished and liveable by now. What must you think of me?'

'I don't mind roughing it a little while longer, but this place better be ship-shape by the time I do move in.'

'Yes, mam,' he said, giving her a mock salute.

She giggled, throwing her pillow at him.

Because it was Saturday, Adam had the day off. Determined to make the most of it, they decided to have breakfast in the local café. They scoured the newspaper for accommodation ads and finally found someplace suitable close to work. A temporary abode until she was ready to move into Adam's *palace*. Tom was delighted she was staying on and offered to help with the move.

An hour later, she went up to the counter insisting on paying for breakfast, only to discover that she'd left her purse back in the bedroom. Adam sorted the bill with the waitress, and they headed home. Him to sort out a few things in his office and her to the house. The front door was open when she returned, but that was nothing new for Adam. Carpet muffling her footsteps, she opened the door of the bedroom and froze, staring in shock at the scene before her.

The blankets were tangled in a heap at the foot of the bed. The wicker chair turned upside down. The wardrobe doors barely hanging. Her bag was on the floor. Lipstick, eye shadow, Vaseline, a small hairbrush, packet of tissues and her red purse were scattered all over the dusty linoleum.

Alice was staring at a pocket-sized photo of Louisa, the one Hannah had given Carrie the last time she was out at the house. Her body language saying it all. She didn't look sorry to be caught out. If anything, anger and hate flashed in her black eyes. Blobs of spit foaming the corner of her mouth. Alice looked up, crumpled the photo in her fist and stepped towards her, radiating hostility. It took all of Carrie's willpower not to turn and flee.

'Put everything back where you found it, right, now! Then get out.'

'You know – you look just like her. A lying, deceitful toad. She betrayed me. I told her everything, my deepest darkest secrets,' her voice hitched in a sob, 'and she flung it all back in my face. What kind of friend does that to someone?'

'What are you talking about?'

Alice's expression changed; the transformation so sudden it was unnerving. She started laughing, tears streaming from her eyes. 'Do you remember that trick we played on them – when I stole the key? They believed us. Boy, weren't we a team?'

'I don't know what the hell's got into you, Alice but you need help. I'm getting Adam,' Carrie said, spinning on her heel.

Alice pounced on her in a flash, slamming the door shut, blocking her escape route. It was like déjà vu all over again. First with Nathaniel, now with her. She was standing so close they were almost nose to nose. This deranged woman had worked with Adam for almost eight months. How could he not have seen the signs?

'Look, whatever it is,' she said, licking her lips nervously, 'we can work something out. There's no need to go all psycho on me.'

Alice's eyes looked wild, fanatical. Carrie couldn't keep up with the constant mood changes. It was like she was on drugs, wired to the moon.

'I missed you,' Alice said suddenly, grabbing her hand. 'Let's run away now before they catch us.'

'Let go! You're hurting me.'

'You're not getting away from me this time, Louisa.' Her voice was low, deadly.

Carrie stiffened in shock as the penny finally dropped. Bile rocketed up her throat. The room seemed to spin, round and round, faster and faster, sucking her into the black hole of its vortex. And for a dreadful moment, she couldn't catch her breath. Desperately trying to get a grip, she held on to the door jamb to steady herself. Staring in disgust at the woman before her, she emitted a raw anguished cry from the depths of her soul that was almost animalistic.

'You evil, twisted bitch,' she screamed, ramming her back against the wall. 'I know who you are. You murdered my mother.'

Alice laughed. The sound like a cackle, was eerie, bone-chilling. 'Yes, I killed Louisa.' She frowned. 'I couldn't let her leave with that boy. It wouldn't have been right. I had to protect her reputation. I was her friend.'

Carrie grabbed her throat. 'Some friend - you're sick, you know that. I'm going to make sure you rot in jail for a long, long time, Carmel.'

'Stupid girl. You've no proof. Who's going to believe something that happened over twenty years ago?'

'I will.'

Both heads turned simultaneously. Carrie almost sagged with relief. Carmel gave a howl of rage, tried to twist out of her grip. Adam had seen her through the voile drapes and overheard everything through the open window. She was going down for a very long time. He bound Carmel's wrists with a rope while Carrie called the guards. Fortunately for them, they were in the vicinity and arrived promptly. The sergeant in charge took their statements.

'We've been searching for this woman for a long time. Take her down to the station,' he commanded the younger guard.

'This is not over, Louisa.' Carmel shot Carrie a final glance of hatred before being bundled out to the waiting Garda car.

Adam touched her shoulder. 'Are you okay?'

She drew a long shuddering breath. Looked at him. 'Finally, some justice for my mother. Maybe she'll rest in peace now.'

'I need to be alone for a while, Adam.'

'Sure, call me when you're ready?'

She nodded. Carrie walked down to a big snow-white horse grazing in the paddock, stroked its neck and fed it an apple. She always found horses therapeutic, now even more so. Max ran beside her, loving all the space and freedom. She took a ball out of her pocket and tossed it to him.

The ball didn't fall on the grass. She searched around but couldn't see where it landed. Suddenly, a small dazzling orb of light floated through the air in her direction. Carrie stared transfixed as it started to move closer and closer, but she didn't feel any fear. The orb grew bigger she had to shield her eyes from the blinding light. It began to fade after a moment, then disappeared. In its place stood a tall girl in a light blue dress, smiling, radiating love, Max's rubber ball in the palm of her hand.

About the Author

Lorraine O'Byrne (née Barry) was an Irish author of children's stories and adult fiction. Inspired by her childhood in rural Ireland, Lorraine distilled her interest in fairies, pixies and other supernatural creatures into her children's stories such as *The Hippity, Dippity Witch* and *Lucy Pebble's Miracle*. Lorraine's first adult fiction was *The Wrath of Voodoo* in 2004, about a young Irish woman who went on an adventure to Kenya. Despite an interest in the supernatural, Lorraine always brought her trademark humour to her writing, as 2015's *Escaping the Prince* testifies.

Lorraine graduated from the University of Limerick with a BA in Languages, History and Sociology, before obtaining a diploma in freelance journalism and an MA in Creative Writing, also from UL, where her tutor was bestselling Irish author Donal Ryan.

Like so many Irish writers before her, from WB Yeats to Edna O'Brien, Lorraine was inspired by Ireland's natural landscapes and succeeded in seeing the ordinary in the extraordinary. Her book *Poppy the Cygnet* was inspired by the numerous swans that visit the beautiful lake of Lough Gur each year, where Lorraine worked as a tour guide.

Lorraine spent her final years working as a carer for the elderly in her community while she lived on a farm in Co Limerick, with her beloved husband Donal, and their cherished family pets. Lorraine enjoyed many outdoor pursuits such as hill walking and horse riding. The rural chimes of farm life proved stimulating for her imagination, as it was here, she completed her final novel, *I Will Find You*, a story of a long-buried secret seen through a supernatural prism.

Dear Reader

Thank you for reading *I Will Find You*, Lorraine O'Byrne's final book. We hope you enjoyed the story as much as we know Lorraine loved writing it!

To help reach out to readers of *I Will Find You* and Lorraine's other books, we have set up a Facebook page. The page contains relevant info and interesting content related to Lorraine's work. Discover more about Lorraine and *I Will Find You*, as well as interesting info on Lorraine's other books, including the novel *The Wrath of Voodoo* and the several fabulous children's books Lorraine wrote, including *The Hippity Dippity Witch, Lucy Pebbles Miracle, Escaping the Prince* and *Poppy the Cygnet*.

The Facebook page is also an opportunity for us to learn more about you. We would love to hear your thoughts on *I Will Find You* and Lorraine's other books, so do visit us and let us know what you think. Simply scan the QR code below, and you will be taken straight to Lorraine's page. You will also find a QR code that directs you to where all of Lorraine's previous books can be purchased.

While Lorraine has sadly passed on, we are committed to celebrating her work and reaching out to both new and existing readers.

Donal O'Byrne

Facebook

Lorraine's Books